CW01240209

STONE COLD

DAVID J. GATWARD

WEIRDSTONE PUBLISHING

Stone Cold
by
David J. Gatward

Created with Vellum

To Kaleem

Grimm: nickname for a dour and forbidding individual, from Old High German grim [meaning] 'stern', 'severe'. From a Germanic personal name, Grima, [meaning] 'mask'.
(*www.ancestry.co.uk*)

1

Hidden by shadow, the edges of which were ragged like ripped paper and frayed cloth, the figure stood in silence. They were not entirely alone, their company, trees; sorrowful sentinels that had stood watch over this place for so long, protecting it from the worst of the weather.

This was a peaceful place, so that was something, and they were glad of such. It gave their mind a welcome moment of respite, not only from the worry and stress of the next few days but also from the memories.

Years had gone past, but the pain had stayed, and running away from it hadn't helped at all. You can run away from a place, from people, from family, from your past, but you can never run away from yourself. That had been a lesson hard learned, which was why they were back, a voice calling them onwards, louder now than ever, that only they could hear, had ever heard.

Wind came, whipping the high branches into a dance, a

frenzied blur of movement, a celebration in anticipation of what would soon be in play.

At their feet, a dark pool lay cold and quiet, its mirrored surface turned to a glittering spray of ripples by the breeze. The water held a memory, and it was here that the voice was loudest. And they listened.

'I know, and I'm sorry,' the figure whispered, a reply to the voice only it could hear. 'But I'm back now. And we will be together soon.'

The wind died, but it felt as though the place was taking a slow, deep breath, before another gust pushed its way through the trees, and the gentle ripples on the surface of the pool grew larger.

Just a step away from the pool's edge, a modest cairn stood as though waiting for something, like a swimmer nervous about taking their first dip into the chill water. It had been hidden from sight when they had arrived earlier that day, found it buried beneath creeping fronds of ivy, hidden behind the thick, splayed hands of ripe, green fern. But they had brought with them the necessary tools to clear the place well enough to allow the cairn to be visible once again. Now that it was clear, the figure was sure they'd heard a faint, joyful cry as the first stones had been set free.

Kneeling, the figure placed a small tin in a shallow hole they'd just dug between the pool and the cairn. They had rescued it only hours before from behind books and papers thick with dust. They had not been surprised to find it in the very same place where it had been left so many years ago. Out of sight, out of mind. That something so small, barely the size of an egg carton, could contain within it all that was left of something so precious, had given it a weight beyond just the physical. They had carried it from its hiding place with gentle hands and felt such a connection with it that their skin had tingled with the cold of the metal. A burning reminder of what once had been.

Standing, the figure took a step back from the strange tableau now at their feet; a guardian of stone, a metal box heavy with memories of love and laughter and pain, and a pool, which had unwittingly been the thief of it all.

They did not blame the pool. It had never been its fault. No. That belonged to others, and they would know soon enough, and it would be their last memory before death took them.

The plan had been long in the making, a thing brewed over years. A career in numbers, in the deeper understanding of disguising things in books and accounts, had led them down dark, fertile paths. Over time, opportunities had presented themselves, and information had been uncovered. Now, they would put it all to good use, though, at the end of it all, and they knew some of that information would have to be shared. They had not returned to ruin the lives of those untouched by the history they were themselves haunted by, and perhaps, sharing what they knew, would be a way of asking for forgiveness.

They read something then, a heartfelt letter to a long-lost soul, which they knew resided here still, because had they not returned here, in those days not long after that awful theft of the other part of themselves, and heard it so clearly say their name? Was it not from here that the same voice had been calling them for so long, a haunting melody beckoning them to return? And hadn't they talked, then, together once again as they had always been meant to be, the connection no weaker despite the finality of the thing that had torn them apart, and the years gone since, now nought by dust?

Other explanations had been given, of course, and misguided help provided, but no one had understood, because no one ever could. No amount of talking or pills had silenced the voice, but those had served together well enough to convince, for a while, that it was all in their mind. Now, though, in the place where the voice was the clearest, peace was at last felt. This was right, they knew, coming back one last time, to do what must be done, before they could finally embrace what they had been running away from for so long, and what they would ultimately do once their work was complete.

Letter read, it was placed in an envelope, then in a zip-lock bag, and finally beneath the tin. Steady hands then blan-keted the tin with soil, tucking it in, safe and warm. All that remained to be done was one last task before they could begin what was, in the end, *the* end.

With hammer and chisel, the figure set to it, as tears of sadness and of joy fell together onto the soft, moss-covered ground, and it welcomed them gladly.

2

Harry woke to the sound of his own roar cracking his skull in two and immediately knew something was very, very wrong. Not because of the yell. And not because his heart was now rapidly trying to smash its way out of his chest. No. The darkness, though, was a bit of a give-away. That, and the reeking stench of whatever the hell had been pulled over his head to cut out the light. He tried to sit up, couldn't, the ground beneath him rough and cold and damp, his hands bound behind his back, his ankles tied together.

The roar that had woken Harry, and which still echoed inside his head, then decided to introduce him to a headache that had clearly been waiting in the wings for him to wake up. Now that he had, it rushed forward to take centre stage with all the tact of a stampeding rhino, the pain of it like having his head in a vice.

Harry's roar returned, only this time it was born, not just from the shock of coming to, but also from frustration and rage. How the hell he had ended up where he was, he had no idea. What bothered him more, though, was that he hadn't the faintest idea where the hell he was in the first place, and that was difficult to judge blind.

With a groan, Harry rolled onto his side, his right shoulder taking his weight, and in the process, finding a collection of jagged stones to lean on. They jabbed into him, sending sharp strikes of pain down his arm, and up into his neck, where they joined in with the throb still pounding away in his head. He rolled on, tipping forwards onto his chest. He tried to keep his face out of the dirt, but water and mud found his mouth anyway and he spat it out as he tried to work out what to do next.

The odd thing about the predicament Harry found himself now in was that it wasn't one he was entirely unused to. Not that he'd been bound and blinded numerous times before, but he'd certainly experienced it. Survive, Evade, Resist and Extract, or SERE training, had been an integral part of life back in the Paras and was very difficult to forget. None of it had been designed to be fun. Quite the opposite, in fact, the aim being to make things as realistic and uncomfortable as possible. Otherwise, what was the point? He'd also ended up in the wrong hands while working undercover on more than one occasion; being blindfolded and tied to a chair, while someone whipped the soles of your bare feet with a length of hosepipe was an experience he wished he could forget, but couldn't, probably never would. So, whatever this was, at least it wasn't that. Well, not yet anyway.

Sucking in a deep breath, then exhaling as he moved, Harry shuffled and dragged his knees upwards, leaning on his forehead as he did so, and bracing his neck. He ignored the pain of grit and stone cutting into his flesh, and was soon on his knees.

From this position, it was easy for Harry to pivot on his hips, and he was soon sitting upright on his heels. A cramp hit, almost sending him back to the ground, buckled and yelling, but he forced himself to see it out, flexing his toes, his muscles to hurry the pain away.

As the cramp eased, Harry managed to rock back onto his feet, then pushed himself up to standing. His legs complained, muscles and joints all joining in together to voice their resistance to being forced to move. Dizziness swept in, and nausea sent Harry's head spinning, causing him to stumble forward, his head thumping into rock. He yelled out, snapped his head back, only to find that whatever was on his head had caught on something. It ripped away suddenly, but if Harry had hoped to find light waiting for him, he was very much mistaken, as one darkness simply replaced another. But at least he could breathe cleaner air, he realised, no longer forced to suck oxygen in through the stench of the hood that had been covering him.

Enjoying the sweeter air for a moment, Harry allowed his eyes to become accustomed to this new gloom and soon, shapes began to appear. At first, they had no recognisable form, were just odd blobs, distorted shadows, fractured sections of darkness leaning against one another as though drunk. Soon, however, they revealed themselves to be what they truly were, and Harry was stunned to see what he was sharing his prison with. After all, that's what this was, a prison, and he had known that as soon as he had come to. And now, the thick, rusting iron bars he could now see blocking his way of escape, made that more than clear, as did the chain that held them fast, and the hefty lock binding it.

Harry, as far as he could tell, was in an old mine, trapped in a small alcove off of a larger tunnel, the floor of which was wet and cut through with a single set of parallel iron rails, which branched off beneath the iron bars and across the floor beneath his feet. At one time, carts would have run up and down those rails, Harry thought, and he glanced at the one that was sharing his tiny space. Perhaps it had been pushed there on the last day the mine had been used? Or maybe it had simply been left and forgotten? Either way, it was as rusting as the rails it rested on, and Harry could see no immediate use to it.

Elsewhere, Harry saw other remnants of the mining life the darkness had been home to; a simple set of wooden shelves leaning against the wall, rotten and melancholy, a single, leather, hobnailed boot upturned in a puddle, even the smashed carcass of a lamp. In direct contrast to this small and impromptu history lesson, however, were other items, and the sight of them made Harry feel both happier about his current predicament, and conversely, even more concerned; their presence indicated a disturbing permanence to where he now was.

A sturdy, metal-framed, folding camp bed was laid out with a sleeping bag. A camping toilet was pushed up against a wall. And the reason the darkness was nothing more than a grey, depressing gloom, was because on the camp bed, a small battery lamp glowed weakly. He saw no food, no water, and that told Harry enough about whoever had managed to imprison him: he would be meeting them soon, otherwise, why bother with the scant comforts designed to at least stop him from freezing to death, or soiling the place and making it stink? That they'd not given any thought to how he was supposed to navigate his new home, bound hand and foot, almost made him laugh. Almost.

Now that he had his bearings, Harry's next task was to do something about the ropes at his wrists and ankles. He twisted his hands away from each other, and realised to his surprise that the ropes weren't all that tight, just tight enough, which was strange. Had he been bound in a hurry? he wondered. And that knot looked clumsy as well, didn't it?

Harry lifted his wrists to his mouth, bit into the rope, and tugged. The rope resisted, so he pulled harder, felt it give a little, then stop again. Frustrating. Maybe something else would work? He had another look around the rocky alcove, saw how it was somewhat lacking when it came to sharp edges. He didn't need a knife, just something to cut into the bonds.

He spotted the hood he had woken up wearing, still hanging from a sharp point of rock in the wall, but that was both too high and probably not sharp enough to cut through what was holding him. Which left the shelf, the smashed lamp, the boot, and the cart. The shelf looked to Harry like it might collapse just by being stared at, the glass from the lamp had long ago been ground away to nothing, and the boot was a soggy thing best left alone. So, the cart it was, and Harry knew this was going to require patience. The edges of the cart were not sharp, but blunt and rough, and their only chance at cutting through the ropes that held him was through a simple process of erosion. But it wasn't like he had anything better to do, was it?

Harry headed over to the cart, turned his back to it, rested a hand on either side of one of its tired edges, and started to rub the ropes at his wrists back and forth. With every stroke, he forced his mind to claw itself back to where he had been before waking up in this dark, dank hole. But no matter how hard he tried, his memories refused to get into any sort of order, and all that he was left with was a jumbled recollection of walking his dog, Smudge, a figure approaching him, then a shadow dropping over his head, an arm clamping itself around his neck, and finally, something sharp jabbing into the side of his neck. And after that, darkness, and the memory of a single, whispered word: sorry.

3

Grace was, in almost every possible way, absolutely knackered. Driving home, her dog, Jess, clipped in beside her and with her head heavy on her lap, she guided her old Land Rover along winding lanes, thinking of little else other than the deep, hot bath she was soon going to be soaking in.

The day had been a long one, up early to get herself sorted for the day, then she'd met up with her dad, Arthur, before heading over together to the shoot they were both a part of. Arthur had been in charge of looking after the guns, a job he excelled at. He knew how to keep an eye on things, make sure the shoot was safe, could yammer on with anyone from a solicitor to a celebrity, and had no qualms at all about speaking his mind. Last year, he'd taken a gun off a loud-mouthed, and very well-known, politician, then personally marched the daft sod off the shoot and back to his vehicle. There had been an awful lot of swearing, and a good few threats chucked around, too, but none of it had bothered Arthur. That he'd hoofed the loud-mouthed pillock firmly up the arse with a muddy boot to encourage him to bugger off had been quite the highlight, and had very quickly become a tale told up and down the dale over enthusiastically drunk pints.

Grace's job had been to look after the beaters, a ragtag collection of people of all ages and walks of life, who were happy to spend their Saturday traipsing across field and fen, no matter what the weather threw at them. Today the weather had been fairly kind, if one ignored the violent downpour that had broken the sky at midday.

Beating on a shoot was something Grace had fallen in love with immediately at the age of ten when she'd joined her dad and his dog. She'd surprised everyone by doggedly marching through drive after drive, waving her flag, and calling out to get the birds shifting and flying over the guns. Having followed Arthur into the business, not for the money that was for sure, but for the love of it, working a dog on a beat had become a passion. Jess, the dog she'd had for enough years for them both to start looking a little tired as the day had worn on, was a wonder. She was never happier than being out in the fields, following her nose through thick grass or brambles, dancing around spinneys and through woodlands, as birds took to the air around her like confetti shot from a cannon.

With the day darkening, Grace was relieved to arrive home before night fell completely; the lights on her Land Rover could sometimes be fickle, and on two occasions had died completely, forcing her off the road to investigate, only to have them come back on once she'd lifted the bonnet.

The house was dark, which meant Harry was probably pulling a late one. He wasn't on duty, she was sure about that, but his was a job that refused to be constrained by the normal working week. It wasn't as though people only got up to no good between the hours of nine to five.

Unclipping Jess, Grace opened her door and slipped out of her seat, then helped the dog down to the ground, unwilling to let the hound's weary legs deal with the jump. A quick stroll across to the front door and they were soon both inside, lights on, and with her boots heaved off, Grace got down to the first job of the evening; lighting the fire.

The wood-burning stove was an ancient thing of strange design, all angles and welding, but it didn't half kick out some heat. It sat against the wall, gazing out into the large room that took up most of the ground floor of the house, and comprised a cosy lounge area directly in front of it, and behind that a very workable kitchen diner.

With the fire laid, Grace touched the firelights with a lit match, and soon flames were licking at the kindling, which popped and cracked. Larger pieces of wood were placed on top, then the stove door shut, its thick, glass windows dancing with orange tongues of fire. Jess, with no invitation needed, slumped down directly in front of it and closed her eyes.

'Been a good day, lass,' Grace said, and gave Jess a scratch behind an ear.

The dog wagged her tail just enough, but didn't move from her spot.

Feeling the heat of the fire already starting to seep from the stove, Grace stood up and left Jess to enjoy it alone as she then headed upstairs.

The house had two further floors, but the main bedroom was on the first floor, with a second bedroom, and the bathroom, and it was there that Grace went first. Sitting on the edge of the bath, she dropped in the plug, then set the water running, the silvery liquid gushing out in a thick plume of steam as it hit the cool air.

Hot water wasn't enough, though, Grace thought, and poured in a generous amount of a muscle soak bubble bath. That done, she popped back downstairs to check on the fire and Jess, found both to be absolutely fine and in no need of further attention, then made her way back upstairs and into the bedroom.

Stripping off her work clothes, Grace was unable to hold back a yawn, and the power of it seemed to pull out of her whatever remaining energy she had. She sat back on the bed, yawned again, and half undressed, sunk backwards onto the mattress, realised that was a very bad idea indeed, and promptly sat up again to try and pull off her thick socks. Neither seemed entirely happy with letting go of her feet, but they eventually loosened their hold and a moment or two later, Grace was naked and walking back to the bathroom.

Having left the door open, the steam from the bath had sent itself off to investigate further into the house in thick plumes worthy of a Hammer House horror movie.

Grace kicked through the steam, sending it swirling off as she stepped into the bathroom to check on things. Bubbles were now peaking over the edge of the bath, and she dipped a hand in to check the water. Scalding was the word that immediately sprung to mind, so she switched the hot water for cold and used a bottle of shampoo as a paddle to swirl the water around until it was at the desired temperature.

Dipping her first toe into the water, Grace sucked in a sharp breath at the heat on her skin, but pushed on regardless until both feet were in, and the water was halfway up her calf muscles. Gradually lowering herself through the bubbles and into the water, Grace closed her eyes, breathed in deep the sweet-smelling steam, and then let out the most satisfied of sighs.

Lying there in the near blistering heat of the water, Grace felt the aches and pains of the day leach from her and into the water, and she realised that really the only thing that would improve the moment would be the presence of Harry. Not that he was ever really keen on sharing a bath, but often half the fun was in just trying to persuade him to give it a go. His grumbling could reach epic proportions as he entered the bath, moaning about water spilling over, that there just wasn't enough room for two people, that showers were more his thing.

Smiling at the thought, Grace checked the clock on the bathroom wall, saw how late it was, and wondered just how long Harry would be. She wasn't worried, because Harry wasn't someone she had ever felt she needed to worry about in any way at all, but he hadn't called her or sent her a message to let her know where he was, and that was a little odd. She was sure there was an explanation for it, though, and got back to focusing on letting the hot bath do its worst.

When she finally decided it was time to get out of the bath, Grace pulled out the plug, wrapped herself in her thick, green dressing gown, shuffled across to the bedroom to find her slippers, and then headed downstairs.

Jess hadn't moved an inch, and didn't even stir when Grace padded over to drop some fresh logs into the stove. That done, she turned to the kitchen, ready for a nice thick bowl of the homemade chicken soup Harry had put in the freezer the weekend before.

Pouring the liquid into a pan, and putting it on a low heat on the hob, Grace checked her phone: no message. She pulled up Harry's number and gave him a call. No answer, straight to voicemail. She tried again, then hung up.

Stirring the soup as it started to heat up, she decided to check in with Matt, Harry's detective sergeant, just to see if he could tell her what was going on. She guessed there was an emergency of some kind, and that was why Harry hadn't been in touch and was unable to get to his phone to answer it.

'Now then, Grace,' said Matt, answering her call in three rings, and she could hear the confusion in his voice that she'd called him at all. 'Is everything okay?'

'I was just about to ask you that,' Grace said. 'Do you know where Harry is?'

'He's not home, then?'

'No,' said Grace, shaking her head even though her only company was a dog happily snoring away on the hearth. 'There's no message, and he's not answering his phone, so I just assumed there was an emergency or something.'

'You're absolutely sure he's not home?' Matt asked.

'I think I'd know,' Grace replied.

'No, you're right; he's not exactly hard to miss, is he?'

Grace breathed deeply, tasting the chicken soup in the air, and turned off the heat.

'So, you don't know where he is, then?'

Matt was quiet for a little too long, and that was enough to twist Grace's stomach.

'No,' he said, 'I don't. But I'll check with the rest of the team and get back to you. As far as I know, he was out this afternoon to meet up with some farmers in Yockenthwaite over in Wharfedale. There's been some funny goings-on over that way of late, apparently, but obviously we need a little more detail than that, because you can't really investigate funny goings-on, can you?'

'No, I guess not,' said Grace.

'I'll give the farmers a call as well; see if they can shed any light on this. They might know something if they were the last to see him.'

'Ring me as soon as you know.'

'Speak in a minute,' said Matt, and hung up.

Grace poured herself a generous bowl of Harry's chicken soup, grabbed some thick slices of bread, then shuffled over to the sofa in front of the fire.

The soup didn't just taste good; every mouthful felt like it was healing her from the inside somehow, feeding her body with just what it needed after the long day.

Grace's phone rang.

'Matt?'

For a moment just the other side of too long, Grace heard nothing but breathing.

'Grace, are you sure you've not seen or heard from him?' Matt asked. 'You've not missed a call, there's not a message on your phone?'

'There's been no call, and there's no message,' Grace replied, snapping a little at the questions. 'Why, Matt? What's wrong? Has something happened? Is Harry okay? What did those farmers say, the ones you were going to call who he'd met up with? Did they know anything?'

'Only managed to speak to one of them, Mr James Horner, but I'll check with the other two when I can. James said that Harry was going to take Smudge for a walk before heading home.'

'Where was he walking her?'

'That, I don't know. I'm going to drive over to where he was, and see if he's not just on the side of the road getting angry.'

'Why would he be doing that?'

'My guess is that he's got a flat tyre in that old Rav of his and probably doesn't have the tools to sort it out. Either that, or he does have the tools, and he's already broken them in frustration.'

'That does sound like Harry,' said Grace, almost managing a small laugh. 'But it's late now, Matt, isn't it? And if it is a flat tyre, why wouldn't he just call to let me know that's what had happened?'

'Phone signal's terrible out that way,' Matt replied. 'He's probably swearing into the darkness and kicking his vehicle hard enough to tip it over. I'll call you as soon as I've got hold of him, okay?'

Grace understood that Matt was doing his best to make her feel that everything was going to be fine, but she wasn't convinced.

'This doesn't feel right, Matt,' she said. 'This isn't like Harry at all.' Then she added,' I'll come with you.'

'No, you won't, because you don't need to. I'm sure it's nothing.'

'You don't know that, do you? Anyway, I can be ready in five.'

'Grace, please ...'

Grace went to reply, but said nothing.

'Stay put, and I'll call you as soon as I can,' Matt said. 'Okay?'

And with that, the call was over.

Grace lifted a spoonful of soup to her mouth, but after talking with Matt it just didn't taste right, so she put the bowl on the floor and gazed into the fire. Jess, meanwhile, stared at her owner. And waited.

4

Matt had done his best to make light of Harry's disappearance, because the last thing he wanted for Grace right then was to have her worrying. But if he was honest, he was a little concerned himself, because disappearing was not something Harry ever did. As their DCI, he kept in touch with the team and made sure everyone else did the same. Communication was key, something they all prided themselves on, so the fact that not only had none of them heard from him at all that afternoon, but that even Grace hadn't a clue where he was, well, that was somewhat troubling.

The story about the flat tyre was one Matt had come up with on the spot. He didn't think it was true in the slightest, because no flat tyre was enough to have Harry out so long past the end of his shift. And yes, the phone signal was bad out that way, but a bit of walking around would soon find enough of it for Harry to have called Grace.

So, just what the hell had happened? Had the gruffest man in the dale driven off the road and into a beck and was now unconscious and hanging upside down as the water slowly filled up the cabin? No, that was just ridiculous, and Matt quickly forced that thought from his mind. But what else could it be? Someone like Harry just didn't go missing. It simply didn't happen. And that meant that there had to be a perfectly reasonable explanation, because anything else was unimaginable.

Like he'd told Grace, he'd called the farmers, only managed to speak to one to see if they could shed any light on his whereabouts, and that was how he now knew where he had been heading, and why. He didn't have a specific location though, but he just couldn't see how, in reality, Harry could be missing.

Locking up the office, and with a message sent out to Constable Jadyn Okri, who was also on duty that night, Matt jogged over to the old police Land Rover. It was sitting out in Hawes Marketplace, and to Matt it looked like it was asleep, so much so, he almost felt bad about having to go and wake it up. Though Jadyn was down the other end of the dale, Matt wanted him back in Hawes at the office, just in case. Just in case of what, he really wasn't sure, but he was now thinking back to what Grace had said, and that she'd been right; this really didn't feel right at all, did it?

Kicking the engine into life, Matt flicked on the headlights, managed to coax the gear stick into first, then headed up through Hawes, turning at the primary school to take him into Gayle and then up Beggermans Road. He did his best to ignore the delicious smells from Hawes Chippy, which seemed to have hooked themselves into the air vents of the Land Rover as he'd driven past, but his stomach still gave a little rumble. Best fish and chips on the planet, and that was a fact.

By the time Matt reached the top of Beggarmans Road,

the night had grown dark enough for the hills and moors to sink into it and disappear, like the humps of vast whales diving beneath the surface of the sea. The view as he crested over the top and then down into Wharfedale was a haunting one. The sense of space yawning open in front of him was eerie, and Matt found himself wondering what ghosts and wraiths called this land home when day was done, and night had come to claim it.

Not that he was one for believing in anything like that, not really, but it was hard to ignore the spooky nature of the Dales when thick blankets of darkness laid themselves across it, and the silence of the place became almost overwhelming. That was half the beauty of it, though, the way the hills and vales seemed to breathe with their history. Living in the Dales was to walk side by side with the deep memory the place had of those who had walked its wildness long, long ago.

Dipping down into Wharfedale, Matt focused on the road ahead, pushing all thoughts of the undead from his mind. The Land Rover's headlights brushed the road clean, and raced him along the dry-stone walls lining his way.

Matt was coming through Oughtershaw, when a call came in on his phone. He would've answered it on the hands-free, but the Land Rover was so loud and rattly that he wouldn't have been able to hear whoever it was calling him anyway. Slowing down, he managed to find somewhere to pull over, and seeing that it was Jadyn who had called, returned the favour.

'Please tell me you're not calling me because you've not got your keys and therefore can't get into the office,' Matt said, immediately trying to make light of whatever it was that Jadyn was calling him about, if only to stop him thinking of all the bad things that could've happened to Harry.

'No, I'm in the office,' Jadyn said. 'I've just taken a call. That's why I'm calling you. Where are you?'

'Oughtershaw,' Matt answered. 'Why?'

'That's good, you're near where it is, then, aren't you? Well, you're heading in the right direction, anyway. Just need to go through Hubberholme and you'll be there.'

'Will I? And where's there exactly? Get to the point, Jadyn! What are you talking about?'

Jadyn, Matt knew, had a habit of either not getting to the point immediately, or skipping right over it.

'Harry's Rav,' Jadyn said.

Matt felt the world around him swoop in as though it, too, was now listening in to the conversation.

'You mean we know where he is?'

'A farmer found the vehicle just up beyond the White Lion Inn, in Cray.'

'Which farmer?'

'Richard Guy.'

The name didn't ring a bell, but then Matt realised why.

'Dicky Guy, you mean? I'm amazed he's still alive, never mind farming. Not seen him in years, for which I'm grateful, I hasten to add.'

Jadyn said nothing for a moment, then, 'He doesn't sound best pleased about where it is. Says Harry needs to learn how to park properly and that if it's not moved before the morning, he'll be hauling it off somewhere himself. I think he muttered something about dropping it into some ghyll somewhere.'

'That sounds like Dicky.' Matt sighed, rolling his eyes.

He couldn't remember the last time he'd had the misfortune of being in the presence of old Dicky Guy, but it sounded like he'd not changed much. It wasn't that he was a bad farmer, far from it, in fact, more that he just had no time for people. Though he'd generally kept himself to himself, when he didn't, fists had been known to fly. Matt had never really got to the bottom of why, and whenever the man was mentioned, most folk simply shook their heads and clammed up.

Thinking about where Jadyn had said Harry's vehicle had been found he said, 'But there's nowt along there for Harry to be looking at, is there? I know he was over this way to meet up with some farmers, but—'

'Actually, I checked on that,' said Jadyn. 'Gave one of them a call.'

'You did?' said Matt. 'So did I, actually. Who did you speak to, then?'

'Tom Sykes. He confirmed that Harry met them this afternoon, them being Tom himself, James Horner, and Tina Hodgson.'

'I spoke to James myself,' said Matt. 'Confirmed the same, so that's something, isn't it? Did Tom mention anything about what they wanted to chat with Harry about, exactly? All I knew was what Harry said, something about funny goings-on, which doesn't exactly tell anyone much. So, my guess is that there was more to it than that.'

'Tom said there'd been sightings of a light in the fields, in a woodland as well, I think, and a figure walking about.'

'Doesn't sound like much, does it? Mind, it's quite a lonely place out that way, isn't it? Understandable that folk get a little jittery and suspicious. Probably just walkers, but always worth checking out, just in case.'

'Tom said they were wondering if it was poachers, or someone checking farm buildings to see if they were locked or not, if there was anything worth coming back to nick. I think they just needed some guidance on security and Tom said that Harry advised them on that anyway.'

'Did he have any idea where Harry was going once they'd finished? I know he was taking Smudge for a walk.'

'Tom said the same, and that Harry was going to head along the river a ways to give Smudge a walk and a bit of a dip in the water, as far as he was aware, anyway. Wanted it done before he headed back home.'

'Which river? Whereabouts exactly?'

If Jadyn had got a location from Tom, then that would make things a bit easier, thought Matt, somewhere definite to start from at least.

'Up beyond Beckermonds.'

Matt almost did a double take.

'You sure about that?'

'Yes, why?'

'Because Beckermonds is nowhere near where you're telling me Harry's Rav has been found, is it?' Matt replied. 'It's completely the other direction! In fact, I've just flown past the turnoff for it!'

'You're right, it doesn't make much sense, but that's what Tom told me.'

'Dicky didn't mention Harry?'

'Only that he needed driving lessons.'

Matt sighed.

'Then where the hell is he, Jadyn? Why's his Rav parked over beyond Cray, and yet apparently he was going somewhere completely different and is now nowhere to be found? It doesn't make sense!'

'Grace hasn't heard from him, then?'

'No one has!'

For a moment, neither officer spoke.

'Oh, I've just remembered something else,' Jadyn said. 'Dicky Guy, he thinks Harry will have to pay for the damage as well.'

'Damage? What damage? To what?'

'The wall. Apparently, there's a load of stone around the vehicle or under it or something, and "walls cost money, too, and that doesn't grow on trees, does it, so what were we going to do about it?"' Jadyn quoted, doing a fair impression of Dicky's heavy accent. 'He made it very clear that he wanted me to understand that they don't just build themselves, and that he was busy enough as it was repairing a hole in another wall, without someone knocking down another.'

Under different circumstances, Matt would've laughed.

'Jadyn, I don't believe for a second that Harry would drive into a wall. What else did Dicky say?'

'Nothing, really; he just sort of swore a lot, then hung up.'

Matt stared out of the Land Rover's windscreen.

'Right, I'm going to check on Harry's vehicle,' he said. 'If it's just up beyond Cray, and on the side of the road, I doubt I'll miss it.'

'Anything you want me to do?' Jadyn asked.

'Yes,' said Matt. 'Call Grace, and let her know Harry's vehicle has been found and that I'm going to investigate. You can tell her as well that I'll call her soon enough, once I've had a look around for myself, and seen what's what.'

'Won't that worry her even more, though?'

'Yes, it will,' Matt said. 'But she's a right to know, hasn't she, like? And I don't know about you, but I, for one, don't want to be keeping any details hidden from the love of Harry's life.'

With that said, he killed the call, and headed off to find Harry's Rav, all the time wondering where the hell their gruff DCI was, and why he wasn't with his vehicle.

5

Grace took the call from Jadyn with her usual air of calm, giving little away in the tone of her voice, her words.

'I really appreciate the call, Jadyn, thank you.'

'Well, Matt told me to tell you, so that's what I'm doing, just following orders. And like I've just said, he'll be in touch soon, for sure. You're okay, though, right?'

'What? Yes, I'm fine. Thanks, Jadyn. Really.'

There was a slight pause before Jadyn responded.

'You know, Grace, I don't think we've anything to worry about though, have we? This is Harry we're talking about. He's just too big to go missing, isn't he?'

Grace actually laughed at that.

'Fair point.'

'I'm sure you'll hear something from Matt soon. Or from me. Or from both of us. One of those. Yes, I mean ...'

'Speak soon, then?' Grace interrupted, just to stop Jadyn from rambling on.

'Yep.'

Call over, Grace stared at the fire. It was still roaring away, and the room was now nice and toasty. Jess had given up on staring at her owner, having now moved from the floor to one of the sofas, where she was stretched out on her back, paws in the air, and was snoring softly. Most likely, it was because Harry wasn't around; he wasn't a fan of having the dogs on the furniture, but both Jess and Smudge knew Grace would let them get away with it if he wasn't around.

The evening was getting on now, and although Grace was weary from the day, and drained because of the bath, she was wide awake, alert. Harry never went missing. It just didn't happen. She knew that Matt and Jadyn were doing their level best to downplay things, but it wasn't working; she doubted they were even able to kid themselves with the reasons behind Harry's disappearance they'd given her.

'Well, I can't just sit here, can I?' Grace said, staring over at Jess.

In response, the dog took in a deep breath, then let out the loudest, most satisfied huff, and wagged her tail once, twice, letting it whump softly on the cushions.

'It's okay,' Grace said, and reached over to give Jess's stomach a scratch. 'You can stay here. Nice and cosy. You've had a long day, you've worked hard, you deserve it.'

Grace stood up.

Jess went from out for the count to ready and alert in a heartbeat, no longer lying on her back, but sitting on the floor, her wide, sharp eyes staring up at Grace.

Grace shook her head.

'You're not coming, lass. I need you to stay here, look after the place for me while I'm gone.'

Jess, clearly not listening, wagged her tail hard enough to cause her to shuffle across the floor.

'No,' said Grace, as firmly as she could. 'You're not. I'll be fine. I'm just going out to see what's what, that's all. You stay—'

Jess was at her feet, sitting on them almost, and staring up at her.

'You're not going to take no for an answer, are you?'

The look in Jess's eyes was enough of an answer.

'You're sure you want to come? You wouldn't rather the warmth of the fire?'

The tail wagging grew stronger, faster.

Grace hurried away from the fire and Jess, taking the stairs two at a time. She dressed quickly, then went back downstairs. Jess was waiting for her, already sitting by the door, that tail still full of enthusiasm.

Grabbing a dry jacket from off the back of the door, Grace heaved on her Wellington boots once again, snatched her keys from a small wooden bowl on a little table to the left of the door, and gave the door handle a twist. Cool air barged in like it had been waiting outside far too long and had grown impatient. She took a flat cap from another hook, then went outside, Jess to heel, and hurried over to her Land Rover. Opening the driver's door, Jess leapt up with the ease of a dog half her age. Grace scooched in beside her, leaning in, a paw on her lap, face forwards, ready to go.

Clipping Jess in, then herself, Grace reversed out of where she'd swung the vehicle in a couple of hours ago, then rolled down the gravel track to the main road. A quick right and she was soon in Hawes, then onwards through Gayle, and up Beggarmans Road.

Where the hell are you, Harry? she muttered to herself, staring out of the windscreen in the vain hope she might spot him wandering the moors, or making his way across a field. She couldn't think of a single good reason why he would be doing such a thing, and so far away from where his vehicle had been found, but that didn't stop her looking.

Racing down into Wharfedale, the Land Rover dancing down the lane just this side of dangerously, Grace snapped the window open, not only to give her right arm a little bit of extra space, but to have the breeze keep her awake. She was still alert, true, but she had already fought back two yawns, so anything that helped her stay awake was welcome.

Hubberholme came and went, and then, a few minutes later, having just passed through Cray, she saw lights ahead. There, pulled into a layby roughly hewn out of the side of the road, was the old police Land Rover, and in front of it sat Harry's Rav.

Grace skidded in behind the Land Rover.

'Stay,' she said, glancing down at Jess and giving the dog's head a scratch. Not that the dog could follow anyway, but reinforcement of commands was one of the reasons the dog was so damned good.

Stepping out into the night, Grace shuddered at the cold and pulled her jacket in tight. She walked past the police Land Rover and over to Harry's Rav. Whether she was imagining it or not, she sensed the darkness closing in about her, sending the faintest of shivers up her spine. She'd never been the skittish type, the kind of person to jump at a shadow or worry what could be hiding in it, but tonight was different, because Harry was out there somewhere, and she half wondered if the darkness itself knew exactly where, and just didn't want to tell.

'Matt?'

Nothing.

Grace called again, still no response. Just where the hell was he? Losing Harry was one thing, but Matt as well, and on the same night? That, she could very much do without.

She walked around Harry's vehicle. When she got to the front, she saw rubble beneath the front wheels, like the man she loved had parked on top of a section of tumbledown wall.

'Matt? Where the hell—'

'Grace?'

Matt's head popped up from the wall beside the road.

'Bloody hell, Matt!' Grace gasped, the shock of seeing his face loom at her out of the dark a little unexpected. 'What are you doing? Nearly gave me a heart attack.'

'I could ask you the same thing, like, couldn't I?' Matt replied. 'We talked about this, didn't we? And I thought I was clear enough for you to understand.'

'You were clear enough, Matt, but I couldn't just sit at home, could I?' Grace replied. 'And I knew where you were, so here I am.'

'Even so ...'

'Even so nothing,' said Grace. 'There's no way you really expected me to just sit at home, is there? So, where is he? Where's Harry? What have you found? If his Rav is here, he can't be far away from it, can he?'

'Just a mo',' said Matt, and Grace watched the odd sight of Matt's head and shoulders bobbing along on the other side of the wall in the dark as he made his way along it towards a gate to her left. A minute or so later, he was back, having walked back along the road to Grace.

'Well?' she asked.

Matt folded his arms, shook his head.

'Grace, I've no idea where he is,' he said, his tone dejected, his voice low. 'He's not here, that's for sure. But why? I can't make head or tail of it.'

'Why do you think he parked here?' Grace asked. 'And what's all that under the front of the vehicle? What is it?'

'Wall, apparently, but as you can see, there's no damage to the wall, is there? Or to the Rav, for that matter.'

Grace looked up and down the wall.

'Doesn't make much sense.'

'None of this makes much sense, by which I mean, none at all. At least we won't have to be paying any money to Dicky Guy for the damage, so that's something. Frankly, I wouldn't have put it past him to have thrown those stones under the vehicle and then claim it's bits of the wall.'

'Dicky Guy? Name rings a bell, but I've no idea why.'

'Best to keep it that way if you ask me,' said Matt. 'He's one of those people who never has anything good to say about anyone or anything, when he's got anything to say at all.'

'Why? Doesn't cost anything to be nice, does it?'

'I'm sure Dicky would disagree on that.'

'Harry doesn't crash into things, though,' said Grace. 'Well, what I mean is, he doesn't when he's driving, does he? He's clumsy on his own two feet for sure, walking into things, knocking things over, like he's no idea of his size or where his arms and legs are, where they end, but behind the wheel? He's safe. Fast at times, that's true, but always safe.'

Matt said, 'We've checked with people he was meeting over this way earlier today, and that all went ahead. Apparently, he was heading off to Beckermonds with Smudge.'

Grace turned back to her own vehicle on hearing that.

'Beckermonds? But that's just back along the road, isn't it?'

'And yet his vehicle is parked right here, and he's nowhere,' said Matt with a baffled sigh. 'I can't put any of it together right now, but I'm sure we will.'

'I'll go have a look for him,' said Grace. 'Won't take me

long to get over there, will it? I can drive up and down the lane, beams on full. Should spot him easily enough.'

Grace opened the driver's door to climb in, but a cough from Matt hooked her back.

'We'll be sending a team out soon enough, Grace,' Matt said. 'One person on their own isn't much good, and we don't want to go losing you, now, as well as Harry, do we?'

Grace hesitated.

'I'm serious, Grace,' Matt insisted. 'Don't go rushing off and doing something that gets yourself in trouble; that's not going to help us or Harry, is it?'

Grace could see Matt was right, albeit reluctantly.

'So, what next, then? What are we going to do?'

'You're not going to do anything,' Matt said. 'And although we're only a few hours into Harry disappearing, I'm calling in the big guns.'

'How do you mean?'

'I've already been on the phone with Mountain Rescue. We're getting a search underway as we speak. Everyone's coming over, and should be here soon enough, like. Jadyn will be over soon as well, and I've called Liz to look after the office.'

'Jadyn didn't mention any of that when he called.'

'That's because this all happened while you were driving over here, instead of staying at home, like I'd have preferred.'

Grace gave a shrug.

'Well, if there's a search going on, I can help, can't I?'

Matt went to say something, but clearly thought better of it.

'I'm sure he's okay, you know?' he said. 'This is Harry we're talking about.'

Grace gave a nod, could think of no reply, then spotted headlights coming towards them, slowing down.

'Looks like folk are arriving already, just like you said.'

'You sure you don't want to get yourself back home?' Matt asked. 'We've more than enough folk coming over to get on with the search. It's what we do, remember that.'

'I'm staying,' said Grace. 'No arguing.'

Matt held out his hand.

'Here, then,' he said.

Grace looked down and saw that Matt was holding out a bar of chocolate.

'You'll need it, good energy boost.'

Grace took the chocolate, then the approaching vehicle pulled in, and Matt headed over to meet the driver.

6

Having anyone other than Grace arrive out of the blue to offer to help and join in the search would have been, at the very least, an annoyance. Matt had dealt with various missing persons cases over the years, and often, close relatives, though they meant well, could get in the way. It wasn't a criticism, not by any means; who wouldn't want to join the search for their nearest and dearest? But it was never that simple, especially so in the Dales. You couldn't just put out a line of people across a section of moorland and set them off looking, that just wasn't the way it worked. The land was as treacherous as it was beautiful, and even the most experienced, well-trained and kitted-out individual could be caught unawares. And being local to the area didn't mean you knew what you were about either.

Rarely was there a time when the Mountain Rescue team were called out and one or two were unavailable due to the hills and moors showing their teeth. But then, that was why they were all volunteers, wasn't it? Matt thought. They all understood that to enjoy the outdoors required a certain acceptance of risk, so why not be one of those who would be on call should the worst happen? After all, a call-out could just as easily be one you were at the sharp end of yourself.

That thought made Matt smile as much as it did shudder, though the smile was a nervous one. On two occasions so far in his life, he had been the one making the call; the first because he and a friend had got into a pickle down a pothole in the Peak District, the second because, despite his own usual over-preparation when it came to what kit to carry, he'd headed out into the hills somewhat lacking in what was needed.

The situation down the pothole had been nothing short of terrifying. He'd been in his early twenties, full of piss and vinegar as his Grandad would've said, his confidence creeping well into arrogance. Having not really taken the weather reports all that seriously, because he'd firmly believed they would be in and out of the cave before the rain came in, he and an old friend, Charlie, had ventured deep into the bowels of the Earth, only to find themselves trapped by rising waters. By sheer good fortune, the pothole had afforded them a decent air pocket, and they'd survived their time underground by eating what scant supplies they'd taken with them in a battered ex-MOD ammo tin, namely a litre of water, a terrifying amount of chocolate and peanuts, and squished into the helmets they were wearing, an unhealthy quantity of marzipan.

When they failed to pop out of the cave at the expected time, an alert was raised by someone they had left their details with, and the rescue team was sent to find them. It was only when the waters abated a little could any kind of rescue be carried out. Matt and Charlie had been close to hypothermic when lights had appeared in the darkness and they'd finally been led out into daylight. That rescue had been instrumental in Matt's eventual decision to become a member of the local rescue team himself.

As for the other call-out? Well, it was an experience that he still shook his head at himself about, and one he was never likely to forget.

On that particular day, a few years into his marriage to Joan, he'd been in a bad mood, for reasons he could no longer recall, and having quickly thrown a light waterproof on, headed out into the hills to try and walk himself out from under the black cloud swirling over his head and into a better mood. Once again, the weather had played its part in his downfall, when, after slipping over and twisting his ankle badly, Matt had found himself utterly unable to carry on with his walk. Though only three or four miles from civilisation, it may as well have been a thousand.

It was only then, when he'd realised that he could go no further, had he had understood just what a predicament he was in. The wind was bitingly cold, and seemingly growing more teeth as the day went on, he had no warm clothes to speak of, no survival blanket or anything else to help him stay warm, and no way to call for help either. Rain had been in the air, too, and had swept in unannounced thanks to the fells being the fells, enjoying their own little weather system, oblivious to what the weather forecast had been.

He had been lucky, then, that having dragged himself over to a dry-stone wall to get out of the driving wind and bullet-like spots of rain riding it, a runner had found him, and because, unlike him, they clearly had a brain, were able to get him warm. Quickly wrapping him in a silvery blanket, the runner had given Matt something sugary to eat, then punched a call in for a rescue.

That was one day the rest of the team took great delight in making sure that he would never forget, and fair enough,

Matt thought. He deserved all the ridicule they could throw at him for being such an idiot.

Grace, however, wasn't just someone who knew Harry. She had as much experience as anyone on the rescue team when it came to understanding the landscape and the weather of the Dales, was exceptionally fit, had turned up wearing all the right gear, and to top it all, she had a dog.

'She's a good nose on her, has Jess,' Grace said, as she stood with Matt, the rescue team gathering around them now. 'There's one of Harry's beanie hats in the Land Rover, so I've given her a good sniff of it. I know she's not a trained search and rescue dog, but if he's out there and within a thousand yards of where she is, she'll sniff him out, you can be sure of it.'

'Well, don't let her go leading you off and away from the rest of the team,' Matt said, saying it more for those closest to them to hear, than for Grace's benefit; he wanted them to know that Grace was going to be following the same rules as everyone else, and that she was being kept an eye on as well. 'I'd not usually have someone close to the one we're searching for along with us, like, but you're different, for obvious reasons.' Then he added with a wry smile and a wink, 'Do what you're told, though, yes?'

'I will,' Grace said, returning the smile and wink warmly. 'I just want him found, Matt, that's all.'

'Well, that's why we're all here, isn't it?' Matt agreed, but said nothing more, because he had a sense that anything he would say could easily be taken the wrong way. Be too positive, and it was easy to come across as insincere, but if you're not positive, then it can easily sound as if you've already given up. Which he hadn't, and never would, either, but that was just the way of things; words were easy to misinterpret, whereas, in situations like this, actions really did speak so much louder.

Leaving Grace to stand on her own for a few minutes, Matt walked over to chat with a small number of the rescue team, and gave a nod to Jadyn, Dave, and Jen, who had now all turned up as well to join in the search.

'Jim's on his way,' Jadyn said, as Matt went past.

'He is? But he's not working today.'

Jim was now part-time, sharing his working week between life as a PCSO and managing the farm with his parents. Everyone knew that at some point, the farm would hold sway, and Jim would stop being a PCSO for good. It was where he belonged, after all, thought Matt.

'Oh, there was no arguing with him,' said Jen, leaning over to join in. 'And I had to pretty much nail Liz's feet to the office floor to have her stay there as a point of contact.'

Matt thought about that for a moment, glanced around at the rest of the team.

'Something on your mind?' Dave asked.

'There is,' said Matt, and looked back at Jen. 'Call Liz, tell her to get kitted up and out here as soon as she can. And apologise for the confused messages as well. We don't want Ben, though; I need people with experience of being out on the hill at night. He'd be keen, I'm sure, possibly too keen, and next, we'd be having to have him stretchered off with a twisted ankle or worse.'

'Will do.'

'The office can look after itself for tonight, I think, don't you? Liz is more use here, especially with how what we're dealing with doesn't make sense, with Harry's Rav here, but as far as we know, and as I've said, he was actually heading up to Beckermonds with Smudge.'

With that agreed, Matt left the team to talk amongst themselves.

By the time Liz had skidded up alongside Harry's Rav on her motorbike, and Jim had arrived in yet another old Land Rover, and with his dog, Fly, beside him, the search had been organised, and everyone was heading off to their designated areas. Liz had arrived with a passenger, one Matt wasn't entirely unsurprised to see, despite his request.

'Now then, Ben,' he said, as Liz walked over with Harry's younger brother beside her.

Liz gave a shrug, rolled her eyes.

'Couldn't really keep it a secret, could I?'

'Didn't expect you to, either,' said Matt, and looked to Ben, seeing stark worry drawing lines on his face. He wondered about sending him straight home again, but knew there was little chance of him listening. 'You okay, lad?'

'I'm better joining in than not,' Ben replied. 'I was out when Liz called, rushed back. Harry's not the kind of person who just disappears, is he?'

'No, he's not,' Matt agreed, 'but before any of us start jumping to wild conclusions, I think it best if we just work this like a normal missing persons case.'

'Harry's not a normal missing person, though, is he?'

'No, Ben, he's not, but then he's not really normal anything, is he?'

Matt couldn't think of a single reason for Harry to have said he was going to one place to then end up somewhere else entirely. And if that wasn't weird enough to begin with, the fact that he wasn't with his vehicle was even more confusing. Had he just abandoned it? And if so, why? There seemed to be nothing wrong with it, though that was hard to tell, as he had no key to start the engine. But a walk around it had shown him nothing out of the ordinary. So, what the hell had caused Harry to leave it? Made no sense at all. Nothing did.

As for tying Harry's possible whereabouts to a specific location beyond where he'd told those three farmers he was going with Smudge, and where the Rav had been found, well that was next impossible, which was why Matt had decided to get Liz over in the end, rather than leave her alone in the office.

Matt felt rather ill at ease considering how little they knew, not that he was going to let that show to anyone, especially the likes of Ben or Grace. What they did know was where Harry had last been seen, where he'd said he was going, and where his vehicle had been found. That gave the rescue team a huge area to cover, but at least they had something to go on.

Grace had actually bought a spare set of keys with her for the Rav, and Matt had grabbed a quick look around the vehicle, but found nothing to suggest where Harry might have gone, or why. The whole thing was a mystery.

With the whole team now at his disposal, and Grace and Ben to boot, Matt had decided to put them to use beyond just walking the moors. Grace and Jess were good for that, and Jadyn, too, seeing as he was a member of the rescue team. After a quick one-to-one with Ben, where he explained just how important it was that he went steady, and didn't go rushing off and getting himself injured, he paired him up with an experienced member of the team, who welcomed him warmly. The other three, he gave specific tasks.

'We've enough boots on the ground for the general search,' he explained, 'so if it's all the same with you, I'm going to make use of you beyond looking, and tap into your actual skill set. Understood?'

There were no complaints from anyone, just attentive faces waiting for their orders.

'Jen, I want you and Dave knocking doors. And you as well, Jim, okay? That way we cover ground a lot quicker; not just with the physical search for Harry, but by getting the news out that he's missing. I want every single person and their dog up and down Wharfedale, keeping an eye out for him. None of us can think of a single reason for him going missing; could be that he's ill, could be that he's fallen while out with Smudge, who knows? But the more folk who know that he's out there, the better chance we have of finding him.'

'You're worried, aren't you?' Liz said, as Matt turned from Jen, Dave, and Jim, to her.

'I'm trying to not be, but I'm not doing a very good job. I know this could be an accident, something quite simple, but …' He shook his head. 'How's Ben, really? I mean, he seems fine right now, but my guess is he's not.'

Liz said, 'Actually, I think this will do him good. He's not been himself these last few days, distant, you know? Snappy. My guess is that work is busy, something like that, anyway.'

'Well, I've put him with Gary, so he'll be well looked after, that's for sure.'

'So, what about me, then?' Liz asked. 'What do you want me to do?'

'That motorbike of yours,' Matt said, nodding at it. 'It's as good off-road as it is on, as are you as a rider. That's why I called you over. We've Harry's Rav here, but we've also been told he was heading to Beckermonds, as you know.'

'You want me to go have a ride up that way, see if I can spot anything?'

'I do. We need to have eyes on that area as well as here, just to make sure.'

'He can't be up that way, though, can he? Otherwise, how

did the Rav get here? Beckermonds is what, five miles away from where we are now? So that means he must've driven it here afterwards, doesn't it?' Liz stopped, frowned. 'Unless someone moved it, right? Though why would anyone do that?'

'I'm just exploring all the options,' said Matt. 'I'll be sending a team that way as well, but you're faster on that bike, and you can cover a hell of a lot more ground. Get yourself up there now, if you could, and have a good old scout of the place. No point in you waiting around. Then, when you're done, report back to me. After that, you can head up Gilbert Lane, then start buzzing the lanes and trails; this whole area is riddled with them. I'm not saying you'll find anything, but maybe you will.'

'I'll be eagle-eyed, I promise.'

'I'm covering all bases here, Liz, but don't go riding around like a lunatic; I can't be dealing with you getting injured as well. I was at school with a lad who lived up that way, who was a keen trail bike rider. I lost count of the number of accidents he had. So, do us all a favour, and take it easy, and go safe, you hear?'

Liz patted the top of the helmet she was carrying and smiled.

'When do I ever do anything else, Matt?'

7

Despite his predicament, Harry was surprisingly comfortable. As damp alcoves went, his prison wasn't too bad, all in all. He'd certainly been in worse places, and in worse scrapes for that matter, which perhaps wasn't saying much, considering some of what he'd done in his life, both in the Police as well as the Paras.

The gloopy light from the small lamp was doing its best to keep the darkness at bay, and the bed and sleeping bag at least afforded him some comfort and warmth. He'd yet to take advantage of those, beyond sitting down to rub the blood back into his hands and feet having freed them; the cool air of the place hadn't yet managed to seep through his clothes to his skin, but when it did, he knew he would welcome the warmth of the sleeping bag.

None of this meant that Harry was going to just sit there and accept his predicament, however. Far from it. He was locked inside a hole down a mine, not banged up in solitary in a high-security incarceration facility. And that meant he was going to do his all to get the hell out.

Having walked around what he was now referring to as his cell at least a dozen times, Harry had found little that would be of use in fermenting an escape plan. He certainly couldn't dig himself out; he didn't have time for that for a start, never mind the fact that the walls were rock and he was deep underground. As for the chain and padlock, he'd wasted no time in having a closer look; their size and strength more than apparent when he'd first laid eyes on them.

The metal bars he was trapped behind were as old as the mining cart he'd used to saw through his bonds. At first, he'd wondered why such a place would exist down a mine, but then he'd found evidence which told him why; in one of the many jagged corners of the small cavern, Harry had seen something sticking up out of the muck on the ground, and given it a kick. Dislodging it, he'd then recovered a single horseshoe.

It sat in his hand now, and its small size told Harry enough; this alcove had been an underground stable for ponies that had worked down in the pit, pulling carts to the surface, perhaps even to power pumps and other machinery. Harry had scant knowledge of the mining history of the Dales, but finding that small horseshoe was, for whatever reason, oddly comforting. So, he pocketed it, a little keepsake of what was already one of the more bizarre episodes of his life. It might even give him a little bit of good luck, he thought, tapping the pocket.

With little else he could do for the moment, Harry decided that a lie down might be for the best. Though he wasn't cold as yet, the sleeping bag was rather inviting, so he kicked off his shoes, unzipped the bag, and slipped inside. To his surprise, he found something stuffed deep inside, which had managed to remain hidden by the bag's soft folds. Reaching for it, he removed a carrier bag, inside which was a selection of squashed items from Cockett's bakery, and a haphazard collection of other snacks. Though he couldn't be absolutely sure of that fact, the smell alone was enough of a giveaway; he'd been left a steak pie, the best in the country if not the world, a couple of pork pies, and some of that famous fruitcake, one he could probably recognise blindfolded.

Tucked up in the sleeping bag, Harry decided that a bit of food would do him good. He would ration it, though, as he had no idea at all when his captor would be back. He was confident that they would be, however, because why else was he being so well looked after? And that sent his mind back to the way he'd been tied up; securely, yes, but not to the point of making escape impossible. The knot had been a bugger to begin with, but as he'd rubbed the rope away at the edge of the mining cart, it had loosened quickly, and he'd been free. The rope at his ankles had been much less of a bother. It was all very odd.

Sorting through the food, Harry put to one side the crisps and chocolate bars, noting that there was one whole packet of Tunnock's Caramel Wafers, a favourite of his since moving to the Dales, something he'd pretty much kept to himself. Yes, folk knew he liked them, but just how much? Well, that was private, wasn't it? And Harry wasn't one for sharing something so personal, except with his nearest and dearest. Anyway, he would save all that until later, because for now, the steak pie was calling.

Biting into it, and once again astonished by just how damned tasty such a thing could be, Harry decided to turn his mind to trying to work out a reason for his incarceration. Escaping was obviously on his mind as well, but that required a little more thought and planning, and he had to consider how he could use his jailer in that process as well. Not knowing who they were or why they'd abducted and imprisoned him was frustrating. However, if he could narrow things down a bit, prepare himself for the visit he was absolutely sure would happen sooner or later, then he might be in a better position to do a little bit of verbal persuasion.

Tucking into the pie, and drinking some of the water that had also been provided, Harry started to think back to anything over the last few days and weeks that would give him some hint as to the how and why of what had happened. And he came up blank. Things had been relatively quiet of late, with the Dales' summer tumbling quietly towards autumn, beneath skies brushed with clouds placed there by a hidden artist's hand.

The roads had been busy with tourists, the hills dotted with brightly coloured spots of colour as wandering walkers explored them. Cafes, shops, and pubs had bristled with business, and every local tourist attraction had been overrun with visitors from far and wide desperate to take selfies, their backdrop the haunting beauty of a castle, the soft chatter of a waterfall, the strangely damning glare of sheep. But in all of that, nothing caught Harry's attention as something that would have led to him waking up in an underground stable.

With that conclusion drawn, Harry stretched back further, leaving the summer behind, and walking his mind back through the year, then further still, into days long gone, and his life before he'd settled in the Dales.

Over the years, he'd been face-to-face with the worst of humanity, of that he had no doubt. Put a good number of them behind bars as well, though not nearly enough of them, and that always played on his mind. Was that what this was about? Was it some historic vendetta by an old adversary? If so, why now, and why here? No, that didn't make sense either.

Frustrated, and more out of habit than anything, Harry went to grab his phone from a pocket, to find that it was missing, because of course it was. It would've been no use at all where he was, but he'd rather fancied playing one of the mindless games he'd downloaded on it, just to kill the time a little.

Finishing off the pie, and ignoring his irritation at the absence of his phone, Harry sat himself back up, shook his head and rubbed his eyes, then sucked in a sharp breath. He held it just long enough as he realised something. Worry, for the first time, reached its thin, bony fingers around his gut, and gave it a painful squeeze; Grace had no idea where he was, and Smudge, the best four-legged friend he could ever wish for, had been with him when he'd been taken, so where was she now?

8

Matt was halfway to nowhere and fighting a tightening knot of worry in his gut, when a call came through on the radio from Gary Chapman, the member of the search party he'd sent off with Harry's brother, Ben. The news was good; Smudge had been found.

'What? Where?'

'Old barn, just up the edge of Crook Gill,' came Gary's reply. Matt knew roughly where Gary was talking about, and it wasn't too far from where Harry's Rav was parked either, so that was something. 'Poor little bugger, being left like that. To say she was pleased to see us is an understatement. Won't leave Ben alone.'

'She's okay, though?'

'Aye, she's fine, like. Whoever put her in there and tied her to the wall cared enough to leave her with water, and there's a good amount of dry hay in there, too, so she wasn't cold. Scared more than anything, if you ask me, and more than a little confused. What do you want me to do?'

Matt wasn't sure. The discovery of Harry's faithful dog, Smudge, tied up in a barn, was on the one hand a good sign. She was alive and well, and judging by what Gary had just told him, she'd been taken care of by someone, but by whom? Harry? If so, why would he go and leave Smudge in a barn, then vanish? The simple fact was, he wouldn't. And that begged the question, if it hadn't been Harry, then who?

Matt stopped his thoughts from spiralling and asked, 'Is there any sign or clue, anything at all that might tell us where Harry is?'

'Not that we can see,' said Gary. 'Ben? You see anything?'

There was a pause, and Matt heard Ben's muffled reply to Gary's question, but couldn't make out any words.

'No, it's just a barn, Matt, that's it, really,' said Gary. 'Smudge is fine, and getting happier by the minute now.'

'So, where the hell is Harry, then?' Matt asked, his voice raised to almost a shout. 'Why's he not with Smudge, Gary? No, scrap that, why's Smudge not with Harry, because she should be, shouldn't she? He's not one for leaving his dog anywhere he's not coming back to sharpish, and then it's usually the Rav, so why wasn't she there?'

'You think he tied her up in the barn and went walkabout?'

'Of course I bloody well don't, because why would he?' Matt replied, a little angrier than he'd meant to sound, but that was the truth of it, wasn't it? Why would Harry do anything like that? Answer: he wouldn't! Smudge never left his side; the suggestion that Harry would tie her up in a barn and just bugger off was patently ridiculous.

'Then who did?' Gary asked.

Matt answered that question with another question.

'You're sure there's no sign there of where Harry might be, where he could've gone? You're positive, Gary; nothing at all?'

'Honestly, Matt, there's nowt. This is just a barn, that's all. Smudge is fine, and whoever left her here obviously wanted to make sure she was alright, didn't they? So, it must've been Harry, surely?'

'But what if you hadn't found her, Gary? What then?'

'Yeah, that thought had crossed my mind as well,' Gary replied. 'She was lucky Ben heard her whining above this wind, because it's fairly picking up at the moment, isn't it? I can barely hear myself think.'

There were no sensible answers to any of this, Matt thought.

'Put Ben on for a mo'.'

There was a rustling sound as Gary handed the phone over to Ben.

'Matt?'

'Now then, Ben; how are you doing?'

'I'm happy I heard Smudge,' Ben said, 'but it's only made me more worried, to be honest; where's Harry? He'd not leave her here, would he? Which means someone else did.'

'Exactly what I was thinking, and what I've just said to Gary,' Matt agreed. 'How does Smudge seem to you?'

'Like Gary just said, happy to see me. She was properly confused, being left here on her own, and she's not easy to separate from Harry, is she?'

That was a good point, thought Matt.

'No, she's not,' he said. 'Happy with those she knows, but usually a bit wary.'

'I think they knew she would be found,' said Ben. 'That's why she was left here, all comfortable, because she wouldn't be alone for long, and they wanted her to be okay.'

Matt hadn't considered that, but then another thought crossed his mind, expanding on what Ben had just suggested; what if they knew that a search would be organised and

Smudge would be found as part of it? But why do that in the first place? Nothing was adding up.

'Well done for hearing her,' he said, avoiding saying anything more because he didn't want Ben overthinking where his older brother was and what might have happened to him. He then added, 'I think we should take this as a good sign, the fact that Smudge is fine, don't you, Ben? If his dog's okay, it suggests Harry is as well, wherever he is.'

Ben stayed quiet.

'Put Gary back on, Ben, if you could?'

Gary came on the line.

'We'll carry on with the search, then, right, Matt? '

'Harry's somewhere, isn't he, so there's not much else we can do, right now, is there?'

'Not really, no.'

Call over, Matt took a moment to think through what he now knew. He didn't believe for a moment that Harry had left Smudge in a barn. That notion made no sense whatsoever. If he was going to leave the dog anywhere, then they would've found her curled up in his Rav, that was for sure. A barn? No chance. But why this barn and not one along past Beckermonds, where he'd had said he was going? What the hell had happened to him?

The answer was glaring and terrifying, and one that Matt really didn't want to give any thought to, because to do so would make it real, but what choice did he have? Someone had, for whatever reason, taken Harry. Whoever it was, they'd left Smudge in the barn for some reason, either to come back for her, or because they knew a search would be sent out for Harry, branching out from where his vehicle had been found, and therefore, Smudge would've been discovered as well.

The whole situation struck Matt as very, very odd. Harry had disappeared, but his dog had been found safe and well. If all they'd cared about was snatching Harry, then they'd have not cared what happened to Smudge, would probably have let her loose to end up wandering the fells then scratching at someone's door.

With dawn soon approaching, Matt had a sick feeling in his stomach from the thought that he very much doubted anyone would be finding Harry, not today at any rate. He wasn't lost wandering the fells, there had been no accident that had left their beloved, gruff DCI swearing in a dell somewhere waiting to be found. No. This was not a normal missing persons case at all; Harry, Matt knew in the very marrow of his bones, had been abducted.

MEANWHILE, with Jess by her side, Grace was keeping her eyes peeled, trying to spot anything that might be a sign as to where Harry might be, when a call came in from Ben. No sooner had it finished, Matt had rung her as well.

'I've heard,' she said, before Matt had a chance to even get a word out. 'Ben's already told me about Smudge. That's good news, isn't it?'

'Well, she's fine, so yes,' Matt said. 'Whoever left her in the barn made sure she was warm and had water.'

'That's something, then.'

'It is, Grace, yes, of course it is, but ...'

Matt's voice died.

'But what, Matt?' Grace asked.

'What? Oh, it's nothing.'

Grace didn't believe that for a second.

'You were going to say something, and don't pretend that you weren't, either.'

A brief pause, then, 'Look, Grace, I can't—'

'Yes, you can,' said Grace, her voice firm. 'Don't go

keeping me in the dark about things, you hear? I won't like it, and I don't think Harry would, either.'

There was a pause as Matt took a moment to decide on what he was going to say next.

'Look, Grace,' he said at last, 'if Smudge has been looked after, then that's a good sign, isn't it? It has to be. It can't be anything else.'

'Yes, but why was she looked after like that? Why was she safe in a barn, but with Harry nowhere to be found? What are you thinking, Matt? You need to tell me. Don't keep me in the dark.'

Another pause, then Matt said, 'I know we're all out here searching for a lost or injured Harry, but finding Smudge, it's got me to thinking that's probably not what we're dealing with.'

'Then what are we dealing with, Matt?'

'Grace ...'

Grace nearly shouted down the phone in reply.

'Matt, please, just tell me, will you? You can't hide stuff from me, not with this! You just can't!'

Matt hesitated, pulled both by his responsibility as a police officer, and as a friend. Eventually, he said, 'I've not even spoken to the team about this. And I need to chat with the DSupt as well. Until I have, I can't be talking about it with you, Grace, I just can't; it's more than my job's worth. I hope you can understand that.'

'You seem to be confusing me with someone who gives a damn about any of that,' Grace snapped back. 'Harry is my only concern, Matt. Nothing else. So, please, just tell me what you're thinking. I'm not about to have a breakdown out on the hill, trust me. Whatever's happened, I know Harry can look after himself, we all do, so get to the bloody point!'

Grace heard Matt take a deep breath, then exhale slowly, clearly preparing himself for what he was about to tell her.

'I think someone's taken Harry.'

Grace couldn't help but respect the man for telling her and stayed quiet to allow Matt the space to keep talking. She knew it would've gone against every fibre of his being to tell her.

'I know that's a jump to make, Grace, trust me, I really do, but they've made sure Smudge is fine, haven't they? So, why do that, if—'

'If they want to harm Harry,' said Grace, cutting in. 'Right? That's what you were going to say, wasn't it?' She didn't allow Matt time to answer, and said, 'But why take him in the first place?'

'I don't have an answer to that,' said Matt. 'They want him for some reason, but my gut's telling me it's not to do him any harm, and that's the only reason I'm telling you this. And I know you want to know more, and rightly so, too, but from here on in, I kind of need to get the team onto things. I think this is rapidly turning from a missing persons case into something more criminal, and with you being a civilian ...'

'I'm not just a civilian, Matt, I'm Harry's girlfriend! No, I'm more than that, aren't I? We live together, we're planning a future together, I'm his partner!'

Grace immediately regretted the anger she used to spit out those words, but left them hanging anyway.

'And you're a friend, so don't you go forgetting that bit, either,' said Matt. 'I'll keep you up to date on things, I promise, but only when I can, and with what I'm allowed to. You understand that, right?'

'I do, of course I do,' said Grace. 'But—'

'No, Grace, there are no buts,' said Matt. 'Not with this, there can't be. You coming out to help with the search, that's fine, because at that point, we all thought Harry was just lost somewhere, didn't we? But with discovering Smudge, there's no way any of us can think that, is there? And this is a police officer we're talking about, remember that.'

'What's that supposed to mean?'

'It means,' said Matt, 'that as soon as the press gets a hold of this, everyone's going to know about it, aren't they? Do you really want to be dealing with that, those vultures knocking at your door, waiting for you round every corner, asking you questions, taking photographs, making stuff up just to get a headline?'

'Maybe that's the point, then?' Grace suggested. 'What if whoever's taken Harry has done so because they want to be noticed? I've no idea what for, but it's possible, isn't it?'

Matt's answer ignored what Grace was suggesting as he said, 'I'm going to let the search run 'til it turns light, just in case anyone finds anything or spots anything of use. After that, well, we'll just have to see, won't we?'

Grace stared out across the moors and saw a thin blade of light cutting a line between the horizon and the sky. Day was approaching, and soon the sun would be staring down.

'Thanks, Matt,' she said, and that was that.

Dropping to her knees, Grace took Jess's warm, furry face between her cold hands and kissed the dog in the soft dip between her eyes.

'He's okay, isn't he, Jess? We both know that, because we both know Harry.'

Jess's answer was a wag of her tail as she then pulled herself from Grace's grip, and got back to trying to sniff out Harry's scent.

9

Matt kept the search going for longer than he'd planned to, letting dawn break to the sound of curlew and buzzard on the wing, and the ever-present bleat of the sheep, which dotted the hills and fields like stubborn patches of ice and snow. He would've kept it going longer, too, but common sense prevailed, and after a chat with various other members of the rescue team, decided enough was enough, that it was time to send everyone home and have a rethink.

They'd found no hint of Harry's whereabouts other than his abandoned vehicle and the very confused Smudge, and there was no sign of him along past Beckmonds either. On the one hand, that wasn't much to be going on with at all, but on the other, he could only think that it was a positive, and would continue to do so, regardless. At least they'd not found a body, he thought, dark thoughts burning bright in his mind suddenly, only for him to extinguish them in an instant. No way was he going to allow any such notion to cloud his judgement; he needed a clear mind to work out what to do next.

With the search over, he'd then called in the Scene of Crime team. There was no need to involve either the pathologist, Rebecca Sowerby, or her mum, Margaret Shaw, who was also the district surgeon. There was no body for them to be dealing with, so they could rest easy for now, and Matt very much hoped things would stay that way; such a call was not one he would ever want to make, and just the thought of it was enough to make his heart stop.

With both Harry's Rav and the barn now classed as crime scenes, he needed them looked over properly, and no one did that better than the people in the white paper suits. He was duly concerned that both sites would have been disturbed too much by the search, but that was just the way of things; they'd set out thinking they were looking for a lost or injured Harry. Now though, with Smudge found, and no sign of Harry, Matt knew something else was going on here, something considerably more sinister. What, though, he had no idea.

Having given himself and the team enough of a break between the end of the search and everyone meeting up again back at the office, Matt was sitting in a chair, absolutely exhausted. The rest of the team was there as well, and they all looked in much the same state; weariness scratched into their faces, but eyes wide with an alertness so sharp it pierced their exhaustion and gave it little chance to envelop them.

Afternoon was already pushing on. Matt had done his best to get some shut-eye in the hours between the SOC team arriving and then making his way back into Hawes from home, but sleep had eluded him. He must've had some, he felt sure, but regardless, it had clearly not been enough, not by a long shot.

'Tea?'

Rubbing his eyes as a yawn broke through, Matt looked

up from where he was sitting to see Liz staring down at him, a huge mug held out in front of her.

'Thanks,' he said, and took the offered drink.

'Dave's just popped along to the Penny Garth; seems to think what we all need is a couple of bacon butties each.'

'He's not wrong.'

'No, he isn't. But then he rarely is about something like that. Some would argue, he's an expert in that area.'

Liz sat down beside Matt as he sipped his drink. She was nursing her own steaming mug, while Jen, Jadyn, and Jim talked in weary tones over by the radiator, with Fly sound asleep at their feet. Smudge had headed back with Grace and Jess; Grace, like Ben, had taken a little bit of persuading to not come into the office, but Matt had managed to help them both understand that it was best for them to be home now, and to get some rest, because they would be no use to anyone exhausted. Mind you, neither would any of them, he thought, so that was something he needed to deal with once Dave returned.

Matt was halfway through his mug of tea when the larger-than-life PCSO returned from the Penny Garth Cafe.

'Food!' he announced, crashing through the office door with an armful of white, grease-spotted, paper bags.

The announcement was met with sleepy enthusiasm, everyone hungry, but almost too tired to close the distance between where they were and the offered sustenance.

Dave proceeded to walk around the office delivering his wares.

'Thanks,' said Matt, taking one of the bags.

'Can't think on an empty stomach,' said Dave.

'Wise words.'

'The most wise, I think you'll find.'

'Says the man who keeps goats for a hobby.'

'Funny you should say that, seeing as they're also very wise. In fact, many would regard them as the wisest of all the creatures on God's green earth.'

Matt frowned at that.

'Goats? Wise?'

'That's why they have those little beards,' said Dave, pointing at his own chin. 'Just so they have something to stroke with their hooves when pondering something important.'

Despite everything that was going on, Matt somehow laughed, and Dave joined in with a playful wink.

Silence settled in the office then, as everyone tucked into their butties, with Fly enjoying a few offered bits of bacon fat from Jim.

Once everyone had finished eating, Matt called them all over and they gathered about him, sitting in a half circle on their chairs.

'First, well done, everyone, for last night,' he began. 'I know you're all knackered, but we've a job to do, haven't we, so we'd best get on with it.'

Those last few words were swamped by a yawn so large that Matt's jaw almost locked in place while he was speaking.

'Sorry about that.'

'What now, then, Boss?' Jadyn asked, his own words riding an escaping yawn as well.

Then everyone was yawning, a swift epidemic sweeping through them with a voracious appetite.

'That's the question that's bothering me,' Matt replied. 'And my tired brain isn't helping none, either.'

'Maybe if I get the pens out,' Jadyn suggested. 'Might help everyone to get a few things down?'

'There's not much, though, is there?'

While Jadyn did as he'd just suggested, Matt had a quiet

word with himself to sound considerably more positive than he had just then. Regardless of how he felt, the team was looking to him, not just for leadership, but reassurance.

With the young constable now poised with pen in hand, Matt thought back over what had happened, what they knew, but decided it was better to give the floor to the team, rather than just take over.

'So, what do we know?'

'Harry's missing,' said Jadyn, which everyone knew was stating the blatantly obvious, but he wrote the DCI's name on the board anyway.

And fair enough, too, thought Matt, because seeing the name there made the situation real.

As Jadyn's pen squeaked against the board, Jen said, 'Last seen over in Wharfedale by three farmers, Tom Sykes, James Horner, and Tina Hodgson. Jadyn spoke with Tom yesterday, and we need to pop out for a face-to-face, but I managed to get a call through to James, and he really only confirmed what he'd said to you, Matt.'

'Which was?' Matt asked, willing his brain into gear, as right then, it just seemed to be coasting along in neutral.

'There was nothing that he could recall that any of them noticed that would make them think something was up with Harry,' Jen explained.

'You asked, then?'

'I did. Not explicitly, like. I mean, I didn't say, *So, was Harry acting funny, and was he being followed?* or anything like that. Just asked general questions, and it was clear that when they met with him, everything was fine.'

'Nothing's ever clear from just a phone call,' said Matt. 'So, you're right, we need a face-to-face with them all. What were the specifics?'

'As we all now know, Harry said he was off along to Beckermonds with Smudge to give her a good walk at the end of the day before heading back home. Tom was adamant, however, that there was no mention by Harry of him going anywhere near Cray. It was Beckermonds, then home to Grace. That was it.'

Matt opened the question out to the others.

'Anything else on Harry's last known movements?'

'Not a thing,' said Jim, and Dave gave that a firm nod of agreement. 'We knocked on every door we could, but no one's seen him. It's like he's just vanished, which he hasn't because that's impossible, but it's still really odd, isn't it? I keep thinking he's just going to walk in at any minute and tell us to stop making a fuss about nowt.'

Matt then asked, 'What about the farmer who called in about the Rav, Dicky Guy, I think, wasn't it?'

'Yeah, we knocked on his door as well,' said Dave. 'And it's not one I'll be rushing back to knock on it again, that's for sure. Not the friendliest bloke.'

'What did he say?'

'"*You moved that bloody vehicle yet?*" was about the gist of it,' Dave replied, having lowered his voice into a more gruff tone, clearly attempting a loose impression of the farmer. 'I know where we found the Rav wasn't exactly an official lay-by or anything, but even so.'

'Any reason for him to be so grumpy?' Matt asked, though he knew that Dicky Guy never needed a reason. It was just his default setting by all accounts.

'Said he parks his vehicles there if his sheep are in the bottom fields and he's out checking them and he can't be doing with anything getting in the way of that. Though, to be honest, I think he just enjoys being a bit of a git.'

'I might have to go and have a word with him.'

'Rather you than me.'

Matt said, 'Don't suppose he mentioned Harry, did he? Maybe saw him parking the Rav, was waiting for him to come back for it, and when he didn't, he called it in?'

Dave shook his head.

'I asked if he'd seen the driver and he said that if he had, he'd have been over to have a word with them instead of calling it in, which is a fair point. Not that he actually needed to call it in in the first place.'

'Moving on, then,' said Matt. 'Anything from you, Liz?'

Liz gave a shrug, shook her head, which struck Matt as a little out of character. Mind you, she was at home with Ben, wasn't she, so she was probably picking up on his worry as well. He knew that with him and Joan, if one of them felt something, the other soon picked it up as well, to the point where Matt had, just occasionally, wondered if his wonderful wife wasn't also a little bit psychic.

'Nowt to report at all, really,' she said eventually. 'I mean, I'll admit that I had a great time racing around on my bike past Beckermonds and then up Gilbert Lane, or I would've done if it had been for a different reason than any of this. But no, I saw nothing beyond the usual dry-stone walls, sheep, and a few deer. Bumped into a couple of farmers out on their quad bikes once dawn had arrived, and they said they'd keep an eye out. That's it, really; sorry.'

Matt waited to see if she had anything else to say, but she'd already slumped back into her seat. He'd have to keep an eye on her.

'Which brings us to Smudge, I guess.'

'At least she's okay,' said Jim.

'I think we should all take that as a good sign,' Matt agreed. 'There's no reason for whoever's behind this to have been that kind to a dog, so I can only think right now that whatever it is they want Harry for, it's not to harm him, is it?'

Those words silenced the team for a moment.

'You think that's what we're dealing with, then?' asked Jadyn. 'That Harry's been kidnapped?'

That last word sent a chill through the room so harsh that Matt was surprised his breath didn't freeze in midair.

'That's a strong word,' he said, 'but I can't see that abducted or taken are any less so, can you? And yes, that's what I think, but I'd rather keep that within these walls for now, if that's okay with everyone. Last thing we need is the press swooping in on a story about a DCI being snatched ...' He remembered something from earlier that morning, his chat with Grace where he'd mentioned the same, but decided to keep that to himself. 'Right now, our priority is to work out what the hell we do next. We've had the SOC team in, haven't we? And they'll have a report to us soon enough I'm sure on what they have or haven't found at the barn and where we found the Rav.'

'Do you think they'll call us?' Jadyn asked. 'The kidnappers, I mean. That's what they do, isn't it?'

'You mean to ask for a ransom or something?' asked Dave.

'Why else would someone take him?'

Jim asked, 'Who, though? Who would drive all the way up here to kidnap Harry?'

'He's probably made a good few enemies in his lifetime, hasn't he?' suggested Jen. 'I can't think that it's anyone up here though. He's settled in really well, hasn't he? Not so much at the beginning, like, but he's part of the community now. He's not been here long enough to provoke someone like this, surely.'

Matt wasn't so sure about that, and went to join in the discussion, mainly to shut it down; it was a huge leap to take, from Harry going missing to Harry being held for ransom, when there was a sharp knock at the door.

Jen got up and went to answer it. As she opened the door, Matt and the rest of the team saw Grace standing there, with the two dogs, Jess and Smudge, at her heels, both wagging their tails and keen to get inside to see Fly. She looked both tired and wired, Matt thought, like she could drop from exhaustion at any moment, yet at the same time head out to spend the next ten hours walking the fells, looking for Harry. And he had no doubt at all that the idea had crossed her mind and perhaps was why she'd turned up at the office instead.

Grace didn't wait to be invited in, and instead just stepped into the room, as Jen closed the door behind her.

'Sorry.' Grace yawned, and once again, another swift epidemic broke out as everyone tried to hold in a yawn and failed. 'I got a bit restless. I can't sleep, that's for sure, and I don't really know what to do with myself, so I thought I'd just come here. Hope that's okay. I'll not get in the way, I promise.'

She let Jess and Smudge off their leads and the dogs trotted over to wag tails with Fly. Soon they settled into a quiet tumble in the corner of the room.

'Not sure this is the best place for you, though, Grace,' Matt said, concern in his voice. 'You're a civilian, you see, and this is ... Well, I know you're Harry's partner and all, but, like, this is a police matter, isn't it, like I explained last night, and—'

Grace cut across what Matt was trying to say by pulling up a chair and sitting down next to Dave.

Matt cocked his head, stared, but Grace was clearly going nowhere.

'Smudge is missing Harry,' Grace said, as though that was reason enough for her to have turned up. 'This is the first time she's actually left my side since I took her home.'

'We're all missing him,' said Jadyn, then added a little too quickly, 'but I'm sure he's alright, Grace, you know? There's nothing to worry about, I'm sure. This is Harry, right?'

Grace smiled.

'It's not me who should be worrying about him anyway, is it?' she said. 'After all, it's not me who kidnapped him, is it?'

There was an edge to Grace's voice then, Matt noticed, hard and keen and angry.

'How do you mean?' Jadyn asked.

Grace turned to the constable.

'Well, would you like to be the one responsible for keeping Harry locked up somewhere? Can you imagine? Think of the grumbling, the shouting, the swearing! And imagine what he'll be like once he gets out, or we find him, and he then gets a hold of who's responsible.'

'Look, we don't yet know what's happened to Harry,' said Matt, 'so we can't go jumping to conclusions.'

The tone of his voice betrayed what he really thought, though, and Matt could tell no one in that room was accepting any other explanation.

'Maybe not,' said Grace, 'but you didn't call that crime scene team in just for a laugh, did you? Anyway, it's what everyone is saying about what's happened to him, isn't it?'

Her words dropped a stone into Matt's stomach so heavy it nearly punched a hole right through.

'What? How do you mean, it's what everyone's saying?'

'I was chatting to Dad before I came over here,' Grace began, 'and before you say anything, Matt, you need to know that he called me, not the other way around. I've not said a word to anyone about what's happened to Harry.'

There was suddenly a lot Matt felt he wanted to say, but at that moment he decided, for diplomatic reasons, it was probably best not to. Instead, he just gave Grace the floor and waited for her to continue.

'I don't know who Dad heard about it from, not specifically, anyway. He was in Campbell's in Leyburn this morning and he told me that someone came over and asked how I was doing. He'd thought that was an odd thing to ask, so he asked why they were enquiring, and they mentioned to him about Harry, if there was any news, and wasn't it odd that he'd been kidnapped.'

'But we don't know that he has been, do we?' said Matt, somewhat exasperated. 'Right now, it's just one line of inquiry, and we could really do without the rumour being spread because it's not helpful at all.'

Dave said, 'Matt, if it's being talked about in Campbell's, then there's bugger all we can do about it now, like, is there? And you know that as well as any of us.'

'I know,' replied Matt, 'but it's still frustrating, isn't it?'

Jen said, 'Matt, if everyone's talking about it, then maybe someone will spot something or remember something they've seen or heard. You never know, it might play to our advantage.'

Matt turned to look at what Jadyn had written on the board.

'Maybe,' he said. 'And it's not like we've much to go on right now, have we?'

'So, what do we do now?' Grace asked.

Matt wanted to reply with, *Well, for a start, you won't be doing anything, because you're not a police officer or a PCSO*, but instead said, 'My hope is that something will come back from the SOC team, and soon. Until then, we need to run this like any other MISPER.' He looked at Grace as he said the next bit, 'We'll need to have a look around your house.'

'What? Why? It's not me that's done this, is it?'

'I'm not suggesting that it is. However, there might be something there that gives us a clue as to what's happened.'

'Like what?'

'I've no idea,' said Matt. 'We need to start somewhere, and with any missing persons, we always go back to friends, family, the home, the workplace, that kind of thing.'

'We'd also look at social media, phone bills,' added Jen, 'but seeing as Harry has no social media presence at all, and has never been one for long conversations on the phone, I think we can count those out.'

'We'll still see if his phone records come up with anything, though,' said Matt, 'if only to count that out as well. And I'll need to have a good chat with you, Grace, if that's okay. There might be something you've noticed without even realising it, and sometimes that kind of detail comes out with a bit of questioning.'

'But what could I possibly know?' Grace asked, though no one provided an answer.

'I'll contact his old detective superintendent back in Bristol,' said Jen. 'Might be there's something she can tell us.'

'Old enemies, you mean?' said Grace.

'For now, that seems the most likely to me,' said Matt. 'Someone with an old grudge.'

'Who, for some reason, is also an animal lover,' added Liz.

Almost as though on cue, Smudge pushed her way through the group and slouched over to Grace to rest her jaw on her knee.

Grace gave the dog's head a scratch.

'It's alright, we'll find Harry, I promise,' she said, then lifted her eyes to Matt and added, 'Won't we, Matt?'

'Count on it,' Matt replied, and despite how little of the day there was left, started to divvy out tasks to the team.

10

Dicky Guy was having about as good a day as he ever had, which meant not at all. He hated mornings, be they cut through with sunshine, covering the fields in gold like spilled grain, or weighed down beneath sodden clouds, solemn and grey. He hated afternoons, because whatever jobs he'd had planned for the morning invariably waded through lunch with little regard for his grumbling belly, and more often than not, had designs on stealing his evening too. And he hated evenings well enough, without work getting in the way, because his house was cold and damp and untidy, and going to bed simply meant that too soon he'd be up once again to face the same god-awful hell of his existence.

The morning had been trampled all over by a bad-tempered cow that, like the rest of his small herd, was nearing the end of her milk production cycle. She was an old beast, and stubborn, but Dicky hadn't the money to go spending on new stock year on year. Most of his herd were older than he would've liked, but that was the way of things, and he didn't see any way to change it all for the better. He was hanging on by the skin of his teeth, drowning in unpaid invoices and bills, and just hoping, as with every year, that he'd get to the end of it without swallowing the barrels of his trusty old shotgun and pulling the trigger.

The cow had lashed out at him, sending a rear leg into his chest hard enough to have him on his arse. Then, as he'd gone to push himself back up and continue with the job, half wishing the hoof had crushed his chest and killed him, she'd emptied her bladder all over his head. He could still smell the stink of it on his skin, despite heading home once the milking was done to wash and change.

Dicky had farmed alone for decades now, and he'd never been able to push enough to grow things to the point where the money he made was enough to lift him out of drudge and hardship. He couldn't survive on just his dairy herd, and had never been able to fix things enough to increase the number of cows, so he had a small flock of sheep, a good number of hens, had years ago attempted and then failed in brutally tragic fashion to establish a pheasant shoot on his land, and had once even had a go at something considerably more exotic; a couple of pairs of alpacas.

For the life of him, he couldn't remember why he'd ever thought that would be a good idea, though the funny-looking animals had certainly been a draw for those who passed the farm by road or trail. Having spotted this, he'd attempted as best he could to monetise the attraction, tried to offer alpaca rides around a paddock, photographs with them, anything that could justify the oddest of all his purchases. But in the end, he'd had to let them go, mainly thanks to one of them buggering off up the fellside with a small child attached to it, holding on for dear life. That the parents hadn't sued him had been a miracle.

With his morning thusly ruined by a cow's hoof and a couple of gallons of hot piss, Dicky hadn't been in the best of moods come the afternoon and a repair job on a wall round the field out the back. Dry-stone walls were, to his mind, bloody useless. They did their job, there was no denying that, and yes, they looked pretty, but the work involved in keeping on top of them, making sure any holes were stopped up before all his animals made a break for it, was an impossibility. Some farmers, he knew, had the luxury of being able to pay for a couple of lads to come and fix the holes, and rebuild the walls like new.

Not Dicky, though. There was no luxury in his life at all. In fact, the closest thing he did get to anything even touching on comfort was buying Imperial Leather soap. The smell always reminded him of his mum and dad, long gone now, who had farmed the same land he was now the steward of. They had been kind, loving, damned good at what they did, and respected. Dicky had grown up hoping to be the same, but events had conspired against him, and like a tree stood alone on a hilltop to face all weathers, he had become a tortured thing, battered, bent, and bruised. The bright light of love that had shone in the eyes of his parents for each other, their affinity with the land they had worked upon, and the skill and care they had in their farming lives, which seemed to come so easily to them, had eluded Dicky.

While working to repair the hole in the wall, he had pondered the deeply hidden, darker memories behind his gradual decline into the mean-spirited old git he knew that he'd become, and that had only served to darken his mood. And how could it not? He was old now, yet a love now over fifty years old still burned a hole in him when he recalled it, and it angered him that he'd allowed such pain to define him. He guessed that was why he'd been so enraged at finding that detective's vehicle being parked where it was, but sometimes, he just needed something to lash out against, and it had been that, for whatever reason.

Where was she now, Dicky wondered, that girl who'd walked into his life to steal his heart, only to run away with it, years later, and never give it back? What she'd wanted with it, he'd never quite understood, nor been given the chance to ask, thanks to the disappearing act she'd done, not so much leaving as abandoning him, just days before they were due to walk the aisle, and with twins to bring up on his own. He had ruined that as well, hadn't he? In ways even his own pain-obsessed, shrivelled heart could not bear to dwell on, so those memories he left buried; they were for other times, not now, perhaps never. Like his parents, his children too were gone; one for good, the other who knew where?

The wedding rings were somewhere, weren't they? Not the engagement ring, because she'd taken that with her, probably sold it. The rings wouldn't be worth much, he knew that, because when had he ever had much to spend on anything? And why had he kept them? For the same reason he'd held on to the pain, he guessed, because to let go of it was to let go of her, and he'd never been able to.

What a fool. Not just for letting the bitterness hack at him like a chisel in the hands of a vengeful stonemason, but for putting all the blame on her, when deep down, he knew he had driven her away. And maybe that was why he'd carried the pain of it all these years, he thought. No, there was no maybe; that was exactly why. Incapable of accepting the part he had played, Dicky knew he'd placed all the blame on her, hoping that in doing so, it would crush the memory. The opposite though had happened, and the memory had burned into his mind as a permanent reminder of what he'd done, not only to himself, but to the family he'd loved, reminding him as well how he'd so utterly failed his own children, a punishment considerably less than the one he knew he truly deserved.

With the ache in his back now the white-hot pain of being stabbed with a poker drawn from a blacksmith's furnace, Dicky rested a while, trying to stretch himself out a little. He heard bones crack, felt some slight relief, and sat himself down on the edge of a water trough he'd had installed goodness knew when for his cows.

Reaching down for a battered and beaten flask from which he would pour not only tea, but another memory—his fiancé's firm belief in tea being the salve to any problem—a cool wind caught Dicky sharp. He gave a shiver, his eyes catching sight of a figure walking along the footpath across his fields. Their stride was purposeful, determined, and Dicky wondered what it would be like to have time so freely available to go wasting it on nothing more than a stroll.

The figure raised a hand in a wave, and to his surprise, Dicky found himself returning it. Then the figure was gone, the path ducking behind a distant spinney where the decaying remains of decades-old pheasant pens lay quiet beneath branch and bow. He hadn't ventured in there in years, never would either. Just couldn't bear it, what with everything else that lay beneath the heavy creaking bows.

With just about enough of the day left to leave him no option but to continue fixing the hole in the wall, and with a tepid cup of tea drunk, Dicky forced himself to his feet and got back on with the mind-numbing task of placing stone upon stone upon sodding stone. He would continue until the hole was filled, or nightfall prevented such, and then back home he would trudge.

The thought crossed his mind to get in touch with a couple of old mates of his, Alan and Brian. They'd not spoken in years, true, but so far as he could recall, they'd loved this kind of work, hadn't they? Mind, they were builders, after all, so that made sense enough. Not that they'd ever take on the job, earning so much more running that building firm of theirs, as they had done for decades. He also wondered if they shot still, because Alan had been able to knock anything out of the sky, and Brian hadn't been too shabby at it himself, either. He doubted they did, and pushed away the creeping thought that threatened to engulf him, as it had engulfed them all that tragic day.

Thinking ahead to the evening, Dicky knew that it held little in the way of a warm embrace for him; a supper of corned beef and onion sandwiches washed down with a very cheap beer, sat in front of an old television set, watching he knew not what. There would be no fire again, just a thick wool blanket, because he'd not fetched any wood from the other small woodland on his land, and he didn't have the money to buy a good bag of it, dry and ready to burn.

Dicky placed a particularly large stone on the wall, his muscles straining with the effort, only to feel a snake slip around his neck. Then he was jerked backwards with such force and violence, his feet left the ground. But, of course, it wasn't a snake, Dicky realised, as he snatched at the arm choking him, crushing his throat, trying to gain some purchase.

His own weight at last played in his favour, and Dicky was back on the ground, but he was being dragged backwards, though where or why, he couldn't guess. A sharp prick in the side of his neck barely registered, as he tried to push himself into his attacker, to unbalance them, knock them off their feet, but instead his old rubber boots just slipped in the grass. With that not working, he moved on to twisting and turning, desperate to wrench himself from the grip so tight now that he was beginning to see stars, needed to breathe, but couldn't. Then, in one sudden moment of shocking violence, he was yanked over onto his front and there he saw where he had been dragged, as the water trough yawned in welcome and the water embraced his gasp.

Pushed beneath the ripples, Dicky was surprised to find that despite the panic, and the abject horror of cool water gushing into his lungs, the only thing he could really think of was the reflection he had caught in the surface of the water, the brief moment before he had been plunged through it, shattering it into a million pieces.

Unconsciousness had come quickly then, and death had followed soon after, Dicky's legs quivering with the last throws of life, as his bladder and bowels relaxed and emptied themselves. The last thing to cross his mind, as the ferryman had approached to guide him into death's final darkness, was that in that reflection, he'd recognised the eyes that had stared back at him. Then, death took him, and Dicky embraced it, relieved that at last, justice had been done.

11

By the time Matt had gone through who was doing what, there wasn't enough of the day left for anything useful to be done. Jen had contacted Harry's previous commanding officer, Detective Superintendent Firbank, down in Bristol, and left a message to say she'd be in touch the following day. There was no point chasing the SOC team for anything, because they'd only just be getting to what they'd found at both sites, and he'd just have to hope for the moment that they'd get something to him sooner rather than later.

A request for Harry's phone records hadn't been needed, because, thanks to Harry not giving two hoots about anything like that, Grace had access to his private account. She'd had to log in for him not too long ago, because he'd never managed to set up a direct debit to pay his monthly bill, and after lots of swearing at his phone, had asked her to sort it out for him. Unsurprisingly, nothing came from that either, with every number recognised, and essentially comprising the team, Ben, Grace, Arthur, and a handful of other numbers easily accounted for.

The three farmers, Tom Sykes, James Horner, and Tina Hodgson, had all been contacted once again, and were happy to meet with someone the following day, though none of them could think why anything they had to say about Harry would be useful.

With all of that done, Matt had been left with a search of both Grace's and Ben's houses, which he had decided to leave till the following day when everyone would be a little more with it. Not that he expected to find anything at either, but still, at least he'd be doing everything by the book. He'd also had enough time before calling it a day to sit down with Grace and have a chat. They went through the days leading up to Harry's disappearance, but Grace was unable to come up with anything that struck her as suspicious or strange. She had noticed no one following Harry, no change in his behaviour, no odd phone calls or people walking past the house; not that they could without being noticed, seeing as where they lived was up a gravel track, their house with a small number of others, huddled together in a field.

The final task of the day had been to call Walker, their own detective superintendent, and on hearing the news, she'd cancelled whatever it was she was in the middle of and driven straight over. Matt had done his best to convince her she didn't need to, but she'd ignored him utterly. On the plus side, she'd not expected him to stick around and wait for her, or to sort out somewhere for her to stay, and had said she would meet with him in the morning; she just wanted to get over straight away in case there were any developments.

With everything sorted, Matt had sent the rest of the team home. He had then said to Walker that if they were to have any chance at finding Harry, and to be prepared for whatever came next from whoever it was that had taken him, they all needed a good night's rest. In light of this, he asked if she could arrange for a couple of Uniforms to be brought in. She'd agreed, made the necessary arrangements, and Matt had left the office happy that they'd all done everything they could so far. All he had to think about now was spending the rest of the evening with his wife, Joan, and daughter, Mary-Anne.

'Evening, Officer.'

The voice took Matt by surprise, mostly because he was almost half asleep and thinking only of getting home.

Having made it halfway across the marketplace to his vehicle, he was tempted to just keep walking, but the fact that he knew the voice was enough to stop him.

'Askew,' Matt said, and forced himself to glance over his shoulder to see the very last person he had any interest in speaking to.

Richard Askew, a local journalist the team had a love-hate relationship with, and which generally leaned more towards the hate side of things, was standing behind him. Pencil-thin, and tall, in the darkness of the evening he reminded Matt of a heron standing patiently by a river waiting for its prey to swim by. A very disconcerting image indeed, and one he pushed away quickly.

'Got a minute?' Askew asked.

'Nope, not even half of one,' Matt replied. 'I'm heading home, and my advice would be to not stand in the way of a man, his family, and the promise of some really good food and a cuddle or two.'

'I know about Harry.'

Matt had suspected exactly as much as soon as he'd heard the man's voice slip into the early evening to ruin what was left of it, but the shock of those words out loud still hit hard.

He closed the distance between them quickly, conscious that he didn't want anyone walking by to overhear them.

'If you know anything at all, it'll be to keep quiet,' Matt said.

'Well, like I said, do you have a minute?'

'No, I don't.'

'You sure about that?'

'Persuade me otherwise, because whatever it is you think that you know, I'd put money on half of it being hearsay, and the other half bullshit.'

That actually made a smile crease the journalist's lips.

'I'll have to remember that one.'

Matt could tell by the way Askew was making no attempt to walk away, that he was either going to have to take the man back to the office for a chat or arrest him; and arresting him was by far the most attractive of the two options. A lot more paperwork, though, and that really would put a dint in his evening.

Without saying a word, Matt gave a nod back up towards the Community Centre where the office was, and led Askew towards it. He let them both in through the main doors, then along to the interview room, making a point of not turning on any of the lights. He knew the way blindfolded, Askew not so much, and the dull gasp of irritation as the journalist tripped over a small bin standing against the wall made him smile, then immediately regret being so petty.

'Here,' Matt said, and quickly flicked on the light, then opened the door to the interview room. 'I've not got long; Joan's cooking tonight, and as far as I'm aware, it's a chicken curry. My advice is to not get between me and the eating of it.'

Askew entered the room, closing the door behind him.

'What are you going to do about it if I do?'

'Not me,' Matt said, sitting down. 'Joan. And don't go

thinking her wheelchair will slow her down when she makes chase; she can't half fly along in that thing when she wants to. Plus, if there's anything to hand along the way to throw at you, she's very, very accurate.'

Askew grabbed a chair and dropped himself into it.

'Right then,' said Matt, eyes now on the journalist. 'You've managed to persuade me that whatever it is you want to tell me isn't going to be a complete waste of my time, so what is it? What do you know about Harry, and why should I care?'

Askew said nothing for a moment or two, and while he remained quiet, he made a big scene out of taking a battered notebook from a pocket, and a well-chewed pencil from another.

'People are talking,' he said eventually, 'and being a journalist, I'd prefer to get the facts straight before I write anything.'

That statement made Matt roar.

'Facts? Really? Come on, Askew, you're having a laugh, aren't you?'

Askew's response was nothing more than a blank stare. 'I know you don't like me, and I can promise you that the feeling's mutual.'

'That's a relief.'

'Isn't it? But then I don't really like anybody. People get in the way. I find them interesting, really, but that's about it. Anyway, I'm not here about you, am I? I'm here about Harry, and, though it will surprise you, I'm sure, I'd like to help.'

Had Matt's mouth been all false teeth, he had no doubt that right then they'd have fallen out.

'I'm sorry, what was that again? And didn't you just say that you don't really like people?'

'I want to help,' Askew repeated.

'Yep, I thought that was what you said. Colour me confused. Go on ...'

'Do you remember when that young couple disappeared from their camper van a while back? They were famous because they'd won the lottery and were big on Instagram because of it and the life they were living?'

Matt shuddered a little at the memory, because that whole investigation had been a horror show, and what they'd uncovered would, he felt sure, haunt him, and possibly the Dales, till the end of his days.

'I do,' he said. 'And what of it?'

'If you recall, Hawes was suddenly rammed with fans and journalists from all over the place, wasn't it? Harry needed a hand to deal with them all, and for a reason he's never given me, he trusted me to handle it. He didn't have to, but he did. And I've never forgotten that.'

'He's a terrible judge of character sometimes.'

'As shown by the company he keeps.'

'Touché.'

'But the fact remains, I'm offering to help. It's that simple.'

'How?' Matt asked.

'Rumour is a terrible thing,' Askew explained. 'It doesn't so much grow, as mutate. And with the little I've already heard and found out, I think it's rather enjoying itself.'

'Go on ...'

'So far, I've heard that Harry's been kidnapped by a London drugs gang, that he's been whisked off into a witness protection programme because of all the undercover work he's done over the years and his life is now in danger, even that someone's snatched him to ship him off to take part in an illegal man vs dog fight. That last one I found particularly amusing.'

'Do you see me laughing?'

'No.'

'Then get to the point.'

'It's about controlling the flow of information,' Askew said. 'Right now, the rumours are ahead of you, aren't they? And they won't be doing anyone any good at all.'

'Why so altruistic all of a sudden?' Matt asked. 'I know you've just explained that Harry trusted you that one time, but even so, this is very suspicious.'

'Believe it or not,' Askew said, 'I actually respect Harry. And before you laugh at that as well, can you think of any reason for me to say that out loud?'

'Not really, no.'

'Here's my suggestion, and you can take or leave it. I know your commanding officer will be down soon. And she'll want to be on top of the flow of information as well. In my experience, in amongst all the noise, you'll often find a thread of something, which, when pulled, leads directly to the cause.'

'I don't understand ...'

'Rumours are useful,' Askew continued. 'Spread enough of them and the truth is hidden.'

Matt realised then what the journalist was saying, thought back to when Grace had turned up at the office and told them what her dad had told her he'd overheard at Campbell's.

'So, what you're suggesting is that what you've heard, some of it, a lot of it perhaps, could've been started by whoever's responsible for—'

'Kidnapping Harry? Yes, that's exactly what I'm suggesting.'

'Bloody hell.'

'All I'm saying is that I'll keep my ears open for anything and everything, okay? I can feedback as often as you want me to, and keep you abreast of any new stories floating around.

Who knows, some of it might be useful in the end. To both of us …'

Matt was, even by his own admission, lost for words.

'I don't know what to say.'

Askew stood up.

'I didn't trust Harry when he arrived here,' he said. 'Figured he'd be a good target, easy to hit, easy to take down. Surely, he'd have a dark past, plenty of dirt for me to dig around in, that kind of thing. A rich seam of stories to mine.'

'And now?'

Askew walked to the door, opened it.

'Oh, believe you me, I've no doubt at all that he's got a dark past, and plenty of dirt for me to go digging in, but I don't want to, not anymore.'

'Why?'

Askew gave a shrug.

'Believe it or not, I don't say this about many, as I'm sure you'll understand, but, if I'm honest? I like the man.'

And with that, he was gone, and Matt was left alone with his own cold, hard disbelief.

12

Matthew Porter loved cheese, which was a good job, really, seeing as he was an artisan cheese maker in the Dales. It wasn't what he'd expected to do, and it certainly wasn't something he'd dreamed of doing since he was a kid. Far from it, in fact.

Back then, when the days had been punctuated by scuffed knees and trying to hit crows with smooth pebbles flung from a homemade catapult, he'd wanted to be everything from a rally car driver, buzzing the tracks worldwide at terrifying speed, to a professional clay shooter, knocking them out of the sky and winning medals. Neither had come to anything in the end, the rally driving because the closest he'd ever got to having a rally car was an old Ford Escort he'd put alloys on and a fat exhaust, and the shooting because it was bloody expensive. Mind you, he'd not shot in years, not since that god-awful accident years ago, but then he wasn't the only one; something like that was bound to stay with you. Still had his gun license, though.

Up early to a late summer's day, Matthew had welcomed

the morning with a coffee and a cigar. It was a morning ritual he enjoyed, and even more so since the divorce. Standing out in the garden, sipping a flat white, and enjoying the woody taste and smell of tobacco was as close to Heaven as he could imagine. The views made it even more so, staring out across the fells, Penhill in the distance.

A flock of geese swept over, honking as they went, and he followed them as they swept down the valley towards the River Ure below. Part of him envied their absolute freedom, though if he was flapping about all day or floating on the river, he'd have no time to make cheese, would he? And that would be no good at all, no matter how relaxing it sounded.

Cigar and coffee done, Matthew grabbed what he needed from the house, locked up, then headed to his car; it was actually a 1971 Mini Van, and a cheese delivery Mini Van no less, and his pride and joy. Restored to near mint condition, the paint job a beautiful cream, the black livery he'd had done down the side by a sign writer, called out to everyone that the Wensleydale Cheese Wheel was driving by.

The journey to work was relaxed and easy, a fifteen-minute ride along lanes dressed on either side with the kind of scenery Matthew guessed God was especially proud of. The beauty of the Dales was hauntingly peaceful, and he knew that he would never leave. Having been lucky enough to be born there, he had at points considered the idea of moving away, even toyed with it a little. A few years in York after university, a few more as far south as Sheffield, but the Dales had called him back. Those years away had been useful, allowing him to make a bit of money in accountancy and investing in property, but he'd woken every morning to the whispering of Wensleydale in his mind, and then, eventually, the whispering had grown to a bellowing call, and he had answered.

The great thing about coming back was that he had stayed in touch with a good number of old school friends, and they, like the dale itself, had welcomed him home with open arms. When he'd said that he was going to open a cheese business, most had thought him mad, not least because there was the Creamery up in Hawes, and did he really want to go head-to-head with that rather larger concern? No, of course he didn't, because that was patently ridiculous and business suicide, which was why Matthew had specialised and gone all artisan.

Arriving at the little industrial unit he worked from, which rested just out of sight on the outskirts of the village of Aysgarth, Matthew parked up and gathered his thoughts for the day. He was here because he'd taken a risk on a hobby which, for some reason, had stirred a passion deep within him he'd never realised he had, and for cheese of all things. Having worked his whole life with numbers, he'd decided to try out various hobbies because he didn't really have one, and as his now ex-wife had pointed out on numerous occasions, drinking good wine and sitting down a lot didn't really cut it.

Over the course of a year or thereabouts, Matthew had tried everything from pottery and oil painting, to woodcraft, gardening, and eventually learning to make cheese. He still couldn't really pin it down as to what had attracted him so much to cheese, but if he was pushed, he would probably say the taste of the stuff. That first go, he'd created something simple, a soft cheese, but it had blown him away with its freshness, and he'd immediately wanted more, not just in his belly, but in his life. That initial course completed, he'd continued his learning, developed his skills, got into researching old cheese recipes, uncovering long lost recipes and discovering how the cheeses we eat now tasted decades, centuries even, ago.

Heaving himself out of the Mini Van, Matthew gave the vehicle a gentle pat on its roof, as though the old vehicle was actually a faithful pet, and walked over to the main door. As he did every morning when arriving at work, he paused for a moment to take in the name above the door, the same one that daubed the van, then slipped the key in the lock and gave it a twist.

Pushing into the building, he was greeted with a smell, which he knew by the end of the day would've seeped into his clothes, his skin. It had been one of the reasons his marriage had failed. Not the main one, but it had certainly been up there. The divorce was a few years ago now, and he still winced a little at the pain of it, but in the end, things had been almost amicable. They'd been able to agree on most things, and the finances had been fairly straightforward as well. Not having any kids had certainly helped with that.

It hadn't been how he'd wanted to start the sixth decade of his life, but sometimes, that was just the way of things, wasn't it? Lonely he was, but better that, than spending the remaining years of his life with someone who couldn't bear to be around him. And now, with his seventh decade not far from snatching him out of the hands of his sixth, he refused to be anything other than positive.

Now inside, and with an hour or so before his four employees turned up, Matthew took a walk. This was his empire, a small one for sure, but it was still his. He had built it, at great personal risk, and it wasn't just surviving, but thriving. His cheeses had a reputation that was hard to beat, with one now being featured in the deli at Harrods of all places, thanks to a contact from his old line of work. He had international customers, supplying not just local pubs, but some really high-end restaurants up and down the country.

He loved it here, and every day he felt excited about the

cheese he managed to create. Which reminded him; there was the cave-aged one for him to go check on at some point, wasn't there? And that was something to really be excited about, not just because it was a new and original product line for him, but because it was completely top secret. No one knew; no one at all! If it was good enough for cheddar in Somerset, then it was certainly good enough for cheese in Wensleydale, wasn't it?

He'd be heading out to check on that later in the day, parking up just far enough away from the secret location, one which he had now owned for four years. He'd purchased it the year the divorce went through, and he guessed there was some symbolism there, but he wasn't about to go looking for it.

With the tour of his little unit over, and excited about the day ahead, Matthew was heading back to the office when something caught his eye. The vat, where the milk was sent to have cultures and rennet added, was full. And it shouldn't have been, which was rather odd. Milk was never left in the vat overnight, because the whole place was cleaned down ready for the next day. That meant there was a problem with the system somewhere, he thought; somehow, milk must've been leaking from where it was stored, and into the vat, though that didn't make much sense either. It didn't just leak; it had to go from where it was kept when it was delivered from the farms, through various other bits of piping and so on, before it got to the vat.

This was not what Matthew needed, not in the slightest. He was surprised to have not noticed it when he'd walked past before, though the sides of the vat were quite high, because the thing was so deep, and he did have a habit of being a bit daydreamy now and again.

Well, it was a problem that needed to be solved, Matthew

thought, and there was no point worrying about it, because worrying about something never helped, did it? Better to just get on with sorting out what had happened so that production could get going again. There would be the cost of getting someone out, the repair, and also the loss of milk, the cleaning, but again, what was the point of worrying? He wasn't about to let a small mishap get him down, not a chance of it, so he marched himself back to the front of the building, where the office and small kitchen were, ready to start making the necessary calls.

Walking into the office, he reached for the phone, only to hear a shuffle of feet behind him. He went to turn around to wish a good morning to one of his staff turning up early, caught a reflection that confused the living hell out of him, and then an arm wrapped around his throat. As his world went black, something sharp jabbed him in the side of his neck.

Panic set Matthew's blood on fire and he reached up to grab at the arm holding him, to kick back against his attacker with his heels, but he was suddenly feeling woozy. He was thinking back to that reflection, not just that he recognised it, but something else, too; was it the eyes? They were, after all, the windows of the soul. So, was that what had shocked him so much, the thing he'd seen behind them staring back?

As his thoughts tumbled and spun, Matthew tried to fight, to stay conscious, to free himself of whatever the hell was now going on, because it didn't make sense, it couldn't, to have someone assaulting him in his prized cheese-making unit. What was the reason? Why would anyone want to do such a thing? He had no enemies, was fairly sure he had no age-old conflicts with anyone who wanted to do him harm, so just what the hell was hap—

Matthew collapsed, unconscious. He didn't feel his body

being dragged across the floor. He had no sense at all of being lifted up, then slowly, and with a fair amount of effort and swearing, tipped into a large vat of milk, face down. He didn't feel the gloved hand making sure that his head was submerged.

Not long after, Matthew drowned. As his heart came to a juddering, desperate stop, an envelope was left in his office, inside which was something he would never read. And he wouldn't have believed a word of it, even if he had been able to.

13

The team all arrived in good time to get cracking with the day. The shift pattern had already been thrown out of the window, with everyone knowing full well they were needed now more than ever. Jim had sorted things with his parents at the farm so that he could be in more and working with the team, but would have to head back at points during the day to help out as needed. The office was loud, everyone talking over mugs of tea, including the two visitors who had turned up to join in, one expected, the other not at all.

'I'm hoping you being here's not a bad omen,' Matt said, going over to talk with the pathologist, Rebecca Sowerby.

'I'm not the angel of death, you do know that, don't you?' she replied, her tone amused, though Matt heard an edge of frustration beneath it.

'No, but I don't think I've ever worked with you on a case where there wasn't a body and usually an awful lot of blood.'

'Makes a nice change, then, doesn't it?'

'Why the visit, if you don't mind my asking?'

'I had a catch-up with the head of the SOC team early hours, because none of us sleep, not really. I requested that an early draft report of findings be sent to me so that I could have a look through it as well, and bring it over.'

'Isn't it easier for the report to be sent to me directly? That's what usually happens. Well, not to me as such, but to the team.'

'It has been,' said Sowerby. 'I've already had a look through it. We can talk through it when we gather round the famous board.'

Detective Superintendent Walker came over to join them, having finished doing her rounds and chatting with the rest of the team.

'They're worried,' she said. 'And I don't blame them either. Do we have any idea yet what's happened, where Harry is?'

Matt stared for a moment into the swirling dregs of what was left of his mug of tea, but there were no answers there. And even if there were, he was fairly sure that tea leaves weren't as wise and all-knowing, as some people professed them to be.

'I think it best if we all gather round and work out what we do next, because, right now?' He gave a shrug. 'I haven't the faintest.'

That said, Matt called the team over, Jadyn going over to the board, pens ready.

'Let's keep this short,' said Matt. 'We've already divvied up the jobs, so we all know what we're on with today. But a quick recap; Jen, you're liaising with Firbank in Bristol.'

'Already on it. She's helping me look through cases where there might be a suggestion that something could come back against Harry. There's a lot to go through, because he was properly busy, and seemed to enjoy getting stuck in. I'll probably be camped out here in the office for most of the next day or two just looking through things, and checking back with Firbank when I need to.'

Matt looked to Jadyn next.

'You're with me, to have a look around Harry and Grace's place.' He then glanced over at Liz. 'And we'll be to yours and Ben's soon after. I know it'll feel strange having us there, and I'm sorry about that, Liz.'

'No, it's okay. Ben and I completely understand. We can't think what you'll find, though.'

'My guess is nowt,' said Matt. 'But it has to be done. How's Ben holding up?'

Liz didn't respond straight away, and when she did, gave only a shrug.

'That good, then?'

'He's worried, I know that, but he's ...'

'He's what?'

'He's worried it's Harry's past that's come back to get him.'

'Well, Harry for sure has a hell of a past.'

'Ben obviously knows a lot about it, too.' Liz gave another shrug. 'And he keeps texting or calling me to check where I am, where I'm going.'

'I wouldn't read too much into it,' Matt advised. 'He's just on edge, that's all. Just keep an eye on him. Dave, Jim?'

The two PCSOs looked up at Matt from where they were sitting and Matt realised that for once Jim hadn't brought Fly with him. No doubt the dog was needed back home and being put to good use on the farm by Jim's parents.

'I want you over to the last people to see Harry, namely Tom Sykes, James Horner, and Tina Hodgson. After that, you're back on with knocking on doors again. I know we've done it already, but I want it done again. Not just over in Wharfedale either; get yourselves around Harry's haunts, see if anyone has noticed anything, seeing something out of the ordinary. I know it feels like we're clutching at straws here, but that's always how things feel early on with an investigation, isn't it?'

'Does Harry actually have any haunts?' Jim asked.

'The Fountain's one,' said Dave.

'He's really doing well with his running,' Jen added. 'I know the routes he takes because I set them for him. There are houses and farms along most of them.'

'We don't have to run the routes, though, do we?' Dave asked. 'I mean, running and me, well, we don't really get along.'

With the horrifying image of Dave running across the fells, Matt turned to Walker and Sowerby, speaking to the pathologist first.

'You've spoken to the SOC team, and you mentioned a report on the two crime scenes.'

'Firstly,' Sowerby began, 'no evidence was found at either site to suggest violence. Smudge, as you all know, was found safe and sound, and had water provided. She was in a barn, so nice and sheltered, and there was hay for her to snuggle up in, which meant she was warm as well. All in all, my guess is that she was quite happy in there.'

'Nothing else found at the barn, then?' Matt asked.

'I didn't say that,' Sowerby replied. 'A key, actually. And guess what vehicle it's for ...'

'Harry's Rav?'

'Give the man a coconut.'

Despite the situation they were dealing with, hearing those words from Sowerby made Matt laugh out loud, and the rest of the team joined in.

'Sorry about that,' said Sowerby. 'Picked that phrase up from Harry. No idea when. Find myself using it now and again, much to the bemusement of anyone who knows or works with me.'

Once the laughter had died down, Jim said, 'If Harry's keys were at the barn, does that mean Harry was there, too, then? How else would they get there?'

'Either that, or whoever took him,' said Matt. 'Remember, we know that Harry said he was going to Beckermonds, and his Rav was found five miles away from that, up past Cray; those two things do not add up to much more than total bollocks, in my humble opinion. By which I mean, Harry can't have done both, can he?'

'Nothing else was found at the barn,' continued Sowerby. 'Fingerprints were taken from the key, and though they're not the best, we've already checked, and they're not Harry's.'

That comment had the whole team looking at each other, confusion in their eyes.

'Who has access to Harry's Rav?' Sowerby asked.

Matt gave his head a scratch.

'Well, I mean, loads of folk have driven it, haven't they? Me included.'

'Grace drives it a fair bit as well,' said Liz. 'So does Ben, because he takes the Rav into the garage for Harry and does all the work on it.'

'Odd then, isn't it,' said Sowerby, 'that we only found one set of fingerprints on the key? If all of the people you've just mentioned have used it, their prints would be on it as well, wouldn't they?'

As he tried to digest what Sowerby had just said, something else bobbed up to the surface of Matt's mind.

'Did you say key or keys?'

'Key,' said Sowerby. 'As in singular. Why?'

'Something else that doesn't make sense then; Harry doesn't have a key on its own for the Rav, does he? He'd only lose it if that was the case. No, his car key is on a fob with loads of others. I don't think he even knows what most of them are for.'

'One of them looks about a hundred years old,' said Liz. 'Huge iron thing. He's never explained what it's for, and I've never thought to ask. When I suggested it was for the wardrobe to Narnia, he kind of just looked at me.'

'Well, regardless of any of that, it's definitely just the one key,' Sowerby repeated. 'New as well, by the looks of it. Maybe Harry lost his keys and had to order a new one?'

'That's easy to check with Grace,' said Matt.

Sowerby now moved the discussion onto the Rav, and Matt noticed a change in the tone of her voice, and it suggested something important had been found.

The team was quiet, listening to what she said next.

'Unlike the key, Harry's vehicle shows plenty of evidence that he's not the only one who's driven it, which matches what you've just told me, clearly. We're on with the fingerprints we've found in the vehicle itself, and they'll need to be checked against everyone you can think of who's at the very least been behind the wheel, just to see if there are prints that shouldn't be there. Not much use until we find whoever's responsible and get a match, I know. Quite a lot of what was found in the Rav was Smudge related; labradors really do shed a lot, don't they? But anyway, that's not the most important thing.'

'Then what is?' Matt asked.

'Two things actually,' Sowerby said. 'First, beneath the Rav, a pile of rubble was found. The SOC team initially thought it was just stones that had fallen from the wall lining the road, but on closer investigation, they found something a little strange.'

'Would that be that they weren't from the wall, because it wasn't damaged?' asked Matt.

Sowerby said, 'They're working on piecing it all together right now, but it looks as though they might all be part of some kind of construction. Hard to tell what it might be due to, with how weathered and broken they are. Looks like there are words carved into some of them as well, a suggestion of a date.'

'That's weird,' said Jadyn. 'Why would there be any of that?'

'Right now, we don't know,' Sowerby answered. 'Bit of a jigsaw puzzle at the moment, but as soon as anything comes up, they'll let us know.'

Matt said, 'Might be worth asking round about that,' and he directed that at Dave and Jim. 'See if anyone can remember anything about carved stones at the side of the road. Might be important, might not be, but we need to be sure. The farmers might have an idea about it seeing as they're from over that way.'

Jen said, 'You said there were two things.'

'I did. The second thing was found down the side of the driver's seat, between it and the door. Easy to miss if you're not on your knees searching, and an absolute bugger to get to with just your fingers. Thankfully, we in the crime scene investigation business have some very long tweezers.'

'And what was it, then, this second thing?'

'A syringe,' said Sowerby. 'Analysis of the contents show that it contained a very strong sedative.'

The office fell silent for a moment as every member of the team analysed that piece of information.

'How strong?' Matt asked, breaking the silence.

Sowerby said nothing for a moment, then looked Matt dead in the eye.

'If the syringe had been full when it was administered, then there was enough in there to knock out a horse.'

Then the office phone rang, and Matt wasn't the only one who had a heart attack.

14

Harry had no idea at all what time it was. He had no watch, no phone, and having turned off the lamp, no light came to him from further up the mine tunnel. His internal clock was usually fairly accurate, but that was only because he was usually above ground and aware of the day passing, and other subtle signs of time rolling on. Underground, there were no cues, nothing that he could look at to tell him how many hours or even days he'd been there.

Days ...

Maybe it had been that long, he thought. He remembered being up in Wharfedale, chatting to those farmers about a few things, then afterwards heading up to Beckermonds to give Smudge a good run. Next thing, he'd woken up where he was now, and the time between those events could've been hours, could've been days, there was just no way of knowing. Mind you, there was the fact that he hadn't soiled himself, so that was as good a sign as any. If he had been out for days, he'd be a mess. He was still in the same clothes, and there were no signs he'd been stripped and they'd been washed only to be put back on him again. That was good enough for him to assume unconsciousness had been hours rather than days.

With little to do right then, Harry had decided that conservation of energy was the best choice for now. He'd finished off the food he'd found stuffed inside the sleeping bag, taken in a little more water, then turned the lamp out and done his best to go to sleep. Not easy under the circumstances, and his mind refused to rest for some time, playing him movies of Grace, of Smudge, and the team. Eventually, though, he had drifted off, and the sleep had been deep.

Waking up, he'd felt disoriented. Unable to fully grasp where he was, the darkness so thick that he couldn't see his hand even when pressed up against his nose, it had taken him a few moments to gather himself. Whatever dream he had been in had done its best to try and drag him back, but as he chased its wispy tendrils away, the sense of it was soon lost, and then, at last, he was fully awake.

Sitting up, Harry unzipped the sleeping bag and twisted around to sit on the edge of the camp bed. He remembered the lamp, but not where he had put it, and it took a little bit of searching, patting the floor with his hands, to find it. When he did, the light it emitted was considerably weaker than he remembered it being, and he hoped that his jailer would be along soon to provide new batteries, as well as more food and water, and maybe even a reason as to why he was there in the first place.

Thinking about that, as he had done before falling asleep, Harry had managed to come up with a list of people he thought most likely to be crazy enough to travel to the Dales, subdue him, and lock him in a mine. All of them were, as far as he was aware, still behind bars, but that didn't mean some mad relative or colleague hadn't been instructed to do something like this. But why, though? That was the thing bugging him more than anything.

The names he had come up with were all frightening and violent criminals, who had themselves terrorised and bullied and tortured their way to whatever power and money and lifestyle they desired. That any of them would kidnap him and then make sure he was comfortable was beyond comprehension. Kidnap him, perhaps, but surely only to then string him up somewhere private to make sure the death they undoubtedly wanted to mete out was slow and painful. So far, there was no sign of any of that on the horizon.

Harry tried to not focus on that particular aspect, just in case all of this led to that in the end, but he just couldn't see it. Whatever was going on, there was just no way a comfortable bed, food and water, and the provision of even a toilet would then lead to many hours in the company of people with wild imaginations and an unhealthy collection of knives, hammers, blow torches, and bolt cutters.

Pushing the thoughts of torture and death deep, deep down, Harry stood up and did a bit of stretching. If he was going to be here for a while, he needed to make sure he didn't start getting stiff, and therefore be unable to react should an opportunity present itself.

After stretching, he ran himself through a quick routine of bodyweight exercises. Not in an attempt to exhaust himself and make himself sweat, but again, just to keep himself moving. Squats, press-ups, star jumps, nothing too taxing, but just enough to make sure his body would stay used to moving.

That done, Harry finished off the water, then paced around his small cell for a while, counting the steps as he did so. When he hit a thousand, he stopped, sat down on the camp bed, and closed his eyes to help his mind focus.

Getting out, right then, wasn't an option. He couldn't bend the bars—he'd already tried—and there was nothing in the small cave that would help him do so. The chain and padlock were hefty things. He couldn't dig his way out, seeing as the walls and the floor were stone. His options, then, were limited to waiting to see what he could learn from whoever had put him here. He had no doubt that they would return; that much had been obvious from the get-go because of the provisions they'd left. If they weren't coming back, then why keep him, not just alive, but comfortable?

Did his memory offer anything of any help at all? he wondered. He cast his mind back to the last thing he remembered, driving up beyond Beckermonds and parking at the side of the road to go for a walk with Smudge. He remembered a lone walker, a few vehicles heading up and down the lane, most of which were farm vehicles, the rest most likely tourists, judging by how shiny the cars were. One had turned around, probably having realised that they didn't fancy taking the narrow, winding road all the way down Langstrothdale to Horton in Ribblesdale.

Walk done, he'd strolled back to the Rav, clipped Smudge into the rear seat, then …

Harry flinched, and his hand went to his neck, as a memory burst onto the scene like a killer breaking through a door; a sharp pinprick to the side of his neck, then something pulled over his head, the hood he'd woken up in.

He'd struggled against it, hadn't he? He definitely remembered putting up a bit of a fight, but that pinprick; someone had injected him with something, and it had got to work too damned quickly for him to do much about it, his legs failing him, and then he'd been on the ground. Smudge hadn't made a sound, no barking, not even a whimper. There had been the scuffling of feet, a voice, too, and a muttered apology, which was really strange. Why knock him out with an injection, drop a bag over his head, and apologise while doing it? After that, Harry's mind was a blank, just a distant memory of fading in and out of consciousness as he was first on the ground, smelling the damp earth, then in the back of the Rav next to Smudge. She'd laid down on top of him, he'd felt the weight of her body. Then unconsciousness had finally claimed him.

Harry opened his eyes, rubbed them, stood up again and started to pace around the cave once more. The memories were a little jumbled, but going over them, forcing himself to remember, had helped. The apology was something, that was for sure, and confirmed to him that whoever was behind this meant him no harm, at least not for now. He had no idea what had happened to Smudge, but considering his current situation he had to believe she was okay. That she hadn't barked at all struck him as a little odd, but then perhaps she simply hadn't understood what was happening, and had, in the end, probably rather enjoyed having him in the back of the Rav with her.

Harry was busy thinking about how much Smudge had come to mean to him, when a sound from down the mine caught his attention. Leaning forward a little, as though closing the distance between him and it by a few inches would help, he wondered if he had imagined it, but then it came again, clearer this time, and as it grew louder, more regular, Harry knew for sure that someone was approaching.

15

Matt was closest to the phone and grabbed it, his heart still thumping hard. The conversation was short. When it was over, he turned to face the rest of the team and read from the few notes he'd jotted down on a scrap of paper as he'd listened.

'Well, it never rains, but it pours, does it?' he said, then quickly clarified that he wasn't talking about Harry, by getting to the point of the call. 'A body's been found floating in a vat at the Wensleydale Cheese Wheel.'

Shocked gasps went off like gunshots; Jen's the loudest of all.

'You mean that place over in Aysgarth?' Jen asked, and Matt heard concern pierce her words as she snapped a quick look over at Liz.

Matt nodded.

'You okay, Jen?' he asked, seeing the shock in her eyes at the news he'd just delivered, and noticing something similar in Liz's.

'A running friend of mine works there; Karen.'

'It was Karen who found the body,' Matt said. 'There was another member of staff with her, Billy McCain.'

'Billy will be making tea, then,' Liz said, rolling her eyes.

'You know him?'

'He's not been there as long as Karen,' said Jen, 'but he's come out to the pub with us a few times.'

'Usually ends up talking with Ben about cars, which is something Ben's more than happy to natter on about, isn't it? I like motorbikes, but cars I'm not fussed about at all because they all look the same, don't they? Ben's happy he has someone he can talk to about them.'

Matt was entirely sure about Liz's comment that all cars look the same. He'd always thought that about motorbikes.

'So, what's this about him making tea?' he asked.

'Karen says that's what he does more than anything, especially if things are a little stressful. That and asking questions, which I've experienced myself a couple of times; before you know it, you've told him what you do, who your friends are, what your favourite television show is, it's quite a talent!'

Matt smiled.

'That's normal enough. When people are nervous, they usually rabbit on a bit, don't they? And making tea is a familiar task to get on with, so doing it can help folk calm down a bit.'

'Do we know who it is, then?' Jen asked. 'Was it an accident?'

'Looks like it's the owner, Matthew Porter,' answered Matt, 'but that'll need to be confirmed. As to it being an accident ...'

Matt looked at Sowerby, who understood immediately.

'I'll give my mum a call,' she said. 'May as well have us both over to see what we think, and if it looks like it wasn't an accident, then we've no delay, have we? I can just call the

SOC team and there's no time wasted.' She stood up to leave the office, then, with her eyes fixed on Matt, added, 'I'd just like to reiterate that this doesn't always happen, you know? I don't just turn up at places and next thing there's a report coming in of a body being found. I'm not a bad omen, Matt, I'm really not.'

Matt got the message and regretted what he'd said earlier.

'Apologies for suggesting that. To be honest, I'm glad you're here; we all are.' He saw Sowerby visibly relax, then looked over at Walker. 'We're already stretched thin; how long can you stay?'

'As long as I'm required,' Walker replied, as Sowerby slipped out of the office and shut the door behind her. 'I could maybe see if I can get someone else down to help as well. Can't promise anything, but you never know. Always a bit like playing Russian Roulette when you put a call in to see who's available.'

'That sounds ominous.'

'Oh, I wouldn't say ominous. Shall we go with the excitement of uncertainty?'

'You mean surprise.'

'If you prefer.'

'Not really that much of a fan of surprises,' Matt said, 'but worth a try.' He looked back at the rest of the team, but before he could say anything, Jen spoke up.

'But what happened?' she asked, the franticness in her voice clearly from the concern she had for her friend. 'All they do there is make cheese; it's hardly a dangerous environment, not unless you've got a serious lactose intolerance.'

'Not sure, not yet, anyway,' Matt answered.

'But if you're sending in the SOC team, then ...'

'I'm not, not right away,' Matt explained. 'Rebecca and her mum will go with us to see if it's suspicious enough to warrant making that call. All we know right now is that where the body was found, it's not somewhere anyone would just end up by accident. But we need to judge that for ourselves, don't we? That means we could have two major investigations going on. And we're going to cover both, because that's what we do, isn't it?'

'Yes.' Jen nodded.

'Good, because I want you in charge of everything we've just discussed about Harry's disappearance,' Matt said, leaving no pause in the conversation for any chance of complaint or confusion. 'You can have Jim and Jadyn with you, and get in touch with those Uniforms Walker brought in for us as well, put them to use beyond just driving around and looking pretty. You know what there is to do, so I'm leaving that in your more than capable hands. Just keep in touch, yes?'

Jen's response was a firm nod, and that was more than enough for Matt. He could see that the responsibility he had just given her had turned her worry for her friend to focus on the job. He turned to Walker, Dave, and Liz.

'Best we get over to Aysgarth sharpish,' he said. 'My hope is that this is a workplace accident, but we won't know until we know, if that makes sense. So, let's get a shifty on, shall we?'

Sowerby popped back into the room.

'Do we have an address?'

Matt handed the pathologist the scrap of paper he'd just written on.

'I know where it is,' he said. 'We'll see you there.'

'I'll follow you,' said Sowerby. 'I'll just give my mum the address and we can head off. I've called the team as well, just to give them a heads up that I may well be calling them again in a wee while.'

As the team got themselves ready, Matt pulled Jen to one side.

'You good?'

'Absolutely,' Jen replied. 'I know what we're on with, so I can't see how there will be any problems.'

Matt didn't reply straight away.

'What are you thinking?' Jen asked.

'I'm thinking that with Harry missing, the last thing we need is our resources spread any more thinly than they already are, and it's not like we're a big city team, is it?'

'That's just the way of things sometimes, though, isn't it?'

'Sometimes yes, sometimes no.'

'How do you mean?'

Matt wasn't sure what he meant at all.

'What is it Harry always says about coincidences?'

'That there's no such thing?'

Matt stayed silent, let Jen mull that over for a moment, and watched as her eyes went wide.

'You don't think ... I mean, you can't really be suggesting that ...'

'That the two things are connected? No, of course not,' said Matt. 'Why would they be? What I am saying, though, is that maybe we just need to be a little more aware than usual, be open to spotting or hearing something that wouldn't usually catch our attention.'

'That's not exactly very specific.'

'No, it isn't,' Matt agreed, then patted his stomach. 'I think we need to listen to this a bit more for a while. Don't be afraid to go with your gut, okay, Jen? If you've a hunch something's off, then ...'

'It probably is.'

'My point exactly. Now, tell me, where are you going first?'

'We'll head over to do a search of Harry and Grace's

place,' said Jen. 'It's the closest anyway, isn't it? I'll ask Grace about that key. Then we'll head to Middleham, to Liz and Ben's place; I'll get the keys from Liz before we all disappear.'

'And after that?'

'We'll meet with those three farmers. Hopefully, something else will come in from the SOC team as well about Harry's Rav, the crime scene, and the barn where Smudge was found. And we could do with that before they potentially get caught up in whatever's happened over in Aysgarth. There's no way Harry's just vanished off the face of the Earth. And with Smudge left as she was, I can't see that whoever's responsible means him harm.'

'Then why take him?' Matt said. 'I know we're assuming someone has, because really there's no other explanation, is there? But it's the motive I'm baffled by; who the hell would want to kidnap Harry?'

'Someone with a death wish?' Jen suggested. 'Imagine being the person who's taken him and locked him away somewhere only to find that he's broken free ...'

'No thanks,' said Matt.

'Exactly. Oh, and we'll see if any of them know anything about those carved stones Sowerby mentioned. Bit of a long shot, but sometimes everything just feels like that.'

With nothing left to say, Matt stepped back and allowed Jen to get Liz's house keys, grab Jim and Jadyn, and get on with the list of tasks they'd all gone through before the call about Aysgarth had come in.

Sowerby was now back in the office.

'We all ready?' Matt asked.

Dave, Liz, Walker, and Sowerby all replied with firm nods.

Matt grabbed his coat.

'Then let's move,' he said, and he led them out of the office.

. . .

ARRIVING IN AYSGARTH, Matt drove past the George and Dragon Inn, then took a right as the main road took a sharp left and on towards the famous Aysgarth Falls. He'd been there so many times, and in all weathers, and he never tired of visiting. His wife had a very soft spot for it. Joan said it was because, after a storm, she found the falls exhilarating and refreshing with the mist thrown up into the air by the terrifying quantity of water tumbling down them. Matt, though, had a sneaking suspicion she liked to go there because it was such a bugger of a place to take a wheelchair; pushing her along the bumpy, puddle-bedecked path would always end up with her giggling away, and Matt cursing behind a smile.

Driving past a garage, he continued a short way before turning into what had once been a collection of old farm buildings. Renovated a few years ago, though he couldn't remember exactly when, they now provided a small number of local businesses with industrial units, which had somehow managed to not make the folk at the National Park panic that they weren't in keeping with the landscape.

Matt often wondered who decided something like that, and why. The Dales were not a museum, and he worried that there was often too much of a drive to preserve the past at all costs, rather than to consider the future of an area, and the people who lived there. What was the point in making sure that everything was kept lovely and pretty if, in the end, no one could live there, get a job, set up a business, or bring up a family?

Surprised by where his thoughts had wandered off to, Matt forced himself to focus, but it wasn't easy. Usually, with any journey in the Dales, he would've spent a good amount of his time behind the wheel feeling like the luckiest man alive, and not just because he would've been thinking about his wife and child, either. No, because he would have been staring out at the world around him, as astonished as ever to be living somewhere so beautiful.

This journey, however, had allowed for none of that. Half his mind was occupied with Harry, and the other half with what he was now going to walk in and find. The green fells were out there, but he'd barely noticed them as he'd driven by, and now there he was worrying about some national organisation's obsession with preserving the past instead of thinking about the future. He really was out of sorts.

First on the scene, but only by a few seconds, Matt was only just getting out of the old police Land Rover, when Sowerby, then Walker pulled in. Sowerby was out first and over to him in a sprint even before the DSupt had climbed out of her vehicle. Dave and Liz were not far behind.

'Any minute now,' said Sowerby, glancing at her watch.

'Any minute now, what?' Matt asked, then the answer arrived like an oil tanker beaching itself on purpose, as a Range Rover was heaved off the road to pull in behind Dave's vehicle.

'Ah,' said Matt, '*that* any minute now.'

'If we need the SOC team, they shouldn't be too long either,' said Sowerby, as the driver's door of the Range Rover was kicked open and someone almost fell out of the vehicle, swearing as their feet hit the dirt. She waved, and the person who had exited the Range Rover returned it, albeit with little enthusiasm.

'Hi, Mum,' Sowerby said, as Margaret Shaw, the district surgeon, approached.

'That bloody vehicle,' Margaret said, as she strode over. 'It's too big, too bloody powerful. I keep telling myself to get rid of it, but do I listen? Do I buggery.'

'Now then, Margaret,' said Matt, trying to hide his smile at her wonderful bluster. 'All well, then?'

'It's the heated seats though,' Margaret said, as though she'd not heard what Matt had just said. 'They're so comfortable, aren't they? And it really is a joy to drive, especially considering it's the size of a bus. Sort of just glides along the lanes, almost like they're not even there.'

'Just sell it, Mum,' said Sowerby. 'Please. It's not a pet or anything like that, is it? It's not important. And you can't feel sentimental about it, can you? It's only a vehicle. Get something more sensible, something smaller.'

That got a piercing look from Margaret, Matt noticed.

'My dear,' Margaret said, stepping close to her daughter and resting a hand on her forearm. 'A Range Rover is never *just a vehicle*.' She snapped her attention back to Matt. 'I hear someone's drowned in some cheese, then? That's a first for me, I have to say. Best we make sure, though, hadn't we, just in case we need to throw in a lifesaver. Where is it?'

Matt glanced over at one of the buildings they were parked in front of and saw a young woman approaching. She was small, Matt observed, though found the word petite might be a better description. Dark hair, pulled back in a ponytail, she was dressed plainly in jeans and a fleece top.

'Karen Chapman?' he said, as the woman came to stand in front of him.

Now that she was closer, Matt noticed that she was pale, and her wide eyes were glazed over with shock.

The woman gave a nod.

'Yes, I'm Karen. It was me and Billy who found him; Billy's in the office making tea.'

Margaret stepped forward and rested a hand on Karen's shoulder, taking over with ease, and without any consultation with Matt. And he was happy to let her; there was something about Margaret that commanded respect, and not a little fear either, though Matt had met few others with such a big a heart as hers. As for Billy, he already liked the sound of him thanks to what Jen had said back in the office, and Karen's words had only served to confirm this.

'How are you holding up?' Margaret asked Karen.

'I don't know,' Karen replied. 'I think it's Matthew, you see, and I wasn't expecting to find him like that, was I? I don't see how it could've happened. It just doesn't make sense. Where he is, you can't, I mean, it's impossible, isn't it? To end up, well, in there? And—'

Karen's voice caught in her throat.

Margaret put her arm through Karen's.

'Well, you just show me where to go for now, and then I can do the rest, okay? How does that sound?'

'Do I need to see him again, you know, lying there? I don't know if I can.'

Margaret shook her head.

'You leave that to me,' she said, then gestured towards the building 'Shall we?'

Matt watched as Margaret and Karen walked away from where he was standing, then he turned to the rest of the team.

'Dave, Liz, I think it best if we get knocking on doors sharpish. So, the two of you crack on with that. If this turns out to be more than an accident, then we'll have the SOC team on their way. And in that case, we'll need this area cordoned off, and a Scene Guard.'

'What are we asking, specifically?' asked Liz.

'Right now, that's hard to say, like, as we don't know what we're dealing with yet. Stick to general stuff for now, ask if they've seen anything strange going on here, vehicles coming and going that they've not seen before, that kind of thing.' He looked to Walker and Sowerby. 'Agreed?'

Walker said, 'That's the best use of the resources we have right now. No point delaying things; someone might have seen or heard something that can help either way. Shall I join in?'

'Yes, that would be great,' said Matt. 'But maybe wait till we know for sure what happened; if this is more than an accident, you can add an extra level of investigation, see what people know about the business, the owner, see if that leads anywhere. Any luck with getting us an extra pair of helping hands?'

'I put a call in on the way over; I'll keep you posted.'

Sowerby said, 'I'll get myself kitted up and follow you over to the building. Best I have a look first before everyone else arrives, then I'll have some idea what we're dealing with, but it'll be down to you, Matt, to make the call on what's happened.'

'I know,' said Matt. 'Having you here, though, means I'll maybe be a little more confident with that.'

A shout from the building caught Matt's attention, and he turned to see Margaret waving at him from the door.

'Best you hurry up,' said Sowerby. 'You know what she's like as well as I.'

And with that, Matt turned on his heels and jogged on over.

16

Harry stepped away from the rusting bars blocking his way out, the padlock and chain catching his eye, and edged back towards the rear of the cave. Assuming that it was his jailer who was approaching, he didn't want to be too close, not right away. The shadows gathered behind him would provide a modicum of cover, and perhaps allow him to get some idea of who had imprisoned him, without giving away too much about how he was doing himself. As yet, he didn't know if it was best to play it quiet, feign illness, or challenge them; time would tell.

With his back up against the rock, Harry ignored the cold as it seeped into his body, and waited.

The footsteps drew closer, each one bouncing around the tunnel with a metallic ring. He saw yellow light dance in the dark, the light from a torch feeling its way underground.

Harry clenched his fists, noticed his heart rate was up, so used slow breathing to bring it down again. If his jailer stayed on the other side of the bars, there would be little that he could do to affect an escape. However, if they stepped inside, well, that would be a different thing altogether, wouldn't it? And he would be ready for just such an opportunity should one arise.

In the gloom of the tunnel, a silhouette stepped into view, giving Harry the impression that a section of the darkness had become flesh. It made its way slowly towards the bars, shining a torch at Harry, and he snapped his eyes shut to stop the bright beam from blinding him temporarily. The figure then paused far enough away from the bars that even if he had been pressed up against them, Harry still wouldn't have been able to reach out and grab hold.

'I've brought food and water. Batteries for the lamp as well.'

The voice was muffled, Harry noticed, and low, but artificially so, he thought; whoever this was, they were trying to disguise their voice. Male, though, that much was obvious.

He said nothing, just watched, listened, the light from the torch preventing him from getting a good look at who was standing behind the glow.

'I'll bring more tomorrow.'

Still, Harry kept himself still, silent, putting the onus on the new arrival to do all the communication.

'I'll leave it on the other side of the bars so you can reach through and get it.'

Harry watched as the silhouette approached, every step steady, careful, cautious.

As the figure drew close to the bars, Harry lurched out of the shadows, causing them to drop the torch. It clattered to the ground, and went out.

'Stay back! Please! It's really important that you stay back! I can't have you get too close!'

Harry heard a thin sliver of panic in their voice, fragile enough to snap at any moment.

Halfway between the wall he'd been standing against and the bars, Harry stared into the darkness, the only light fighting the gloom was coming from the lamp on his side of the bars. He watched the figure drop to the ground and scrabble around for the torch. He noticed that their face was hidden behind a scarf wrapped around their head, only their eyes showing, a jacket hood pulled up over their head.

The torch was found, the light cutting through the dark at Harry.

'So, who are you, then?' Harry asked, his voice calm. 'And why am I here? What's this all about? What do you want?'

'I can't tell you why you're here, but it won't be for long, that much I do know.'

'How's that, then? I mean, if you put me here, then you must have a reason, right?'

A pause; thinking, Harry guessed.

'All I know is that you will be released soon, he pro—I mean, *I* promise.'

Interesting change of tack, there, Harry noted, the *he* becoming *I*.

'Can't say I hold much truck with the promises of a man whose face is hidden by a scarf, and who's keeping me locked in a cave.'

'Here's the supplies,' the figure said, and quickly dashed over to the bars with a carrier bag, before ducking away from them once more.

Harry took a couple of steps closer, caught sight of the figure again, in more detail this time, not that he was going to learn much from a black jacket, jeans, and Wellington Boots covered in thick, grey mud from the cave.

The figure shuffled further away, pulling in the shadows around them like a thick cloak of black felt.

'Are you okay? Is there anything else you need?'

'To not be locked in a bloody cave is what I need,' Harry said, though noticed a note of concern in the question. 'Tell me why you put me here; there has to be a reason. You know people are looking for me, don't you? You can't just disappear someone like me, that's not how this works. I'm a police officer; something like that gets noticed.'

'You just need to be here for now, then you will be let out.'

'Well, I can't see that going too well, can you?' Harry replied. 'I mean, the only way to do that, is to walk down here again and unlock that padlock, at which point, I'm probably going to do my damnedest to chase and grab hold of you, aren't I? By which point, I might be none too careful about how I deal with you, if you know what I mean.'

'I don't mean you any harm. I promise. I'd never hurt you.'

'Again, I'm not a fan of a jailer's promise. Who are you? How do you know me? How did you get me here? And what the hell have you done with my dog?'

Harry's voice had grown gradually louder as he'd spoken, to the point where the final question was a shout.

'I can't tell you anything,' the figure said. 'I just can't, you have to understand that. I'm not allowed. It's too much of a risk.'

'Can't say that I'm understanding anything right now, but then it's a little hard to, isn't it, when you think you're taking your dog for a quick walk, and next thing you know, someone's grabbed me, injected me with something to knock me out at a guess, driven me somewhere in the back of my own vehicle, and dumped me in a cave. There's not even a good book to read, is there?'

'You don't like to read.'

That statement caught Harry sharp, but he didn't respond. He'd been asking questions, talking, to see if the person hiding behind the scarf would let something slip by accident, tell him something he didn't want to.

'I'm sat on my arse in a cold, damp cave; I need something to do.'

The figure started to back away from the bars.

'I have to go now. I'm sorry. I hope the food's okay. This will be over soon.'

'Why do you even care?'

Soon, the figure was lost to the darkness, hidden from view by the torchlight glaring at Harry.

As the footsteps started to fade, Harry called out one last question.

'And what did you do with my dog?'

'Smudge is fine,' came the reply.

It wasn't until a while later, when Harry had grabbed the carrier bag of food, and munched on yet more tasty delights from Cockett's butchers, that he realised what had actually been said.

17

'So, what exactly is it that we're looking for?'

The question was from Grace, and Jen was keenly aware of the edge to it, sharpened by the woman's teeth as the words had slipped from her mouth. At first, she wasn't sure how to answer, what to say, but then she remembered one of Harry's little gems of advice.

'We don't know, not specifically,' she said, 'but I guess it's about trying to spot something that shouldn't be there, or something that should be, but isn't. That's what Harry says, anyway.'

Grace frowned at that.

'Harry said that, and you actually understood what he meant? I'm impressed.'

'Well, when he said it, it was a lot clearer, I'm sure,' said Jen. 'But you know what I mean.'

'Ish.'

'And just so we're all working from the same page,' continued Jen, working hard to add a firmness to her voice, 'it's not *we* as in inclusive of you who are looking for something; this is police work, Grace, okay? I need you to just let us get on with it. I know it's hard, though, I get that.'

'And I'm not in the police.'

'Not that I'm aware of, no.'

'Not even by association?'

Jen shook her head.

'Neither you nor Jess or Smudge can claim to be in the police. Sorry about that.'

'Should I be asking you for a search warrant?'

'You're right in that usually we would need one to search a private home,' Jen said. 'But there are occasions where we don't need to.'

'Such as?'

That edge again, Jen noticed, but she understood why it was there, and apparently getting sharper still, if that was at all possible; she could see why Grace and Harry were so well suited to each other.

'Well, there's your relationship to Harry, isn't there?'

'What if it's me who's kidnapped him, though? Then what?'

That wasn't a question Jen was going to take in any way seriously at all, so she ignored it.

'There's also an urgency to this,' she said. 'As far as we are aware, Harry is okay. And by *aware*, what I mean is, we're basing that on what we've found so far; no evidence of a struggle, Smudge being found safe and well; none of that point to Harry not being okay.' She decided to keep the information about the syringe to herself for now; Grace didn't need to know that level of detail. 'However, we don't want to have any delay in trying to find what's happened to him, where he is, anything, and applying for a warrant can cause that.'

'Makes sense,' said Grace with a shrug. 'I'd best let you get on with it, then, hadn't I?'

And, to Grace's credit, that's exactly what she did, stepping back, and letting Jen, Jim, and Jadyn check through the house.

A couple of minutes later, Jadyn followed Jen up to the first floor, leaving Jim downstairs to continue having a look around the living area downstairs.

'This doesn't feel right at all,' he said, keeping his voice low so that Grace wouldn't hear. 'Searching Harry's house? It's invasive, isn't it? He's our boss, we shouldn't be here.'

'I know it doesn't,' Jen agreed. 'But we have to, and you know that. We're not being disrespectful and we're not searching for evidence of a crime, are we? At least, I can't see how we would be. We're just looking for something which might give us a clue as to what's happened to Harry, that's all. Grace understands that, I'm sure.'

At the door to Harry and Grace's bedroom, Jadyn stopped dead.

'No,' he said, 'this is going too far; I'm not searching through Harry and Grace's clothes and stuff.'

Jen gave the constable a smile, and though she wasn't one for open displays of affection, reached out and gave Jadyn's hand a squeeze.

'I'm sorry,' he said. 'You know what I mean, though, don't you?'

'I do,' Jen replied, and called downstairs for Grace to join them. When she did, Jen explained as best she could why this was all feeling so awkward.

Grace smiled.

'You know, it is a bit, isn't it? Are you really so sure that I can't help at all? I felt useful helping with the search, but now? I just don't like sitting on my hands, like, that's all.'

Jen understood completely.

'I think, with this, I'd feel easier about it if you were in the room with us,' she said. 'I'll look through your stuff, and leave Jadyn to Harry's, that work? I know it's not much, but that's the best I can do.'

'We've nothing to hide,' said Grace. 'We're all grown-ups after all, aren't we?'

For the first time since they'd arrived, Jen felt Grace's usually very apparent warmth return. At the same time, she noticed not just a flicker of a smile, but also something else in the woman's eyes; mischief, perhaps?

About half an hour later, and with the bedroom searched, Jen and Jadyn checked the rest of the house, then met Jim back downstairs. Grace was sitting at the dining table, with Smudge and Jess snuggled up beside her, their heads resting on her lap.

'Find anything?' Grace asked, as Jim finished looking through a few final things, including the post, which had just arrived.

'Nothing,' Jen replied. 'I'll be honest, I didn't expect that we would; I don't think any of us did. But at least we're covering every avenue by doing so, aren't we?'

'It's not Harry's birthday coming up, is it, like?'

The question was from Jim, and Jen and Grace looked over to see what he was talking about.

'No, why do you ask?' said Grace.

'Fancy looking envelope, that's all,' Jim replied, and held up an envelope. 'I didn't think it was, but I had a bit of a panic; can't go missing that, can we? I know he doesn't like fuss, especially when it comes to his birthday, but I reckon he'd be more upset than he realises if we all forgot, if only for the fact that there wouldn't be one of Matt's delicious home-made cakes to demolish.'

Grace took the envelope from him.

'You're right, this is fancy,' she said, holding it out in front of her. 'Well, it's something for him to open when he gets back, isn't it? I tell you, if it's some fancy woman ...'

Jen laughed at that, not least because it was a phrase she'd not heard in years, and only then on the lips of older relatives.

'You're the only fancy woman in Harry's life, that's for sure,' she said.

Grace smiled and started to look through the rest of the post.

'Thanks for being so good about this,' Jen said. 'I know it's not been easy to have us here, looking through everything. We needed to though, just to be sure.'

'It's not a problem,' said Grace. 'I get it. Off over to Middleham to Ben and Liz's place, now, I guess?'

Jen answered with the shallowest of nods, then led Jim and Jadyn to the front door.

'If we hear or find anything, we'll let you know, I promise,' she said, opening the door, then remembered she needed to ask something. 'Don't suppose Harry lost his keys to the Rav at all, did he?'

Grace frowned, shook her head.

'Not as I'm aware, no. Why?'

'A key to the Rav was found in the barn where Smudge had been left. Looked new as well.'

'That's odd.'

'Isn't it?'

As Jen made to leave, Grace spoke again, her voice betraying the concern perhaps more than she realised.

'Just get him back soon, will you, Jen? And safe? That's all I ask.'

Jen didn't reply. Instead, she just held Grace's gaze long

enough to reassure her, then headed outside to join Jadyn and Jim, pulling the door closed behind her.

THE JOURNEY over to Ben and Liz's place was a quiet one. No one spoke, all of them lost to their quiet concerns about Harry. Jen wondered how things were going over at Aysgarth, and was tempted to stop by and see if they could help, but forced herself to carry on down the dale. She also got to thinking about what Sowerby had said back in the office, the syringe found in Harry's vehicle, the strange stones found beneath it.

A bright sun was scything the clouds into tufts, the wind coaxing them along in a slow, dreamy dance, but Jen wasn't really taking any notice. Neither was she thinking about the run she had to do that evening, the events she had in her diary that she was training for, any of it; Harry's disappearance had set them all on edge and the urgency of finding him twisted her stomach and kept it there in a tight knot.

'How's Steve?'

Jim's question caught Jen by surprise, mainly because she had grown so used to the quiet in the car that the low thrum of the tyres on the road had become almost hypnotic.

'My lizard?'

'He's the only Steve I know,' said Jim.

Jadyn said, 'Wasn't there another animal called Steve? Way back when Harry first arrived?'

'Was there?' said Jen. 'Can't say that I remember.'

'You're right, there was,' said Jim. 'Still is, as far as I know. A huge labrador, over in Oughtershaw. How did you remember that?'

'No idea,' said Jadyn. 'Not exactly the most useful piece of information, is it? My brain has a habit of forgetting useful things, but refusing to let go of stuff it just doesn't need.'

Arriving at Ben and Liz's place a short while later, Jen really didn't want to go ahead with what they had to do, and was tempted to stop by at her own place to check in on Steve, even though she knew he was fine, probably chilling out on the sofa as usual. Searching Grace and Harry's place had been troubling, and this was going to feel no less so, she was sure.

Leading Jim and Jadyn up the path towards the house, which was a neat bungalow that had been left to Liz by an elderly relative, Jen pulled the front door key out of her pocket. She slipped the key into the door, and went to give it a twist, when the door was pulled open, catching all three of them by surprise.

Jen jumped back, stumbling into Jadyn, whose solid mass kept her from ending up on her arse.

'Ben?'

Standing in the doorway was Harry's younger brother. And he looked rough, Jen noticed. He was wearing a dressing gown, hugging himself to keep warm, and his hair looked damp, with sweat, she assumed.

'Sorry, didn't mean to surprise you like that,' Ben said, his eyes flitting between them as they stared at him. 'I heard someone at the door and came to see who it was, and then I heard the key, thought it was Liz, so I opened it. Just had another visitor as well.'

'What's wrong? Why aren't you at work?'

'What? Oh, I'm ill,' said Ben.

'Liz didn't mention it,' replied Jen.

Ben hugged himself and to Jen, he looked not just ill, but really on edge, though that was understandable. How could he be anything else?

'Wasn't till Liz was gone that it really hit. I feel rotten.'

'What is it you've got?' Jadyn asked, and Jen noticed the police constable deliberately put a little extra distance between him and Harry's younger brother.

Ben gave a shrug, then stepped back to let them in.

'No idea. Just feel like crap. Started in the night, but I kept it to myself, didn't think it was much. Thought it was just a headache, that kind of thing, then it just got worse and worse. I've called in sick, so Mike's going to be up against it today with me not there, poor sod. The other person woke me up, not you.'

'Who was it?'

'That journalist,' Ben said. 'Said he wanted to ask me some questions.'

Jen clenched her jaw for a moment, then said, 'What kind of questions?'

'About Harry, which was no surprise. Said he'd heard something about Harry's disappearance being linked to some event or whatever in his past, and that of everyone in the Dales I was best placed to know about that.'

'What did you say?'

'Sod off, I think.'

'The best response, Ben,' she said, then led the way into the bungalow, edging past Ben, brushing against a wet jacket hung up on the wall, and nearly tripping over a pair of Wellington Boots grey with mud, which were standing beneath it.

Once they were all inside, Ben hushed the door shut.

'What is it you actually need to do, then?' he asked.

'Exactly what we've just done over at Harry and Grace's,' Jen explained. 'Have a look around, see if there's anything that might give some clue as to where Harry is, what's happened to him.'

Ben's eyes flickered from Jen to Jadyn and Jim, then back again.

'Like what? There's nothing here, you know that, don't you?'

'We still have to do a search, just to be sure.'

Ben turned away and walked down the hall.

'Do your worst,' he said, calling back to them over his shoulder, and disappeared through a door into the kitchen.

'Whatever he's got, I hope I don't catch it as well,' said Jim. 'I can't do with getting ill; gets in the way, doesn't it? You try working on a farm when your head feels like it's going to burst; not good. Mainly because my Dad's one of those people who doesn't believe in illness. Thinks it's all in the mind and that the best way to deal with it is to just get on with the day. He's a tough old bugger, I can tell you.'

'You should try being ill with my mum around, then,' said Jadyn, and Jen heard the smile in his voice; she'd met Jadyn's family a few times now. They had welcomed her with such warmth that she genuinely enjoyed when they got together. Jadyn's mum, though, she was a force to be reckoned with.

'Why?' Jim asked.

'She's got a remedy for everything,' said Jadyn. 'No matter what you've got, she'll be making you some special broth, telling you what you should and shouldn't wear, whether to rest or not, handing you steaming mugs of her secret cure-all recipe, which tastes like you've been punched in the face by a gang of rare herbs and spices, and an angry chilli or two.'

'Sounds amazing,' said Jim. 'Fancy a swap? Next time I'm ill, I'll go see your mum, and next time you're ill, you can ask my dad what to do about it?'

'Next time they're over, we should get everyone together,' Jen suggested. 'Right now, though, we need to get this done.'

She split them all up, and after checking in with Ben

again, headed through to the bedrooms, while Jim and Jadyn got on with looking through the lounge, kitchen, and bathroom. It was only when she had doubled back on herself having looked through one of the bedrooms, that Jen realised she'd tramped mud all the way along the hallway, and everywhere else, by the looks of things. She quickly took off her shoes, then went to find Ben, careful to not step in any of the marks she'd already trod into the carpet and make a bad situation worse.

'Ben?'

Harry's brother came out of the kitchen and looked over at Jen as she held up her shoes.

'I'm really sorry,' she said. 'I've put mud everywhere. Made a right old mess. You got a rag or something? Must've picked it up from your boots.'

'Don't worry about it,' said Ben. 'I'll sort it.'

'No, you won't,' said Jen, frowning. 'You're ill, and the mess is my fault. I'll have a look under the sink, shall I? That's easiest. Anyway, Liz would never let me live it down, would she?'

'Honestly, Jen, it's fine.'

Jen ignored Ben's protestations, found a few rags, ran some water into a bowl, then, having placed her shoes outside the front door, proceeded to clean up after herself. The mud was thick and grey and smelled almost sour, perhaps even metallic, she thought, but what bothered her most was just how resistant it was to being shifted at all. However, after a good amount of dabbing and gentle rubbing, she managed to get the worst of it out.

With everything cleaned up, Jen continued the search in her socks, but found nothing. And the same was true for Jadyn and Jim.

At the front door, Jen stepped back into her shoes.

'Thanks,' she said. 'And get yourself better, okay, Ben? You can't be welcoming Harry home by giving him the flu, can you? He'd not be happy about that at all.'

Ben's response was a rather pathetic shrug, then he shut the door and they were alone.

'Now what?' asked Jim. 'Can't help feeling like we're not getting any closer to finding Harry.'

'Time to talk to some farmers,' Jen said, and dropped to the ground to pull on her shoes. She got some of the dark, grey mud on her fingers, quietly swore to herself, then stood back up. 'And we are getting closer to finding Harry,' she added. 'Because we have to be. I refuse to believe anything else, and so should you, understood?'

Jen's sharp tone took her by surprise, as well as Jim and Jadyn. She went to apologise, but wasn't given a chance.

'No, you're right,' said Jim. 'Sorry. Farmers then, right? That's my world.'

'Then we'll follow your lead,' said Jen.

As they headed back to their vehicle, Jim pointed at someone just a ways down the road and said, 'Who's that?'

Jen looked, saw a tall, thin, man standing, watching. He waved.

'There he is,' she said. 'Askew.'

'Busy sticking his nose in, as per usual, no doubt.' said Jadyn. 'I'm surprised Ben didn't punch him.'

'I'm surprised *everyone* doesn't punch him,' laughed Jim.

Jen decided she'd make a note of Askew's appearance, just in case. With journalists, trouble always seemed to follow, she thought, then closed the distance between her and their vehicle, opened the driver's door, and dropped in behind the steering wheel.

Harry was out there, somewhere, she thought. Probably not scared though, and that thought was almost enough to make her laugh. Bored was probably more like it, and frustrated, and increasingly angry.

And with the thought of Harry trapped somewhere, his anger bubbling over into hot rage, she only hoped they found his jailer before he got his hands on him.

18

Over in Aysgarth, Matt was outside the Wensleydale Cheese Wheel industrial unit and trying to will away two smells from his nostrils, one of which he knew was borne entirely of his imagination, and yet still it lingered. The body hadn't been there long enough to start decomposing, as had been pointed out by both Margaret and her daughter, Rebecca, yet his brain told him that it had, and the smell had hit him immediately.

'It's enough to put you off cheese for life, isn't it?'

Matt smiled at that, because Margaret Shaw was blessed with a simple and effective ability to lighten up even the worst of situations. Never disrespectfully either, but always just enough humour to help remind everyone that real life should never be allowed to be utterly overshadowed by darkness.

Matt gave his head a firm shake.

'Put me off cheese? Not a chance of it. I mean, it's close, like, but I think me and cheese are still good. I'll never abandon it. Cheese is life, after all.'

Margaret raised an eyebrow.

'Is it?'

'Can you imagine life without cheese?'

'Easily. Well, maybe not easily, but I'm fairly sure there's more to life than eating it.'

'Oh, there is, for sure, like,' said Matt. 'There's toasting it, grilling it, grating it, deep-frying it in breadcrumbs, and what about fondue? I'll be honest, though, there's something about a body floating in curds and whey that does put me off it a bit.'

Having caught up with Margaret, who was being led into the building by Karen, Matt had followed them in, past the small office, inside which they'd briefly met Billy McCain, before heading into the main mechanics of the place.

'Tea? I've made it. Probably too much. But tea's good in a crisis, isn't it? That's what my mum used to say, anyway.'

Billy had held out a mug, and Matt, just to help put Billy at ease, had taken it, while Margaret simply stood with Karen, holding her arm. Half a dozen other mugs of tea were quietly steaming away over by a large kettle.

Billy, Matt figured, was late thirties at least, though possibly pushing his head up into the very early forties. His beard was absolutely enormous, and currently held at bay by a massive blue net, which was hooked over his ears. The beard suited him, though, Matt thought, as Billy was a big chap, and the way it was contained in the net reminded him of how farmers sometimes provided hay for animals in their barns, hanging it from the walls in a similar fashion.

'How are you doing?' Matt asked.

'You're based over in Hawes, aren't you?' replied Billy, a mug of tea in his hand that he was stirring frantically with a teaspoon.

'What? Oh, yes, that's right,' answered Matt, stuttering a little at the unexpected response.

'Do you like working for the police? Must be stressful. I don't think I'd handle it well, if I'm honest.'

From the way he was going at it with that teaspoon, Matt had to agree.

'It's a good job, means I'm useful,' he answered. 'And yourself? Do you enjoy your work?'

'It's different.'

'Been here long?'

'Not too long,' Billy replied. 'Fancied a change, saw the job, and here I am. And yourself? Have you been in the police your whole life?'

Jen was right, Matt thought; Billy really did ask a lot of questions.

'I've been in long enough to almost forget what my life was like before it, that's for sure. You were with Karen when you found the body, yes?'

Billy gave a nod from over his mug of tea, which he held close to his lips as he blew the steam away in small, disappearing plumes over towards the door.

'You arrived at the same time?'

'We entered the building together. Was quite a shock.'

'We'll need to have a chat, over at the office in Hawes, if possible,' said Matt, 'so that we can get a witness statement from you, contact details, that kind of thing.'

'Okay. I'm allergic to dogs, though.'

'Pardon?'

'Dogs,' Billy said. 'Ben's brother has one, doesn't he?'

'You mean Harry?'

'The dog's called Harry?'

'No, Harry's called Harry. We can always meet somewhere else, I'm sure.'

'Thanks,' said Billy.

That conversation over, Matt asked if either Karen or Billy could take them to the body. Karen answered by simply heading out of the office and deeper into the building, her hands clamped around Margaret's arm.

Catching them up, Matt did his best to have a bit of chitchat with Karen, if only to keep her mind distracted from what she'd found early that morning when she'd arrived for work, but it was clear that Margaret was doing fine with looking after her. And she had been keen to talk as well, the process of telling them about herself clearly a much-needed distraction.

He'd discovered that she'd worked at the Wensleydale Cheese Wheel for a year now, having returned from a few years of travelling, most of which had been spent crewing tall ships. Billy, she told them, had been there six months and, as if to confirm what Jen had said and what Matt now knew himself, asked a lot of questions. She had an air about her of wildness and adventure, and it was no surprise to Matt that she was a friend of Jen's. Indeed, it was because of Jen that she had turned up in the Dales in the first place.

They'd bumped into each other in a bar abroad somewhere a few years ago, where Jen had just completed some mad ultra marathon, the likes of which Matt simply couldn't imagine. And as how it sometimes is with complete strangers, they'd hit it off completely, their friendship absolutely sealed within those first few moments of accidentally spilled drinks due to Jen not being able to move her legs properly, and Karen asking her why she was walking like a giraffe. They'd stayed in touch, met up a few times, and then, when her time chasing sunsets on the decks of huge ships had come to an end, Karen had found her way to Wensleydale and sorted herself a job. She now rented a little flat in Leyburn, and though hailing from the Devon coast, could never see herself ever moving away. Which meant, she was immediately one of Matt's favourite people.

'It ... I mean, he's just down there,' Karen said, pointing deeper into the building.

Sowerby had joined them by now, fully dressed in the white paper overalls of her trade.

Matt glanced around, saw lots of things made of stainless steel, various pipes, and not one bit of it did he understand.

'Clean, isn't it?' he said, unable to think of anything else to add at that moment.

'Can you be a bit more specific?' asked Margaret. 'Save us having to go poking around too much.'

'Yes.' Karen nodded somewhat frantically. 'Just down there, you'll find a large stainless-steel thing, which is where the milk is stored when it's delivered from the farms we use. After that, there's a vat, which is where the milk goes once it's been pasteurised. Though we do make unpasteurised cheese as well, but that's in another part of the building. The vat is where all the cultures are added, to help the cheese get its flavour, then the rennet, to separate out the curds and whey.'

'And that's where the body is?' Margaret asked.

More frantic nodding from Karen.

'Matthew doesn't usually get things going so early in the morning, so I don't know what happened.'

'How do you mean?' asked Matt.

'The vat's full,' answered Karen. 'That's not usually done till everyone's here, because there's a process to go through, isn't there? Maybe he just wanted to really get a lot done? He's the boss after all.'

'Well, I'm sure we'll be able to find our way,' said Margaret. 'Karen?'

'Yes?'

'Is there somewhere you can sit and wait for us? Back at the office, perhaps, with Billy? He's certainly made enough tea.'

'Okay. It's where I'd go anyway to check emails, the post, that kind of thing, before getting on with anything else. We're releasing a new cheese soon, but that's all a bit hush hush at the moment. I've a few things I can check for that, I'm sure.'

'A secret cheese?' said Matt, perking up. 'Really?' Then he caught a stern look from Margaret. 'You go through to the office, Karen, and we'll be along soon enough, I'm sure.'

Karen's answer was to turn around and walk back to the office.

'Let's go and see what we've got, then, shall we?' said Margaret.

Matt was about to remind her that he was the one in charge of things, but she was already striding off with Rebecca at her side.

Catching them up, he followed along behind until they came to the vat Karen had mentioned. And there, floating face down in more milk than Matt had ever seen in one place in his life, was a body.

For a moment, the three of them just stared at the spectacle, unable to take it in.

'How on earth did he end up in there?' said Margaret, leaning over the edge for a closer look.

And she had a point, thought Matt, the edges of the vat were just below chest height.

He looked around to see if there was anything that could in any way at all have sent the man, who they were assuming was the owner, Matthew, falling in such a way as to end up where he now was, but there was nothing. Not even a step ladder to climb up and tumble off.

Matt said it first. 'Not an accident, is it?'

'No, it isn't,' agreed Margaret.

Matt looked at Sowerby.

'SOC team it is, then,' he said, but she was already on her phone.

19

As the day wore on, Matt's strong feelings about the importance of cheese in his life had started to fade. Witnessing a body being removed from a vat of milk had got him thinking about what else might end up in cheese, and then his imagination had rather run away with itself. He understood, of course, that the process was all very hygienic, that things really didn't just end up in cheese, because it was a very controlled process. He wasn't entirely sure, though, if he'd be able to view a nice slab of Wensleydale in the same way ever again, even if it was resting on a delicious slice of Cockett's fruit cake. Obviously, the only way to be sure, was to put in some serious research, and he'd be doing that once everything had settled down a little. Or, failing that, perhaps this evening, because there was always cheese and cake at home.

The SOC team had arrived and, under the guidance of Rebecca Sowerby, had quickly got on with the job in hand, like an army of giant, white overall-clad ants. The identity of the victim had been easy to establish, though Matt had avoided Karen being the one to do that; a quick check of Matthew Porter's photo on the company website against the body once it was out of the milk had been more than good enough.

With everything going on, Matt had decided it was best to have Karen out of the way, so had taken her to the old Land Rover and had her sit inside, wrapped in a blanket for good measure. He'd also asked her to call the other members of staff who worked for Matthew to tell them to take the day off, and tomorrow as well, just to be safe. As to the reason, he'd suggested that for now it was best to keep things simple and say that there was a problem at the unit, and that she would be in touch.

The truth about it all could be revealed by either himself or the team when they popped out to see them. He didn't want Karen having that responsibility, or to risk things being said that shouldn't. Though, even then, he would be doing his best to keep any suggestion of murder out of the public eye, at least until they knew a lot more than they did right then. They certainly didn't need Wensleydale lighting up with panic about both Harry's disappearance and now a suspected murder. He'd even been able to provide her with a small bar of chocolate as a distraction, and to also help with the shock she was no doubt suffering from.

The ambulance had eventually swung its way into the crime scene, and once Sowerby had been happy with things, that enough evidence had been collected, Matthew Porter's body had, with as much respect as possible under the circumstances, been hauled out of the vat, placed on a stretcher, and taken away, back to the mortuary.

Matt had watched it trundle across the parking area in front of the building, milk dripping from beneath its covers to spatter on the ground. It had reminded him of an ice cream left out in the sun. Sowerby, Matt knew, would follow the ambulance along soon enough, to see if there was anything else she could learn from the body, if there was clear evidence of foul play.

There had to be, Matt thought, because there was no way that Matthew had ended up in the milk of his own accord. Just because he had been found facedown in the milk, didn't mean drowning was the cause of death.

Matt had overheard a couple of the SOC team briefly chatting over whether or not he could have decided to take his own life in a dramatic and almost poetic way, but that didn't make sense either. After chatting first with Karen, and then with Billy again, as far as Matt was aware, there were no problems in Matthew's life that would have caused him to do something so drastic. There was a divorce, but that was long enough ago not to be a motive, the business was doing well, and there was even this promise of a new secret cheese on the horizon. It was something to consider, he supposed, and with Karen's help, he now had a list of family and friends for them to get in touch with to see if there was anything else going on.

By the time the SOC team were done, the afternoon had rolled in on a bank of cloud thick enough to block out the sun, its rays no longer powerful enough to cut through.

Matt called the team together.

'So, what do we have?' he asked, looking at the others, hoping for something.

'Nowt,' said Dave, somewhat dejectedly. 'We've knocked on every door in Aysgarth I think, and there's nothing anyone's said that seems to suggest anything weird was going on.'

'They've all got nothing but good things to say about Mr Porter,' added Walker. 'The business is seen as good for the area, provides a little bit of employment, brings money in; it's what they want, after all, isn't it?'

'So, no one's seen or heard anything out of the ordinary?'

'No,' said Liz. 'I mean, this is Aysgarth, isn't it, so the folk who live here are used to traffic flying by, seeing as it sits either side of the main road. Plenty of questions about getting people to slow down and obey the speed limit, but that was about it, really. I don't think anyone really takes much notice of who's coming and going.'

Matt had been hoping for more, but wasn't surprised by the answers.

'Anyone got any suggestions or bright ideas?' he asked.

'I think,' said Walker, 'that for now, we just wait on Sowerby and the SOC team. What about family?'

'There's an ex-wife,' said Matt. 'Lives away in Barnard Castle now. Other than that, we don't know.'

'Do we have an address for her, and for Matthew?'

'We do,' said Matt. 'Karen was able to provide both of those.'

'Even the ex-wife's?' asked Liz, surprised. 'Why would she have that?'

Matt paused before he told them.

'Apparently, since the day of the divorce, Matthew's sent her a hamper of cheese every Christmas and birthday.'

That drew a collection of baffled looks.

'What? Why?' asked Liz.

'To prove a point. Karen said that she'd asked Matthew the same question, and his answer was that his ex-wife had never believed the business would be a success, and he took rather too much delight in proving that she was wrong.'

'By sending her cheese,' said Dave, clearly baffled.

'Seems like it, yes.'

'Do you think she could be involved, then?'

The suggestion almost made Matt laugh.

'You mean she drove over here to stop him sending her free cheese, and in the process made sure it was permanent?'

'People do the oddest things.'

'Well, it's something we will have to check up on.'

'I'll head over to meet with her,' said Walker. 'As we have her address, do we have a contact number as well?'

'No, just the address,' said Matt. 'Getting over there today would be good though, I think. I've sent both Karen and Billy home now, and will check in on them both tomorrow to get witness statements. Billy's allergic to dogs, so will have to do that somewhere that isn't the Community Centre. Rest of the staff have been told to take today and tomorrow off as well. There's only three of them, so Dave, Liz, would you be up for contacting them and going over for a chat? Remember, that we really don't know anything yet, beyond Matthew Porter's death, so I would suggest we don't even go near what actually happened, because we don't yet know, do we? So, just explain as best you can what's been going on, but without saying too much, and then see if a little bit of gentle questioning can give us anything.'

A breeze caught Matt sharp and it made him shiver a little.

'What about yourself?' Dave asked.

Matt gave his chin a scratch, then looked at Walker.

'Mind if I join you?'

20

The three farmers had been a little reluctant about meeting up for a chat with Jen, what with all the work they had to be getting on with on their farms, which they were all keen to point out. They were concerned about Harry, yes, but none too sure what else they could offer or say and thought the whole thing to be a waste of their valuable time, because there were sheep to deal with, cows to move, bills to pay, tractors to repair. Still, with a little persuasion, which had included seeing them all at the same time, she'd managed to get them to agree to meeting up. The sweetener of doing so at The George Inn, in Hubberholme, had also gone a long way to helping.

Stepping into the inn, Jen had the impression that she had, unwittingly, stepped back in time. The room containing the bar was small and cosy. The ceiling was low, held up by thick, black beams, candles were lit on the bar, and the air was rich with the scent of wood burning in the stove in the wall. To the left of the stove, pinned to a wall, was a somewhat extensive collection of toasting forks. Jen could see the need for one, perhaps even two, just in case one went missing, but the sheer number here was edging towards disturbing. How much bread did anyone really need to toast on some flames, and how many people at once needed to do it?

The last time Jen had been at The George, she'd parked around the back and headed off on one of her longer runs, getting in a good amount of hill work, too. The weather had been rough, and by the time she'd arrived back at her vehicle, she'd been soaked through, her legs on fire, and her feet covered in mud. She'd gone to sit in her car and get changed, but then a waft of hot food had caught her attention, and she'd stumbled inside and ordered a pint and a fish finger sandwich with chips. The urge to stay overnight, despite it really not being that much of a drive home, had been almost too much, but somehow, she'd managed to persuade her legs to take her out of the pub before another pint was ordered and a room booked.

'My dad loves this pub,' Jim said, as they all shuffled inside.

'Impossible not to,' said Jadyn. 'Last time I was here was with the mountain rescue team, when we had that lad go missing from over in Marsett, remember? I've never actually had a drink here, though.'

'And you won't be today, either, I'm afraid,' said Jen.

The bar room contained five other customers, and with Jen, Jadyn, and Jim turning up as well, it seemed busy.

'You're late.'

Jen turned to the corner of the room displaying the toasting forks to see three pairs of eyes staring at them. It was the woman who had spoken, Tina Hodgson. She had a weathered face, and Jen would've put her at anywhere between fifty and seventy. It was hard to tell in the sallow light, and the farming life was an expert at eroding a person's true age.

Jen led Jim and Jadyn over to meet Tina, and the two she was sitting with. She was about to make introductions, when one of them said, 'How do, Jim! How's your dad? Not seen him in a while. And your mum?'

At that, Jim took the lead, and Jen was happy to let him do so, as he walked over and shook one of the farmers' hands.

'Now then, Tom,' he said. 'Dad's grand, thanks, and so's Mum. And yourself?'

'Surviving.'

'Much the same, to be honest,' said Jim. 'But that's farming, isn't it?'

The farmer leaned over and gave Fly's head a scratch.

'Bonny looking dog, this one, isn't she? And you're right enough about farming, like. No one gets into it for the money, and most only ever get out of it by dying.'

On that happy note, Jen introduced herself and Jadyn, and thanked them for their time.

'Not sure what use we can be,' the third member of the party said, who Jen now assumed was James Horner, seeing as Jim was speaking to Tom Sykes. 'Any news on Harry?'

Jen took a seat, and Jim and Jadyn did the same.

'We've found his dog, Smudge,' said Jen. 'She was left in a barn not too far from where we found his vehicle.'

That got a laugh from Tina.

'Dicky was moaning about that,' she said. 'But then he does like a good moan, doesn't he? Can't say as I blame him, but that's by the by now, really. Keeps himself to himself, and that's the way he likes it.'

The three farmers were dressed much the same, Jen

noted; tattered and torn waxed jackets, beneath which sat a varied collection of thick shirts and woollen jumpers.

'Aye, he's not happy unless he's griping, that's for sure, like,' said Tom, then added, 'Just out of interest, where was that barn exactly?'

When Jadyn told him, Tom cast a look at both Tina and James.

'There a problem?' Jen asked.

'Way back, my lad used to go and play over at Dicky's,' Tom explained. 'Back when he was trying all kinds of things to get a bit more money in. He was even one of the first to have a go with alpacas, would you believe! Anyway, my lad would go over and build dens with his two lads, that kind of thing, like, before, well …'

Tom's voice drifted off and Jen saw a faint shadow of sadness not just in the man's eyes, but in the eyes of Tina and James, as well.

'I'm not sure I understand. Did something happen at the barn?'

Tom shook his head.

'No, nothing happened at the barn, but it is on Dicky's land,' explained Tina, resting a hand on Tom's leg for a moment. 'I just think it's odd that you'd find Harry's dog there, of all places.'

Yes, it was odd, wasn't it? thought Jen. They'd have probably established that already, if it hadn't been for the sudden splitting of resources with the incident in Aysgarth; it was easy for the small things to get missed.

'We'll speak with Dicky as well, for sure,' she said, then looked again at Tom. 'You were going to say something, though, then you stopped yourself, about how your son used to go and build dens?'

'Nowt much to say, really,' Tom replied. 'Dicky's a grumpy

old git, everyone knows it, but he's a good reason to be, really if you think about it.'

'How so?'

'His son drowned in a pond. Can't remember exactly how old he was, like. Eleven, maybe? Tragic. And just a year after his fiancé left him. No idea what happened to her. She was from down dale though, so ...'

Tina huffed and puffed at what Tom was implying.

'And my Malcom's from down dale, too,' she said, 'so don't you go bringing in your nonsense about how folks are weird down that way, and can't be trusted like those from the top of the dale!'

James said, 'She ran off with someone, that's all, and whoever they were, they probably provided something a little bit more promising than a life caught up in farming. Can't blame her for that, now, can we? The way she did, maybe, but we don't know the reasons, so my thinking is we're better sayin' nowt about it. And I think she always struggled being a mum of twins.' He paused for a minute, took a deep draught of his beer. 'What was the lad's name, again, the one who drowned?'

For a moment, no one spoke, then James said, 'Michael, I think it was. His brother was Andrew, remember? He was the sickly one, wasn't he?'

'That's right, he was,' nodded Tom. 'Fussy with his food, always getting colds, or whatever.'

'Regardless, we just let him be, basically,' Tina said. 'Dicky's harmless, just likes to gripe most every hour of the day. That kind of pain, some folk just don't recover from, do they? Dicky never has, never will, probably never really wanted to; my guess is that it kept her alive for him.'

Jen decided to move on to something more relevant.

'Now, about your meeting with Harry.'

'There's really nowt much to add to what we've already told you all,' said Tina. 'He came over, because we asked him to, we had the chat, he said he was off walking that lump of a hound of his, and that was it, really, last we saw him.'

'He said he was going up Beckermonds?'

'What he actually said was that he wanted to take the dog for a walk,' said James, 'but didn't rightly know where was best. So, we all suggested a few places, didn't we?'

'There's loads of footpaths around, aren't there?' said Tom. 'Not sure which of us it was who suggested Beckermonds, though, are you, Jim?'

Jim looked momentarily confused that he was being asked a question by Tom, then realised it had been directed at Hodgson.

'Maybe we all did,' James replied. 'That, and Middle Falls, like, and a few other nice spots to go for a stroll.'

'What was it you wanted to talk to Harry about?' Jadyn asked.

'People being silly buggers, that's what,' said Tina. 'Folk on motorbikes not sticking to the lanes they're allowed to use, some on quad bikes as well. Make a right mess, scare our stock, it's not on.'

'Most of them come in from the city,' said James, and Jen wondered at how there was still an inherent distrust of outsiders by some in the Dales, especially those who supposedly came from some nameless city far off. 'No idea about how things are here. And it's not like we can protect ourselves, is it?'

'From what?' asked Jim.

'And that's the question, isn't it?' said Tom. 'From what? Some come over to have a jolly, like, don't they? Go and have a mess around on the fells. But others? Well, this last week or so, we've seen torch lights, haven't we? Up in the fields, around and about, like someone's out snooping around.'

'Harry was over to advise us on security,' explained Tina. 'He's due to come back later in the week.'

'So, you'd best get him found, and quick,' said James. 'It's a lonely life for us, and it's easy to get frightened by funny goings-on. We can't afford to have things go missing; stock, tractors, all kinds of things can just disappear, and there's only so much we can do to prevent it.'

Tom looked at Jen.

'How's Harry's brother doing? Ben, I think, isn't it? Works over at the garage in Hawes, Mike's place.'

'Worried, like the rest of us, and ill. Same goes for Harry's partner, Grace, as well, but they're both taking Smudge being found safe and well as a good sign.'

'Do you think it's someone from his life down south?' asked James. 'He must've dealt with some serious people down that way, criminals that would love to get their hands on him.'

'I've heard that,' said Tom. 'Someone mentioned it when I was in Kettlewell.'

That the news was spreading so quickly was no surprise, but that the gossip about what had happened had followed hot on its heels? That was quite something.

'Right now, we're following up on a number of leads,' she said. 'We'll find him, I'm sure.'

'How someone could get the jump on him is beyond me,' said Tina. 'He's a big chap, isn't he?'

'It's beyond any of us,' said Jen, frustrated suddenly that they'd learned nothing new. Actually, no, that wasn't true, was it? They knew about that other farmer, Dicky, being the owner of the barn Smudge was found in. Worth investigating further, not least because it was all they had to go on. And they also had a reason to explain his surly nature, so that would perhaps help them manage their communications with him a little better.

'Well, thanks for your time,' Jen said, and pushed herself to her feet.

'Not staying for a pint, then?' Tom asked, and Jen could see from the glint in his eye that he already knew the answer.

'If you think of anything else, hear something, whatever, call the office.'

'We will,' said Tina. 'Hope you find him; the Dales need people like Harry around, don't they? Can't be having them just disappear for no reason.'

As Jen led Jadyn and Jim to the door, she remembered something else.

'Don't suppose you know anything about some carved stones, do you?'

That question drew very confused looks in return.

'How do you mean?' asked Tina. 'What kind of carved stones?'

'Not really sure; they were found under Harry's vehicle. We thought they were from the wall, but there's no damage where it was parked.'

'Could be someone's just dumped them there,' suggested Tom. 'We don't get much fly tipping round here, but there's still some who would rather leave something at the side of the road rather than not, aren't there?'

Outside the pub, Jen checked the time. The day was really drawing on now, but there was still time to go and find Dicky Guy and have a chat with him. So, she sent a message through to Matt, to let him know what they were doing next, and asked Jadyn to pop back inside to get Dicky's address.

'You sure we don't have time to stop for a swift one?' Jim asked, as Jadyn returned and gave Jen the address.

'In,' Jen answered, pointing at her vehicle, and they all climbed in. She slipped the key into the ignition.

'So, where are we going next, then?' Jim asked.

'To see a man about a barn,' said Jen.

Then, with a little too much power sent through to the wheels, and in a dramatic cloud of grit and dust, they headed off to their last visit of the day.

21

Matt was sitting with Walker in the front room of a very pretty cottage. They were both staring at a large wooden crate. Matt was wondering if he could take it home with him to fashion into a coffee table. On the other side of the crate was a woman dressed entirely in denim. She was holding a lit cigarette but had yet to take a drag. Matt put her in her mid-sixties.

'And you said this arrived when?'

'Two days ago. I was out when it arrived. Couldn't get in the front door without emptying it first.'

'And you didn't order it?'

'Are you kidding me? Why the hell would I do that? And even if I did, why would I order it from him, of all people?'

They'd arrived late afternoon, the journey had been peppered with numerous traffic jams caused by tractors and trailers. Farmers, Matt knew, were making the most of the good weather, and they didn't give two hoots about other road users when they did, which was fair enough, he thought. If farmers didn't work mad hours, and in all weathers, people would soon complain when food started to disappear or go up in price, so as far as he was concerned, they were well within their rights to snarl things up a bit now and again. And frankly, the roads could do with being slowed down a bit, couldn't they?

Having rung the bell, the door had been opened moments later by Matthew Porter's wife, Rachel. She had invited them in, and in doing so, given neither Matt nor Walker sufficient time to explain why they were there. Instead, she'd whisked them through to the lounge, then disappeared, only to return struggling a little with the weight and size of the wooden crate as she'd dragged it across the floor to where it now lay.

'Ms Porter?' Matt said, only to have Rachel cut in.

'It's Duffy,' she said. 'I went back to my maiden name as soon as the divorce came through. Please, just call me Rachel, though; I'm not your teacher or boss, am I? Now, can you tell me what it is you're going to do about this, please?'

'About the crate?'

'Yes, of course about the crate!'

'Rachel,' Walker said, 'we're here because of your ex-husband.'

'Yes, I know that,' Rachel replied. 'I called about this yesterday and I still haven't heard anything back, though I was informed someone would be in touch. That's why you're here, clearly. I mean, Christmas and birthdays? I've let that slide. But this? It's too much. And where's it going to end, answer me that!'

Matt took a deep, calming breath, in and out.

'Rachel,' he said. 'I'm afraid we need to tell you that your ex-husband is dead.'

'Don't be ridiculous.'

'Rachel ...'

'He can't be, can he? He sent me this ... this idiotic crate of cheese! Honestly, when I get my hands on him, or my solicitor does, then—'

'Rachel,' said Walker, her voice calm, almost comforting, 'the body of your ex-husband, Matthew, was found this morning at his industrial unit by one of his staff.'

'Which one?'

'Which industrial unit? I thought he had only one.'

'No, I mean, which member of staff. Was it Billy? He's new, I don't know anything about him. Or was it that young thing, Katie or Katnip or whatever she's called? I've seen her photo on the website. I bet he's all over her, isn't he? Pretty young thing that she is. Who can blame him, really? I keep a tab on things, you see, still have friends over that way, despite moving over to Castle Bolton just to get away, try and start again. No one expects a divorce this late in life, do they? Not sure Castle Bolton was a good choice, though; not exactly a hotbed of dating for retirees like me.'

'There's no Katie,' said Matt. 'Do you mean Karen?'

'Yes, that's her. Willow thin, pale as skimmed milk.'

Matt threw a glance at Walker, unsure how best to proceed.

'Rachel, we really do need you to understand that Matthew ... he's dead, Rachel. Karen and Billy found his body this morning when they got to work. We don't believe it was an accident.'

'Are they dating, then?' Rachel asked, ignoring the really important bit of what Matt had said, and he wondered if it was on purpose, just to avoid dealing with the news, even for just a few seconds more. 'Makes sense, I suppose. Explains why they'd be there together, doesn't it?'

When Rachel stopped talking, Matt decided to give her a moment, and to see if the news really would settle in her mind. He then watched as her eyes flickered between him and Walker, as though she was searching for some kind of sense in what she had been told.

'So, what exactly are you saying, then?' she eventually asked. 'That he was killed? Someone murdered him? Is that why you're here? And you think I did it? You think I killed him because of ... because of this?'

Rachel gestured at the crate of cheese with a wave of a hand.

'We're here to ask some simple questions, have a chat, that's all,' said Walker, 'and to offer you any support we can in this difficult time.'

'Difficult? How is this in any way difficult? Matthew's dead, isn't he? Means I won't be receiving cheese every sodding Christmas and birthday, doesn't it?'

Matt understood the venom, the pain of a broken relationship never something easily healed, but there was something else there, too; disbelief, shock, even a faint note of sadness.

'We have to ask you where you were early this morning,' Walker said, her voice steady, calm.

'Here,' Rachel said. 'Where else would I be? And before you ask if I can prove it, no, of course I can't. I live on my own, thankfully; after what I went through with that man, I'll be staying single for a long, long time, I can tell you. The sex just isn't worth it.'

'And last night?'

'Let me just check my very busy diary ... Oh, I don't have one, do I? And even if I did, it would be empty. So, once again, I was here, on my own. Probably watching reruns of some cookery show or something. Pathetic really, isn't it, how your life ends up? I was sure I'd be sorted by the age I am now, but here we are, and I'm very much not.'

Matt was beginning to see through the anger and sensing something else; loneliness, perhaps. He wondered sometimes how he would be if he didn't have his wife and daughter to go home to, if he'd go mad listening to the deafening sound of his own solitary existence.

'Do you know if Matthew had any business troubles at all?' Walker asked. 'Any disagreements with people? Is there anyone you can think of who might have had a grievance with him?'

Rachel opened her mouth to say something, then, without any warning at all, she seemed to just deflate in front of them.

'I'm sorry.'

'There's really nowt to be sorry for,' said Matt. 'There's no set way to deal with the kind of news we've just given you.'

Rachel leaned back in her chair and stubbed out the unsmoked cigarette in an ashtray in her lap. Then she just sat there for a moment, shaking her head ever so slightly.

'He's really dead, then?' she said at last. 'Matthew, I mean? He's ... he's gone?'

'Yes.'

Rachel sat forward, elbows on knees, hands together.

'Bloody hell, Matty ...'

She closed her eyes for a moment, shook her head again. When she opened them, all the rage and bitterness had gone.

Matt also noticed the name she'd called her ex-husband; a pet name, perhaps, because it had been said with more affection than she may have realised.

'How did it happen?'

'For the moment, we need to keep such details to ourselves while we conduct the investigation,' said Walker. 'I'm sure you can understand.'

'Dead though? I mean, it just doesn't make any sense,

does it? Yes, Matthew was a royal pain in the arse, and our marriage really did just fall apart in the most spectacular fashion, but ...'

'It's a very difficult thing to accept,' said Matt. 'News like this only ever comes as a shock.'

Rachel sat forward.

'Why the hell did he send me this cheese, then?' she asked.

'Didn't you say that he's been doing that for some time? That's what we understood from Karen.'

'Birthdays and Christmas, yes,' Rachel replied. 'And we're definitely nowhere near Christmas, are we? Well, not near enough to be this far ahead in getting presents posted.'

Matt was beginning to understand.

'Not your birthday either, then?'

Rachel shook her head.

'That was back in April. My sixtieth. It was so memorable that I can't remember it. Like, at all. Except for the cheese Matthew sent. I give it away, you know? I don't let it go to waste. Friends, neighbours, Kirsty who delivers the post, that kind of thing.'

'You've no idea, then, why Matthew would have sent you this?' Walker asked, pointing at the crate. 'Did it come with a card at all?'

'It did,' said Rachel. 'Wait one, I'll go and grab it for you; I put it in the recycling without even opening it.'

Then she stood up and left the room.

With Rachel gone, Matt leaned back and stared at the crate again.

'Bit odd, isn't it? Why would he send her that?'

'Doesn't mean it has anything to do with what happened to him,' said Walker.

Matt wasn't so sure, and could tell from Walker's tone that she wasn't either.

Rachel returned to the room and sat down in her chair.

'Here,' she said, and handed Matt an envelope.

'Fancy,' he said, turning it over in his hands, before handing it to Walker, who pulled out an evidence bag and slipped the envelope inside.

'Something else for the SOC team,' she said. 'Just in case.'

'Just in case of what?' Rachel asked.

Matt ignored the question and asked, 'When was the last time you were in touch with Matthew? When did you last see him or talk to him?'

'We're never in touch,' she said. 'No reason for us to be, is there? No children. We divorced, and that was that. Quite brutal really, if you think about it, isn't it? There you are, your whole life shared with someone else, then boom!' Rachel mimed an explosion with her hands. 'It's over, just like that, and you're left picking up the pieces for years. What a bloody waste. Do you have any idea how many photos I've got of our life together? The hell am I supposed to do with them? I can't just throw them away, can I? And I can't bear to look through them, either.'

Matt watched Rachel reach for another cigarette, light it, then just rest it between her fingers. He wondered if it wasn't the smoking that helped so much, as the act of almost smoking, just having it lit, ready if she needed it.

'We had a dog, though,' Rachel said then, 'and Matthew said I could have her. Died last year, poor little thing. Cancer. Can't bring myself to get another. Not yet. Wouldn't wish myself on any little creature that just wants walks and cuddles and to play.'

'Have you asked him to stop sending you the crates?' Walker asked.

'Trouble is, that would mean talking to him, wouldn't it? I don't have his personal number, and I'm not about to call his office. Better to just let him keep sending them, hope he gives up eventually, and in the meantime, let others enjoy a few freebies. Nothing wrong with that, is there?'

Matt really couldn't see that there was, and neither could he think of any reason to continue the discussion. Then his phone buzzed in his pocket, and with a glance at Walker, he quickly excused himself from the room and took the call.

'Detective Ser—'

'Matt?'

'Now then, Jen,' Matt said, recognising the detective constable's voice. 'Anything to report, then?'

'Yes,' Jen replied. 'I have.'

Matt noticed a heaviness to Jen's voice, as though she had something she needed to tell him, but really didn't want to because it weighed so much.

'What is it?'

Another pause. Matt felt a sinking feeling in his stomach.

'Jen ...'

Jen's reply was succinct. 'Matt, we've got another.'

22

Harry had never been best known for having much in the way of patience. Yes, he could be calm, and yes, he could be organised, but as for patience? He just didn't have time for it. Which meant that right then, having met his jailer at last, and after having tucked into the replenished supplies they'd brought him, it was time to get moving. Easier said than done, what with being locked in a mine, goodness knew how deep underground, but he wasn't about to let a few million tons of rock get in the way of things, or his absolute ignorance of geology. The time had come to make a plan.

To begin with, the visit from the stranger with the hidden face hadn't given Harry much to go on. Not really a surprise, he thought, because something like that often needed a while to percolate. That way, things he'd maybe not noticed right away would start to float to the surface and maybe prove useful. Because of that, and because he'd had long enough to consider everything that had happened to him since taking Smudge for a walk, Harry went right back to the beginning.

Something like this, it was a mini-investigation, so he was going to conduct it like one, look at the evidence, draw up a timeline in his mind, and see where he ended up when he got to the end of it.

Thinking back to when he'd been taken, two things bothered Harry. First, and most obvious, was twofold: why-the-hell and who-the-hell? The who-the-hell he ignored for the moment, because he wasn't entirely convinced that he'd be able to work that out until he was free—and he would be free; there were no ifs, ands, or buts about that, that was for damned sure—so, instead, he thought about the why.

Revenge had been his first thought, because why else would someone knock him out, bag and tag him, then dump him in a mine other than to meter out some deep-seated need to get their own back, make him pay. For what, though, that was the thing, wasn't it? If it was for doing his job, for putting them away and ruining some dark criminal scheme, then why go to the trouble of locking him up in relative comfort?

Next, he'd wondered if it was some kind of ransom, but had quickly ditched that idea as completely ridiculous. Anyone who knew him well, and anyone who didn't, would know or at least guess that money wasn't exactly flowing in the family. And as to friends, work colleagues? Once again, he didn't hang around with the monied types, and never had. He came from a rough background and the only money he'd ever seen as a kid had been in the hands of his now dead criminal father, and that had never been for him, his brother, or his mum. Adulthood had comprised military life then the police, neither of which paid the kind of money that would have allowed him to save up enough of it for someone to think they could benefit from trying to get their hands on it. So, ransom was out of the question.

That was it, really, Harry had realised; in all the kidnapping cases he'd dealt with over the years, revenge or ransom had been the driving force behind them. The kidnapper wanted to hurt a rival, wanted money, wanted to negotiate by using the victim as a pawn. And yet, here he was, stuck underground, the victim of an honest-to-God kidnapping, so there had to be a reason! No way would anyone do this just for the hell of it! Throw in the way he'd been treated, and a few other things he'd noticed or recalled in the silence of the dark, and Harry knew there was something very odd going on indeed.

So, if it wasn't for a ransom, and it wasn't to do him harm in some way, then what was it? Why was someone making a point of keeping him out of the way? Because that's what this all boiled down to in the end, didn't it? Him being trapped down here, meant that whoever had put him there was potentially free to get on with doing something else; but what?

Harry realised that he'd probably not know fully until he was out of the mine why someone wanted him out of the way, but at least he'd managed to narrow things down to that. It wasn't much, but it was something.

As to who-the-hell, Harry had gone through a list of usual suspects in his mind at least a dozen times, if not more, and no single name had come out trumps as someone who would do any of this. They were all violent types, hardened, seasoned criminals; keeping him fed and watered just wouldn't be on their tick list when it came to kidnapping him. And as he'd thought to himself before, they were mostly all serving long sentences, and those that weren't were probably dead.

Having persuaded himself that he wasn't about to end up having his nipples attached to a car battery or having a hammer taken to his fingers and toes, Harry moved on to trying to pick apart the things that had seemed out of place with what had happened to him. Not easy to spot, considering being kidnapped is, in and of itself, hugely out of place, but he figured it was worth a go.

Starting with when he'd felt the sharp prick in the side of his neck when he'd taken Smudge for a walk. Harry remembered two things; one was that a car had passed him by only to turn around and drive by once again. Yes, that happened in everyday life because people could easily end up going the wrong way and need to turn around, so there was an explanation for that. But even so, that it had happened a few minutes before he'd found himself with a bag over his head? That had his attention. He tried to remember the vehicle, closed his eyes to force himself to focus, remembered that it was blue, then ... It had been a hatchback, that much he was sure of. It probably meant nothing, but he'd log it, just in case.

The second thing he remembered was Smudge, because she hadn't made a sound. Not a growl, a bark, nothing. On the one hand, that made Harry a little bit peeved that the dog he'd thought saw him as the centre of her world had obviously not been bothered in the slightest by what had happened. On the other hand, there had to be an explanation for it, didn't there? Had his kidnapper turned up with some fresh steak as a bit of bribery while they saw to him? Or was it something else, something altogether more odd? With that thought in mind, Harry moved on, because a third thing had revealed itself as he'd thought back over those moments, and that had been the mutter of an apology just before he'd lost consciousness. Why would his kidnapper have said sorry? Why feel remorse?

All this thinking was making him hungry, and he was also getting cold, so he grabbed himself a couple of the Tunnock's wafers, then slipped inside the sleeping bag. The bag was warm and those wafers really were quite delicious. It was no wonder they'd become such a favourite of his, and he just hoped that Grace hadn't eaten them all by the time he got home.

Laughing to himself about that, Harry thought back to when he'd woken in the mine. He'd been groggy at the time, disorientated, confused, and his focus then had been to get free of his bonds, then rest a little. The ropes at his wrists and hands hadn't been all that tight, as though they had been put on in a hurry, rather than to keep him restrained indefinitely. He wondered as well if he'd allowed himself a little more time if he'd have been able to pull them apart with a little bit of work with his teeth. At the time, though, he'd been desperate to be free, and with some effort, had managed.

The discovery of the supplies, the bed, the sleeping bag, even a lamp and toilet, were all positives, and again reinforced his belief that he wasn't being imprisoned to then have harm done to him. No. He was being kept alive to then be released, but if Harry was going to have anything to do with it, he wasn't about to wait.

This, then, all led Harry to his encounter with the figure in the scarf. They had seemed nervous, he recalled, not the behaviour he would've expected of someone who had got the jump on him and had him locked up. Then there had been that misstep when he'd asked them why he was there. The stranger had said that he couldn't tell him, just that it wouldn't be for long. Harry had challenged him, tried to make whoever it was give something up without realising, and maybe they had; about his being released soon, the reply had quickly changed from *he* promised to *I* promise. So, who was this he, then, this other person? It certainly made him sure that the one who had brought him his supplies was not the one who was pulling the strings.

Two other things came to Harry's mind, then, both things that the stranger had said. The first, was when he'd asked for something to read. He'd only do that to push back a bit, show that he was still fine, and that he wasn't going to just sit there and accept his predicament. It was a cheeky call as well, its aim to unnerve as much as anything else. The reply from the stranger had been most odd though, he had realised; *You don't like to read*.

How did they know that? It was true, to a degree. He tried to read, he really did, and it was never a case of the old excuse of not enough time. It was simply that reading was a habit he had never got into as a child, and because of that, it had never followed him into adulthood. He very much wished that it had, because he knew settling down with a decent novel would probably do him the world of good and help him to relax and switch off. It just wasn't that easy.

Those thoughts reminded him of Gordy, and how she'd done her best to encourage him to read, bought him books even. He'd have to give her a call once all of this was sorted out, see how she was doing down in Somerset, maybe even pay her a visit. After all, she was now living in his old stomping grounds, and it might be fun to go back, for a little while, at least.

As to the second thing that had come to mind, well, that was even more strange. Worried about Grace, about Smudge, Harry had gone so far as to ask what his kidnapper had done with his dog. He'd not mentioned her name at all. And yet the reply had been, *Smudge is fine*.

That was the bombshell, Harry thought. Those words, *Smudge is fine*, told him so much, almost too much really, and yet also not enough.

His kidnapper knew the name of his dog. Ergo, Harry would happily put his meagre life savings on him knowing his kidnapper. That brought his whole situation so close to home that the pain of it quickly morphed itself into a sharp stab at the front of his brain, causing him to wince.

Sitting up, Harry kept himself in the sleeping bag, but swung his legs over the edge of the camp bed. He rubbed his temples, rocked a little, waited for the pain to go away. As it left him, he reached for another Tunnock's wafer. Biting into it, he was once again reminded of just how much he liked them. And, as he swallowed that first mouthful, he knew in his gut something else; their presence in this room was no coincidence either, was it? After all, there really was no such thing.

23

Matt had been rather looking forward to going home. He was in desperate need of the company of his wife, Joan, and their daughter, Mary-Anne. With Harry still missing, and now the situation in Aysgarth, he'd felt the weight of responsibility keenly. The team was looking to him now, and that was fine, but he felt sure he was overcompensating. Harry was a tough act to follow, and Matt would never even consider trying to, but that didn't mean he wasn't doing exactly that without even realising.

Having Walker there probably wasn't helping matters in that respect, but her presence and experience was needed. As was the fact that, against the odds, not only had she managed to sort them the extra Uniforms early on with the mystery of Harry's disappearance, she had also found someone to step in where Gordy had once stood. Not permanently, for sure, Matt thought, because he didn't think they really needed anyone else. And no one could replace Gordy, could they?

Plus, what if she decided to come back? What then? He doubted that she would, but still ...

The call from Jen had been a shock. Dealing with Harry's disappearance alone was hard. With the suspected murder of Matthew Palmer in Aysgarth, their lives had become exponentially more complicated. But with this, and so soon? It was almost too much. Almost, because Matt wasn't about to let it become that. He had a good team to lead and depend on, and at home, he had the kind of loving support most wished for, and few ever truly experienced. He was a lucky man in a tough place right now, and he was going to make absolutely sure he didn't bugger anything up. No one would be getting much sleep anytime soon, though, that was for sure.

Having concluded the chat with Matthew's wife, Rachel, Matt had given Walker a quick tour of what Jen had told him, which wasn't much.

'What do you mean, another?'

'We think it's a farmer, Dicky Guy. Can't see it being anyone else, considering where Jen found him.'

'And that was where, exactly?'

'In a water trough. One used by his cattle. They're quite big.'

'Cattle are quite big? What?'

'No, the trough, but yes, cows are quite the size, like. Did you know they're the most dangerous animal in the country? More people are killed each year by cows than by any other form of wildlife.'

'Not sure I know what to say to that.'

'Not sure I should've said it.'

'It's not like they've much in the way of competition, is it?'

Matt gave that statement perhaps a little too much thought before he answered with, 'No.'

And with that, he led Walker to the old police Land Rover, and drove them all the way back to Wharfedale.

The route was a cracker, and even with the seriousness of the situation which awaited them, he found himself enjoying it.

Having threaded through the centre of Richmond, one of the few larger towns Matt was genuinely happy to go shopping in, if only for the pies at the aptly named Noted Pie Shop in the cobbled marketplace, the route took them on towards Leyburn. Sitting at the bottom end of Wensleydale, there was a healthy rivalry between it and Hawes, with teams from quoits to darts to football going head-to-head throughout the year. If Matt was in the mood for some posh food to impress Joan, he'd often head to Campbell's, usually spending far too long wandering around the wines upstairs.

Leaving Leyburn, he followed on through West Witton, behind which Penhill slumbered, an iconic silhouette which had stared down on the Dales for millennia. A few miles later, he turned off Temple Bank, and swept along towards and then skirted the edges of West Burton, a village so utterly perfect that Matt was of the quiet opinion that God himself might well have had a hand in its creation. The village's green lay restful and safe, protected as it was on all sides by cottages, houses, and grander dwellings still, and at night, their windows lit by the lives inside, would stare at each other as though caught in some quiet, mysterious communion of secrets and whispers.

Through Bishopdale he then drove, the road a thoroughfare that stubbornly refused to leave behind its once rich life as a conduit for cart and horse; narrow to the point of having Matt hold his breath at points, it bumped and bounced and weaved and bobbed between wall and tree and field, until it eventually caught sight of the River Wharfe and followed it all the way to their destination, Yockenthwaite, and beyond.

'We're here,' Matt said.

He slowed down and turned off the road, crossing the river to bring them past a small collection of houses and farm buildings, then along a track into the fields beyond.

Jen, Jadyn, and Jim were waiting for them, and Matt spotted the telltale sign of cordon tape flapping and twisting in the breeze behind them.

'Ready?' he asked, rolling the Land Rover to a stop, and killing the engine.

'That was quite the journey,' said Walker.

'Oh? If I drove too fast, then ...'

Walker smiled.

'Not in the slightest. It seems strange, though, doesn't it, to have been swept through such beauty to then be faced with this?'

Matt climbed out of the Land Rover and, with Walker alongside, headed across the field to meet with the team.

'This week is going from bad to worse too quickly for my liking,' said Jen as they came to stand with her.

'It is a little odd, isn't it?' Matt agreed, happy to go along with Jen's marked understatement. 'Where is he, then?'

Jen made a gesture with her chin over her shoulder.

'Witness?'

'A walker found him,' she explained. 'He was making his way along to The George Inn for the night after a day out on the fells, saw something floating in the trough and strolled over for a look.'

'Where is he now?'

'At The George,' said Jen. 'He's booked in there for the night anyway, so Jim drove him down while Jadyn and I cordoned the place off, called Rebecca and Margaret, the usual. Jim got his contact details and a witness statement, but I've already said I'll want to speak with him tomorrow; he was fairly shaken up. He's going to pop into the office tomorrow morning.'

'When's the SOC team arriving, then?'

'Well, Rebecca and her mum are probably only a few minutes behind you; I called this all in after speaking to you first. The SOC team will be a while longer, I suppose. Ambulance is on its way as well, but that could be much later; there's been a football match over in Darlington and the fans have got a bit rowdy.'

'Throwing fists as well as insults?'

'You guessed it.'

'Let's have a look, shall we?' directed Matt, and allowed Jen to lead him and Walker over to the cordon tape.

Jadyn was waiting for them.

'Scene Guard, then?'

'No clipboard, though,' Jadyn said, 'so I'm just using my notebook. Only visitors I've had so far have been some inquisitive sheep, a squirrel, and half a dozen crows.'

'You got their names, though, right?'

'I did.'

'Good lad.'

With a wink, Matt lifted the cordon tape, and with Jen and Walker, made a beeline for the water trough a few metres ahead. It was sitting just away from a wall, which bordered the field they were now in, and it was only when they drew closer that Matt caught sight of the body. It was floating face down, the surface of the water mirror like and still. To Matt, it was as though the body had been half set in glass.

'We got an ID at all?'

'Not sure we need it really,' said Jen. 'My money's on it

being Dicky Guy, seeing as we're on his farm. But we can't be sure until everyone else arrives and we can recover the body.'

Matt scanned the area, his eyes coming to rest on the wall.

'Looks like he was busy repairing it,' he said. 'I once did a course on that, you know; dry-stone walling? There's an art to it, and it's not an easy one to master.'

'And did you?'

'God, no,' said Matt. 'I was bloody awful at it; knocked down more rocks and stones than I was able to set down.' He turned his attention back to the body in the water trough. 'If this is Dicky, what do we know about his family? Does he have one, any relatives? I know him by reputation only, rather than his actual background and history. And I'm never over Wharfedale enough to know folk over here as well as I do in Wensleydale. The Dales, they're small, but it's still possible to come across people you know nowt about.'

'I've been down to the farmhouse, knocked at the door, and there's no answer,' said Jen. 'I was going to give one of the farmers I met with earlier a call, just to see, but I didn't want to send the hares running. They mentioned that he was nearly married once, but that was years ago; she left him just days before they were due to walk the aisle.'

'Ouch,' said Matt.

'They mentioned two sons as well,' Jen continued. 'Twins. Said one of them drowned in a pond. He was only eleven. Can you imagine that? They said they don't think he ever recovered from his fiancé leaving him and his son dying. No idea about the other one. I don't think he works the farm or even lives in the area, or they'd have mentioned it.'

'We'll still need some way to ID Dicky, though,' said Matt, 'assuming that it's him. And we'll need to trace the other brother. Was the house open at all?'

'It was, but I didn't feel right just going in for a nosy. I shouted out, like, but there was no answer. A dog barked, and that was about it.'

'Can't really depend on that, though, can we?' said Matt, as the sound of an engine slipped into the moment. 'Not sure procedures allow for the IDing of a body by canine.'

Turning around to look back at the gate into the field, Matt saw two familiar figures, Margaret and Rebecca, climb out of Margaret's Range Rover. He paused his chat with Jen and waited for them to arrive, Rebecca taking a few minutes to first get changed into her PPE, before they made their way over.

'Long time no see,' he said, when they came to stand in front of him.

'What on earth's going on?' Margaret asked. 'Harry's missing, and now two bodies? It's almost like somebody knows and is making the most of it.'

'Beginning to wonder the same myself,' Matt agreed, though really, up to that point, he'd not given the notion much weight. Now, though, to hear someone else mention it?

'Don't start looking too much into it, Mum,' said Rebecca, interrupting Matt's thoughts, 'or before you know it, you'll have come up with your own little conspiracy theory.'

'She's got a point though, hasn't she?' said Matt, still thinking about what Margaret had said. 'And between you and me, this green field we're all standing in, I'm starting to develop my own little conspiracy theory about it all as well, if I'm honest.'

'Could just be a coincidence,' said Margaret.

Matt gave her a look that said more than words ever could.

'Come on, then, Mum,' Rebecca said. 'No point standing here gassing, is there?'

And with that, off she walked, her mum beside her, their grisly destination drawing them on.

24

The following morning, Matt arrived at the office exhausted, but utterly unable to wind down. With everything that had happened over in Wharfedale, the team had all ended up leaving much later in the evening than anyone wanted. Switching off afterwards had been impossible, and Matt was not at all impressed with how he had behaved when he'd arrived home.

Instead of explaining to Joan how he was feeling, he'd simply shut down, slumping into the sofa with a mug of tea, and, quite inexplicably, no appetite for the cottage pie she'd made. She'd left him to his thoughts, where he'd stayed into the early hours, with the television on and the volume low, lights off, and the cottage pie cold on a plate in front of him. He'd eaten it eventually, unable to enjoy the taste, his mind too preoccupied with a week that seemed intent on becoming the worst for the team in living memory.

Arriving early enough to make sure he would be first in the office, despite so little sleep, Matt was surprised to find the doors already open, and even more so when the face that welcomed him into the room wasn't one that he recognised. It belonged to a dark-haired young man with a very precise beard. Maybe early thirties, Matt guessed. He was tall, slim, and wearing clothes clearly bought with considerably more care and attention for how they looked together than anything Matt had ever bought for himself in his life. He was wearing tortoiseshell glasses, and a hairstyle cut with a precision that must've cost considerably more than the ten quid Matt paid someone to take scissors to his own unruly mop.

'You must be Detective Sergeant Dinsdale,' the man said, rising from the chair he had been sitting in, with his legs all bent like a giant, thin-limbed spider. He had a mug of tea in one hand, and the other was outstretched for a handshake.

'There's no must about it,' replied Matt, accepting the offered hand, noting the man's soft, almost musical accent. 'You've got me at a loss, though.'

'Ethan Morgan,' the man said, and now Matt was able to place the accent.

'You're Welsh.'

'The accent is a bit of a giveaway, isn't it?'

'And you're here because ...?'

Matt waited for Ethan to reply, then the office door opened and he glanced over to see Walker step into the room.

'Ah, you've met already, that's good.'

'It is?' said Matt. 'Why?'

'This is Detective Inspector Morgan.'

Matt gave a shrug.

'Nope, I'm still at a loss.'

'The extra pair of hands I promised? Remember?'

Realisation dawned and Matt looked from Walker to Morgan, who, having rested his mug on a table, lifted his hands in front of his chest, and gave Matt a jazzy little wave.

'Hi,' he said.

Matt made a point then of looking Morgan up and down as though inspecting him.

'How are you with dogs?'

'What?'

'Dogs.'

'Dogs?'

'Yes, dogs.'

Morgan glanced nervously around the office, as though expecting one to pounce on him from some hiding place.

'But there aren't any dogs.'

'We've kind of got two adopted as members of the team,' Matt explained. 'Fly's a sheepdog, And Smudge is a black lab.'

'Well, I don't have a problem with them, if that's what you mean.'

'No allergies? It'll be a little rough on you if you have them. I don't mean just to dogs either. Someone yesterday said that they were allergic to dogs I mean, and I'm having to meet up with them out of the office. Bit of a hassle, that, really, but fair enough.' Saying that, Matt realised he hadn't actually arranged anything with Billy McCain, so he'd be getting on with that just as soon as everything else was sorted, and the rest of the team knew what they were on with. 'And we eat an awful lot of cheese. Oh, and one of the cases we're dealing with right now involves a body found at a cheese maker.'

As Matt waited for Ethan to try and come up with a reply, he had to quietly admit to himself that the young DI's dress sense really was very impressive; he clearly had a wardrobe that he'd spent time on and was proud of. As for his shoes? Well, they looked expensive, that was for sure. The shine on them was bright enough to catch the light and almost blind him as he stared at them.

'What about goats?'

That question, Matt knew, was a little unfair, and he couldn't hide the smile at the wide-eyed response it received.

'Goats? What, as in, like, real goats? I thought the Dales were all sheep and cows?'

Matt could feel Walker staring at him.

'How long are you here for?' he asked.

'For as long as you need him, actually,' said Walker. 'Morgan is based in Richmond for the next six months at least. Obviously, he'll have plenty else to be getting on with, as staffing is never easy across an area such as we cover, but I've no doubt he'll be of great use.'

'Oh, and I know I'm a DI,' Morgan said, 'but I'm not here to pull rank; I'm simply here to work as part of the team, learn, that kind of thing. If that works? It'll be a really good learning experience.'

'That's good to hear,' said Matt. 'First things first then, eh?'

'Of course,' Morgan replied, his voice cut keenly with enthusiasm. 'Is there an aspect of the case you want to discuss, something we need to get on with?'

'Aye, something like that,' said Matt, then gestured over at the small kitchen area in the corner of the room. 'How's about we see if you can make a good brew? Because that's the ultimate test, isn't it?'

By the time the rest of the team had all arrived, most of them bringing with them enough yawns to see them through the next month alone, Matt was already getting antsy. Sowerby was there as well, and he was very keen to hear from her. The absence of Harry was playing on his mind something terrible, and now with two deaths to investigate, he rather wished he had considered another career back in the day. Though what that career would've been he hadn't the faintest.

'First things first,' Matt said, gathering everyone around. 'I know you've all now met our newest arrival, but to make things official, I'll do the same on everyone's behalf.' He then looked over at Morgan, who was sitting next to Dave, whose size only served to magnify the man's slim frame. 'Welcome to the team, Detective Inspector Morgan, it's a pleasure to have you here.'

Matt expected to then just crack on, but before he had a chance to do so, Ethan was on his feet and speaking.

'Thank you, DS Dinsdale, for the welcome,' he said, then proceeded to spend a couple of minutes giving the team a not very quick summary of his career and experience. It was all very impressive, Matt had to admit, and he found himself warming to him as he gave them the highlights of all that he'd done so far, but when Morgan finally sat back down in his seat, he wasn't entirely sure how to proceed himself, the young DI's speech having rather stolen the limelight.

'Well, yes, thank you for that, Ethan,' he said. 'Great to have you here as well.'

The team was quiet, all eyes still on the new arrival, though they were also waiting for Matt to guide them with what to do next.

Matt provided a very quick run through of everything so far, from Harry's disappearance to the deaths of Matthew Porter and Dicky Guy. Not just as a reminder for himself and the team, but to make sure that DI Morgan was up to speed on it all as well. He felt sure that Walker would have already done the same, but it was still worth going over again.

'Right, let's start with Harry,' Matt said. 'We still don't know where he is, who's taken him, or why. We've got nothing other than Smudge being fine.' He looked at Jen. 'Do we have anything from Firbank in Bristol?'

Jen shook her head.

'We've been communicating a lot by email, and so far there's nothing to suggest that anyone from Harry's life down south has got it into their head that kidnapping him would be a good idea.'

'How can we be sure?' Jim asked.

'Well, for a start, anyone who's anyone who would want to have a go at Harry, is in prison and serving long sentences. She's had nothing from anyone working undercover either to suggest that Harry is on a hit list, or in any trouble at all. In many ways, his name has been forgotten, replaced by new detectives doing what he did and causing just as much trouble. I think it's safe to say that the criminal fraternity in Bristol has better ways to be spending its time than tracking down Harry. To do so would be a waste of resources, both manpower and money.'

'And that's what Firbank thinks, is it?' asked Matt.

'It is,' said Jen. 'And I agree with her.'

'So, we're no closer, then, are we?' said Dave, voicing the whole team's frustration. 'It really is like Harry's just disappeared off the face of the Earth! And I know that's not true or possible, but there must be something, surely; how can we not have found anything yet?'

In answer to that, Matt decided that it was time to hear from Sowerby.

'Well then, Rebecca,' he said. 'Anything you can tell us that might help?'

Sowerby opened a file and stuck a number of photographs on the board.

'Remember those carved stones we found under Harry's

Rav? Well, this is them. As you can see, they're not much to look at, are they?'

'No, not really,' agreed Matt.

'Tom wondered yesterday if they were just from someone doing a bit of fly-tipping,' said Jen.

'We thought the same, to be honest,' said Sowerby. 'Well, that was until one of my team pieced the whole thing back together. Volunteered for it, too, would you believe? Loves a good puzzle apparently.'

She then placed another photograph on the board.

Matt narrowed his eyes.

'And what's that supposed to be?' he asked. 'Looks like a pile of stones.'

'It is,' said Sowerby, 'but it's more than that, isn't it?'

'Is it?'

'Looks like a cairn,' said Jen. 'It's small, but that's what it is, isn't it? Like those piles of stones you find on top of hills.'

'Spot on,' said Sowerby. 'The stones were all piled up in a certain way, cemented together, too. Looks like someone smashed them apart before putting them where Harry was parked.'

'Was that done before or after Harry's Rav was put there?' Jadyn asked.

'That we can't say, but we do know that they're not from there.'

'Then where are they from?' asked Liz.

'We found plenty of evidence of shade-loving plants, moss, that kind of thing on the stones, fungal spores, too, all of which points to this cairn having originally been built in a woodland, or in the presence of trees at least.'

'I'm struggling to see how this is relevant,' said Jadyn. 'I want it to be, but I can't see any connection. What does a cairn have to do with Harry?'

Sowerby proceeded to place another photograph on the board, this one showing a closeup of some of the stones. 'Here you can see the carvings,' she said. 'They're quite rough, as you can see. Not anything that's been done professionally or anything like that.'

Matt leaned in closer for a better look.

'Not easy to make out what any of that says, though, is it?'

'The carvings have been badly eroded over the years,' Sowerby explained. 'We've had a go at making the best of what's there, picking out what we can from what's just too badly gone, and this is what we've come up with ...' She proceeded to stick another photo to the board. 'We don't know what the first part of the first word is, but we know we've got a K and a Y next to each other. There are definitely letters before, though what they were we just don't know. And it's impossible to say if there were letters after those as well, the stone is just too eroded. The next word begins with an A, ends in L. Then we've some numbers; twenty-something or other, then a one, I think. Not so sure about the next one, then an eight and a two. After that, we've more letters; an S, an E and a P, then some more numbers, another one, then a nine and another nine, but the last number is impossible to make out..'

'You're right,' said Jim. 'They really have been badly eroded, haven't they? How are we supposed to make sense of any of that?'

'Or even that we need to,' Jadyn added. 'Might not be relevant at all.'

'The second word could be April,' Jen suggested, 'which makes me think we've got dates in front of us.'

'My thoughts exactly,' agreed Sowerby. 'Especially as the next word, S-E-P, is most likely September.'

'Looks like something someone would build in memory of a pet,' said Dave. 'I've done the same myself.'

'That would make sense,' said Matt, and then something about the dates became clearer. 'What if the first numbers, the one, eight and two, were nineteen-eighty-two, and the next numbers were actually nineteen-ninety-two?'

'Not a bad guess,' said Sowerby. 'But there's no way of knowing for sure.'

'Or having any idea what, if anything, it's got to do with Harry's disappearance,' said Dave.

'What about Dicky's son?' Jen said. 'We know he was still young when he died; maybe this was just something that Dicky put together as a little memorial?'

'Would explain why he was pissed at Harry being parked where he was, if he managed to drive over a memorial to his lad,' said Matt.

'No reason for it to be at the side of the road, though, is there?' said Jadyn. 'And anyway, Harry's car didn't drive into it, did it? There was no damage. More likely the stones were just placed under his Rav after the fact.'

Matt took a moment to stare hard at Jadyn, impressed with the way he was thinking.

'Anything else?' he then asked, looking to get things moving again after his brief pause.

'Well, you know about the syringe, and we've matched the DNA on it to Harry. There's the new key found in the barn, this cairn thing or whatever it is, but as yet the SOC team have had nothing else to look at with regards to that, not specifically, anyway. I'm sorry.'

The weight of those last two words seemed heavy enough to put a hole in the floor, so Matt pushed on.

'What about Mr Palmer? And what do you mean by not specifically?'

'Sowerby removed the photographs of the cairn and replaced them with ones considerably more grisly.

'This is Mr Palmer,' she said. 'The body shows signs of a struggle, with bruising around the neck, and various other markings suggesting he was attacked from behind.' She pointed at another photograph. 'And this is Mr Guy. His body shows the same in many ways, that being that he was attacked from behind, lots of bruising around the neck, and so on. However, I'd like to draw your attention to these next two photographs.'

Matt, like the rest of the team, was on the edge of his seat now, sensing that Sowerby was about to show and tell them something which could have a huge impact on what they'd been dealing with these past few days.

The photographs were close-ups, that much was clear, but of what, he couldn't say, each one just being sections of pale, dead flesh.

'Both victims drowned, as we know,' said Sowerby. 'Mr Palmer in the vat filled with milk, and Mr Guy in the trough filled with water. Now, what do you see here?'

Sowerby pointed at each photograph and to begin with, Matt couldn't make anything out at all. Eventually, though, something came into focus.

'That's a needle mark,' he said.

'Yes, it is,' said Sowerby. 'Both victims received a jab to the side of their necks.' She looked at Jadyn. 'Now, about that connection you weren't able to see … Chemical analysis shows that each victim was injected with—'

'The same sedative as Harry,' said Matt, cutting in and finishing off what Sowerby was going to say. 'Correct?'

'Correct.'

25

The revelation about the sedatives shot through the team like a bolt of electricity, burning off any of the weariness they had left over from the previous days. The link between Harry's disappearance and the two deaths was now clear, but to what end, none of them knew. Nothing else had come from either of the crime scenes, but the link had been made.

'Which means,' said Matt, 'there's a connection not just between what's happened to Harry, but also between the two victims. This is not random. There is a reason behind them being killed, a plan even.' He saw worry reflected at him in the wide eyes of his team. 'We will work under the assumption that Harry is alive. We have no reason to believe otherwise. At all. Is that understood?'

In reply, all he received were some shallow, unconvinced nods.

'Judging by what we found at both crime scenes, if Harry was dead, we would know it, wouldn't we?' he explained, pushing the point home as hard as he could. 'Both victims were killed, not in secret, but in places where they would be found. My gut tells me the same would be true with Harry.'

'Why sedate him and kidnap him, then?' Jim asked. 'What's the point?'

Matt had been thinking about that for a good while now. The conclusion he had drawn was one he'd kept to himself, and it couldn't be proved at all. Not yet, anyway. He decided now was as good a time as any to share it.

'My best guess is that they want him out of the way.'

There was an audible gasp.

'Out of the way?' repeated Liz. 'Why? What's the point of that? Out of the way of what?'

'It's a distraction, isn't it?' Matt explained. 'Yes, we've got two murders to be dealing with, but we're also trying to find Harry, aren't we? And I don't know about anyone else in this room, but I don't mind admitting that sometimes I'm finding it hard to focus. I'm doing the best I can, but it's not easy. Harry's the one we all depend on, there's no getting away from that fact; without him around, things feel a little undone.'

'You mean that whoever's taken him thinks we can't do our job without him, is that it?' asked Jadyn.

'Something like that, yes,' Matt replied.

Jadyn was on his feet.

'Excuse my language, but bollocks to that, Sarge, if you don't mind me saying so. I know Harry's our boss, but that doesn't mean we're helpless without him, does it?'

'Far from it,' said Matt, unable to hide the smile at Jadyn's response. 'In fact, as far as I'm concerned, Harry's kidnapping has only made me more determined to prove to whoever's behind all this that they're wrong, very wrong.'

Jen asked, 'What do you want us to do next, then?'

'You're meeting the witness from over in Yockenthwaite in

a few minutes, aren't you? Get what you can from them, a nice, clear, witness statement, then I want you and I to run a team each, so that—'

A cough caught Matt's attention, and he turned to see that Detective Inspector Morgan had a hand raised.

'Yes, Ethan?'

'Why don't we have four teams? You run one, Walker runs one, Detective Constable Blades another, and then me? Like I've said, I'm not here to pull rank, just to help.'

'Makes sense,' offered Walker, supporting Ethan's suggestion. 'It's clear now, isn't it, that there's a connection between Matthew Palmer and Dicky Guy? Right now, as far as we are aware, they have nothing to do with each other; one's a farmer, one produces cheese, and that's it. But there has to be a connection, and if we're all working on finding it, there's a better chance that we will. Was anything else found at Dicky's farm? Anything that would give us a way to trace the other brother?'

'There was a dog,' said Sowerby. 'The house was fairly run down. I think the victim lived in the kitchen most of the time, as the rest of the house was thick with dust.'

'A dog's not going to tell us much, is it?'

'We contacted the local vets and they've taken it in for now. There were piles of papers all over the place, receipts, that kind of thing. He must have had a shotgun at some time or other, as we found a box of very old cartridges, a gun cleaning kit, but no gun in the cabinet. No photos anywhere. The place is just a shell, really. The whole house felt very sad, like it just wanted to crumble into the ground and be forgotten.'

'We can check on Dicky's gun license,' Matt said. 'As to the gun, if it's that long ago since he did any shooting, then it probably wasn't even kept in the cabinet most of the time. It was open when you found it?'

Sowerby gave a nod.

'My guess, the gun is broken down, and the pieces hidden about the house. The number of farmers I've dealt with who still think that's fine to do is quite something.'

Sowerby said, 'Anyway, I'd best head off. But if the SOC team finds anything else, I'm sure you'll be the first to know.'

With Ethan's suggestion now in play, Matt divided the team up into pairs and gave them all specific tasks. He tasked Jen and Jim with seeing what else they could find out about Dicky Guy, his family, the farm, his life in Wharfedale. He paired Jadyn with Walker, and gave them the job of getting witness statements from Karen and Billy, and then seeing what phone records they could get a hold of for both victims, their internet history, anything at all they could find that might be useful. It would probably involve lots of phone calls and frustration, but Walker had the patience for that, he was sure. Jadyn, not so much, which was why he had put them together. Liz would accompany him to search Dicky Guy's house and farm. DI Morgan and Dave were to do the same with Matthew Palmer's business and home. And once all of that was done, or even while they were on with it, he wanted more doors knocked, more people asked about what they knew of the victims and their lives, to see if somehow they could find a connection.

'We need to find out anything and everything about both victims,' he said, as he sent everyone off. 'And I mean everything. I want to know about their families, their friends, their interests, their history. I want to know where they shop, where they drink, major events in their lives. I want to know where their paths might have crossed, their phone records, internet history, what they had for dinner last Friday night … You get the picture.'

And with that, the team took off.

Having given Jim half an hour to take Fly out for a walk, Jen waited for the arrival of the walker who had found the body of Dicky Guy. He walked through the main doors of the Community Centre at the time they'd agreed, and keen to waste no time, she led him straight through to the interview room.

'Can I get you a drink?'

The man shook his head. He was wearing the kind of clothing someone who knew what they were doing would pack a rucksack with, Jen noticed. Tufts of black hair poked out from the edges of the red wool beanie hat he had pulled down onto his head.

'Thanks for coming in.'

'It's not a problem, really,' the man said with a sniff, before wiping his nose with the sleeve of his jacket. 'It makes sense as well, considering what I … Well, you know.'

'Before we go any further, can I take your name?'

'Anthony,' the man replied. 'Anthony Booker.'

'Do you have any ID with you?'

'What? Oh, goodness, no,' Anthony replied. 'I've left that all back at The George. I can bring it over later in the week if you need me to?'

'That would be great. Where was it you'd been walking yesterday before you found the body?'

'Just out and about really,' Anthony said, sniffing again. 'There's so many footpaths around. It's easy to get a bit carried away, isn't it, and to just go off exploring?'

'It is,' Jen agreed. 'I'm a runner, long distance, ultras, that kind of thing, so I know exactly what you mean.' She then slid a sheet of paper across the table, along with a pen. 'All I need you to do is fill this out. It's a witness statement, nothing more. There are sections for you to fill in your name, date of birth, address, contact details, and so on. Then all you need to do is just write in the main section what happened.'

'Well, nothing really happened,' said Anthony, wiping his nose again. 'Well, I say that; I think I've caught a bit of a cold from the walk yesterday. It was fairly blowing up on the tops.'

'It does that,' Jen smiled. 'I've been knocked off my feet a few times, I can tell you.'

'So, what do you need me to write again?'

'Just what you found, that's all. Nothing fancy. Just any details you can remember.'

'Not much to say really,' said Anthony. 'I was out walking, and I saw something floating in that trough. Next thing I know, I'm staring at a body and calling the police. It was quite the shock.'

'That's really all we need to know,' said Jen. 'Honestly, just put in as much detail as you can, explain what you were doing, where you were coming from and going to, where you were when you found the body, time of day, that kind of thing. Then you can be on your way. Is that okay?'

'Sounds fine, but I warn you, my writing is truly terrible.'

'Don't worry, I'm sure it'll be fine. Like I said, just put in as much detail as you can. Even if you don't think it's important, get it down, because you never know.'

With that said, Jen sat back and allowed Anthony to get on with filling out the witness statement. As he'd finished filling in the personal details and was about to get on with the statement in full, there was a knock at the door.

Jen stood up, went to answer.

'Matt?'

The detective sergeant was staring back at her, his expression a confused mix of frustration, anger, and bemusement.

'You're not going to believe this ...'

'Believe what?'

'Got a minute?'

Jen glanced over to see that Anthony was busy writing.

'Looking good,' she said. 'I'll be back in a few minutes.'

Jen followed Matt out of the interview room, laughing quietly to herself as a muffled sneeze from Anthony chased her down the hall. Then they were through the main doors and outside.

'What's going on, Matt?' she asked. 'What's happened?'

Matt didn't answer, just kept walking. Then, when they reached the marketplace, which was busy with people milling about, tourists funnelling from coffee shop to deli to pub, he came to a dead stop.

'Look,' he said, and pointed at the tyres of the police Land Rover.

For a second or two, Jen had no idea what it was she was supposed to be looking at. Then she spotted it.

'You've a flat tyre,' she said.

'No,' said Matt. 'I haven't. I've actually got four flat tyres. And I'm not the only one, either ...'

Jen looked around and saw that the rest of the team's vehicles were similarly stricken. They were all either talking together, their faces riven with the frustration about what had been done to the vehicles, or on the phone; Jadyn was looking particularly animated on his, no doubt trying to sort official assistance to get everyone back on the road, and Liz, Jen noticed, looked oddly still, her phone pinned to her face, her eyes staring into the middle distance, but at what?

'They've all got punctures?' she said, her focus back on

Matt now. 'But how? How is that even possible? It doesn't make sense!'

Matt lifted a hand up in front of Jen and opened it. Sitting in his palm were two large nails, bent in the middle, then welded together so that no matter how it sat in his hand, a point of a nail was raised.

'What the hell is that?'

'This,' said Matt, holding the strange device, 'is a homemade caltrop. Primitive, true, but the Romans were big fans, and they've been used across the centuries all over the world. Very effective, you see, against horses, against people ...'

'And against tyres,' said Jen.

'Exactly.'

Then a yell cut across the marketplace, and everyone turned to see Liz running towards them.

26

Back in the cave, and sitting on the edge of the camp bed, Harry had, in every possible way, had enough. He'd finished the food, put new batteries in the lamp, had another nap, and was now not just frustrated, but bored.

Harry didn't do bored.

He'd been going over and over all the things he'd learned from the visit of his jailer. Though *learned* was probably stretching it, he thought, but he'd certainly picked up a few things, which in situ, didn't really point to anything. Together, however? Well, the conclusions he had drawn were, he felt sure, wrong. Because they just had to be.

He had not been kidnapped by anyone who wanted to do him harm, that much he was confident about. Having once again run through the list of potential suspects who would, given the chance, do anything this ridiculous and brazen, he knew that none of them were responsible. And the simple reason was that they would not have been able to resist coming down to see him and crow about it all. Rubbing his face in it, in his predicament, would have been half the fun for them. They would've wanted him to know it was they who had snatched him, they who had imprisoned him, they who had made him comfortable, and they who, soon enough, would be returning with a gaggle of goons to subdue him, and a toolbox full of pain.

As the inescapable fear of such a conclusion to the last few days had faded, which had only been hurried along by the arrival of his jailer, Harry's mind had got to work. He'd sifted through the evidence, re-examined everything a dozen times over, and in the end, been presented with a conclusion so baffling, so hurtful, so utterly and completely wrong, that even now, he could not give voice to it. Indeed, as the name he was sure he could pin to the person who had put him in that cave burned star-bright in his mind, he refused to acknowledge it. And he wouldn't, either, not until he was with them face-to-face, and could finally, hopefully, understand why.

The why was the thing that really held him fast. Whatever reason there was to him being imprisoned, whatever grand design there was behind it all, the simple conclusion he had drawn, was that he was being kept out of the way. Someone, somewhere, didn't want him around just long enough so that whatever they were doing, they didn't have to deal with him getting in the way of it and buggering it up. Which, Harry mused, was a little bit foolish, really, because once he was out, he'd be buggering things up for them good and proper, that was for sure.

Another thing had started to nag at him as well, the realisation that the person behind it all held his team in such low regard that they figured without Harry around, they would be lost, unable to function. Not that he was one hundred percent convinced that the intent of having him out of the way was supposed to render his team useless, but his gut was telling him strongly enough for him to accept it as the most obvious reason. His disappearance would have been a shock, and the resultant search for him all consuming, so what better time to then get on with whatever else it is that they had planned?

That thought horrified Harry more than anything else. He knew that Grace would be worried, because of course she would be, that the team would be doing everything they could to find him, but it was what the person behind his abduction was now up to that had his full attention.

Harry stood up. He took a couple of steps away from the camp bed and, for a moment or two, just stood. He didn't move, just allowed everything to swamp him, drown him, become him.

He took a breath in deep, forced his lungs to expand to their fullest, pushed further, then exhaled. Did it again, then once more.

Now it was time to do something.

Turning to face the camp bed, he carefully rolled up the sleeping bag, and stowed it on the floor on top of the carrier bag that his food had been in. He then examined the bed, how it was a simple construction of canvas and metal poles, strong enough to hold his weight with ease. Then, with a violence he kept locked down, and with very good reason, he tore into the construction, stamping on it until hinges and brackets snapped, the canvas little more than ripped patches of material. He grabbed it with his hands, braced his feet, pulled and heaved and wrenched and tore, the rage at his imprisonment ripping from his lungs in a war cry.

The bed lay in pieces at his feet. He ripped off the remnants of the canvas, and was left with only the metal poles. Grabbing the strongest of the poles, each about the length of his forearm to clenched fist, he separated them from the rest of the frame, then rolled them in a stretch of the canvas, using a thinner ripped strip to hold it all in place. That done, he turned on his heels and walked calmly over to the chain and padlock.

'Right then,' Harry growled through gritted teeth. 'Here goes nothing, you bastard ...'

Shifting the chain so that the padlock hung free from the iron bars, he slipped the canvas-wrapped poles through the loop of chain and wound the poles anticlockwise. The chain tightened, the slack disappeared, and soon the padlock was trapped in the middle of it. Whether it was the point of weakness, he had no idea, but the chain was thick and welded, whereas the padlock had enough moving parts to offer some degree of potential failure, if sufficient stress was placed upon it.

Harry continued to twist, the chain resisting as he did so. Soon, the poles from the camp bed started to bend, but the canvas held them fast, allowing them to be stronger together than alone. It also gave his hands something more to gain purchase on, the sweat on his hands absorbed easily, his grip firm.

The chain complained, the padlock started to buckle. Harry kept on twisting, forcing metal and against metal, wondering which would give first. He roared, swore, braced his whole body and forced each and every muscle to become a part of what he was doing; this was not a job merely for arms, but demanded chest and back and core and the thick, corded muscles of his legs.

Harry wanted to give in, his body screamed at him to stop, to give it a reprieve, but the pain was only in his mind, and he stamped on it, silencing it.

A sharp cry of pain rang out. The padlock buckled further still, and then somewhere in the chain, that one weak link was found despite it doing its best to stay hidden, and Harry was sent tumbling, as the full-body force he had been putting into freeing himself of his prison suddenly had nothing against which to push. He tried to stop his fall, but the momentum was too much too soon, and he shot forward, crashing into the rotting, wooden shelves, splintering them. Then he was on the ground, face full of wet grit and dirt, knuckles bleeding from taking the full force of his fall into the shelves, the wall, the floor.

Silence.

Harry lay still for a moment, at first concerned that he had, in his fearsome haste, done himself some harm, broken something.

Deep breaths, waiting for the pain.

Nothing.

Harry rolled over, sat up, and saw that the chain was a broken thing on the ground beside him, the padlock still in one piece. Then a whining screech of metal on metal razored its way through the still, damp air, and Harry watched the iron bars swing open. And he would've made a run for it right then, if a shadow hadn't immediately stepped through the space he had brute-forced into existence, stared down at him, and held out a hand.

27

Matt stumbled back a little as Liz threw herself at him, eyes wide, wild, her face bloodless.

'It's Ben! Matt, he's ... it's him ... and ... shit-shit-shit!'

Jen had just been thinking back to Anthony in the interview room, because as she'd followed Matt, something had started to scratch at the back of her mind. She had no idea what it was, beyond, perhaps, because of how he had been dressed, that she'd almost felt like she recognised him. Hearing the fear and concern in Liz's voice, however, she quickly stopped thinking about the witness and rested a hand on Liz's arm.

'Liz? What's happened? What's happened to Ben?'

Liz snapped around to stare at Jen, but stared right through her instead.

'He's not making any sense! He said something about Harry, about everything that's been happening. He wanted to know that I was with the team, that I was safe, because he had to do something. He was very, very insistent that I was safe. He kept saying sorry. He was crying, I could hear it in his voice, the words just breaking up.'

'Where is he?' Matt asked. He saw the rest of the team starting to make their way over, but with a look, a shake of his head, he held them at bay, for now.

Liz tried to speak, but couldn't.

'Liz?' said Jen, her voice calm as she spoke to her friend. 'Whatever's going on, whatever's happened, you need to tell us now, so that we can help, okay?'

Into the marketplace rolled a recovery truck; Mike had come to the rescue. Matt guessed from the thumb raised in the air by Jim that he'd been the one to contact him.

Matt glanced at Jen.

'What about the witness?'

'What about him? He's writing his statement.'

'Well, whatever we're dealing with here, go make sure that's all done and dusted, because there's more going on out here right now than any of us understand yet.'

Jen gave Liz's arm a squeeze, then turned towards the Community Centre and ran towards it.

'Now, Liz,' said Matt. 'Take a deep breath, relax as best you can, and go over what Ben said. We need to know. You said he mentioned Harry, yes?'

Liz gave a nod.

'He just kept saying sorry, Matt. I don't understand. Why did he want to make sure I was safe? What's he done?'

'What did he say, exactly?'

Behind Liz, Matt could see that Mike was busy with the police Land Rover; he'd rocked up with four wheels of varying colours, all wearing tyres, and was rolling them over to the vehicle while Dave was on with jacking up the rear axle. The rest of the team was on with the other vehicles as well. Matt had no idea how Mike planned to fix so many punctures, but he wasn't going to be distracted by worrying about that.

'Liz?'

Liz was quieter now, calmer, and Matt could see that the tension had slipped from her body a little, her shoulders had slumped, and the wide-eyed shock in her face had slackened just enough to make her look less terrified.

'Right, yes,' Liz said, breathing with purpose as she spoke. 'Let me think ...'

'Take your time. I'm not going anywhere.'

'First, he said he was sorry, and he kept repeating that, saying that he'd had no choice, that I was in danger, that he couldn't risk that, which was why he did what he did. He sounded terrified, Matt; I've never heard him like that, ever.'

'Did he say why he thought you were in danger?'

'Not exactly, not specifically, no, just that I was in danger and that was why he'd had no choice but to do what he had done.'

'Which was what?'

Liz didn't answer the question, just kept on talking, and Matt didn't think interrupting would be a good idea, so he just listened.

'Said he'd been shown things, photographs of me, that they knew where I was, and that if he hadn't done what he'd done, then ...' She blinked away tears, as though refusing to let them fall. 'He said if he'd known what was going to happen, he wouldn't have done it, but he didn't know what to do, didn't have any choice. He mentioned Harry's past, the people he's put away, that they do things, bad things.'

'I'm trying to make sense of what you're saying, but I'm struggling,' said Matt. 'Was he saying that he or you or both of you were threatened, and because of that, he was forced to do something?'

'Yes.' Liz nodded. 'I think so. That's what it sounded like. But he wasn't making much sense. I could just hear the terror in his voice, the panic.'

'What else did he say? Something about Harry, wasn't it? Does he think someone Harry had dealings with in the past is here now? Is that it? But if that's the case, what is it that Ben's done? And where did he say he was going?'

'He said ... He said that he didn't want to go back to prison, that he wouldn't, and he didn't want the people he loved to be hurt, to be hurt himself, killed.'

'He said that?'

'Yes.'

'Bloody hell, Ben, what's going on?' Matt muttered to himself.

Mike was already onto the front axle of the Land Rover, the rear one now resting on new wheels with hard tyres. For now, Matt was going to ignore that the one he could see looked to be half-bald in places.

'He must've said something else.'

'I'm thinking ... It was all really garbled, Matt. I couldn't make sense of it.'

'Does he know where Harry is? Is that what this is about?'

'Askew,' said Liz. 'He mentioned Askew.'

'What? The journalist? The hell has he got to do with this?'

'That was it! He said he'd told Askew everything he needed to know, and that Harry was fine, but then ...'

'Then what?'

'He just said he had to go, Matt. That's what he said. That he had to go, get away before something bad happened to him. Then he told me he loved me, that he was sorry, and hung up.'

Matt already had his phone out and was pulling up a contact he'd only added over the last few days.

'Who are you calling?'

Matt didn't answer Liz's question, just waited for the call to connect.

It didn't.

'Voicemail,' Matt said, his eyes on Liz, then he spoke into his phone. 'Askew, I know that Harry's brother has been in touch with you, and that he's told you something about Harry. Wherever you are, whatever you're doing, whatever it is you know, call me. Now. We both know you'll regret it if you don't, I can promise you that.'

'Matt?'

The shout was from Mike.

'This one's done,' he said, pointing at the Land Rover. 'I'll get the others fixed quick as I can, I promise.'

'How?'

'Let me worry about that.'

'Don't suppose you've heard anything from Ben?'

Mike shook his head.

'He was off ill for a day or so, then, when he came back to work, he wasn't himself at all. Worrying about Harry, right?'

'Yes, that'll be it.'

Mike frowned.

'Don't suppose you'd know why he took a chain and padlock from the workshop, would you?'

That question caught Matt off guard.

'What?'

'I've a few hanging on the wall. Useful to add a bit of security to things if I need to, like a bike or something. I keep the place locked, obviously, but a chain round a wheel and locked into a ring of steel cemented into the ground helps with the insurance costs.'

'And you're sure Ben took it?'

'No one else there to do so other than me, and I'd remember if I'd done it myself, I think. Well, I hope I would, anyway. I assumed he took it for Liz's bike or something. It's not a problem, just struck me as odd, that's all. He'd usually ask, like.'

'Odd's not the half of it,' Matt said, and he was about to ask if Mike had noticed anything else odd about Ben's behaviour these last few days, when Jen skidded to a halt beside him and handed him a sheet of paper.

'What's this?'

'It's supposed to be a witness statement.'

Matt looked at the sheet of paper, but couldn't really take it in.

'And it isn't?'

'Read it,' said Jen.

Matt could see that the sheet of paper had been filled with writing.

'What, all of it?'

'Yes.'

Matt started to read, stopped, glanced at Jen, then up towards the Community Centre, then back to Jen again.

'You're kidding me ...'

'And before you ask, he's gone,' said Jen. 'He left that behind. He clearly wanted us to read it, didn't he?'

Then Matt's phone rang.

'What?'

'Hello, Detective,' came the reply. 'I've got someone with me who I think would like to speak to you ...'

28

Harry hesitated, staring at the outstretched hand, then up to its owner and saw a face smiling down. Though, perhaps, to describe it as a smile was an injustice to smiles, Harry thought; there was a knowing smugness behind it, a look, which under normal circumstances, he'd have happily slapped right off.

'Askew ...'

'I'm probably the last person you expected to see.'

'You'll always be the last person I expect to see,' Harry replied. 'Or want to, for that matter. What are you doing here?'

Askew wiggled his hand.

'You want to stay down there for the rest of the day, or are you going to actually get up out of the dirt? But, if you're comfortable, don't let me get in the way of that.'

Harry gave it a moment, then finally stretched up and grabbed the offered hand. It felt unnaturally long, the fingers thin, and he had a horrible feeling that if he gripped it too tightly, he might break Askew's fingers like dried spaghetti.

Once he was up on his feet, Harry immediately put some space between himself and the journalist, distrust and suspicion pushing themselves to the front of his mind with consummate ease.

'Why are you here, Askew?'

'I could ask you the same question.'

'If I knew the answer, I can't imagine rushing to give it to you.'

'And there was me thinking our relationship had developed beyond simple mutual dislike, through indifference, and into the strangely uncharted territory of something akin to a neutral zone, where, when need called, a degree of trust could be offered and maybe even accepted.'

'You don't half talk some bollocks,' said Harry. 'Now, if you'd be so kind; answer the bloody question.'

'You won't like the answer,' Askew replied.

'True, but I've had a lot of time to think things through, and there might even be the thinnest of chances that I already know what it is.'

'Then why don't you tell me why I'm here, instead?'

'Because my answer would probably begin with *you're a nosy bastard* and finish with *anything for a story*.'

'There's some truth in that.'

'Some?'

Askew laughed, and his narrow face seemed unsure how to deal with it. For a moment, it was as though the rest of the man's features were trying to ignore the smile and look the other way.

'I followed him,' Askew said.

'Who?'

'The person who put you in here.'

'When?'

'The last time he was here.'

That answer both confused and angered Harry, and he had to forcibly resist the urge to lunge for the journalist and throttle him.

'That was forever ago, Askew! Maybe a day or longer, not that I know, as I've no way to keep track of the time down here. But it was definitely way longer than it needed to be, don't you think, if you knew that this was where I was?'

'But I didn't know that this was where you were,' Askew replied. 'I'd no idea. In fact, I only found that out a few minutes ago, when I heard something metallic snap, and rounded a corner to find you lying on the ground. I followed their vehicle, but I had no idea where they were going. Then they parked up just off the road and headed off across the moors down a thin path. I couldn't follow them because I wasn't exactly dressed for it.'

'Dressed for it? That's the sound of a man digging shallow ground for excuses.'

'I'd have been no use to anyone if I'd have slipped and broken an ankle, would I? I certainly wouldn't be here now, that's for sure. And for all I knew, they weren't alone, perhaps they were meeting someone. Don't know about you, but I don't really fancy meeting strangers on the moor with no way to escape. Not something I'd describe as fun.'

'So, you came back.'

'The clue to the answer to that question is me actually being here, don't you think?' Askew then held his arms out to the side. 'See? I'm right here, Harry, I came back. Not because I knew I'd find you, or anyone, actually, but because I am, as you rightly pointed out, a nosy bastard. Proud of it, too. I'd be a useless journalist if I wasn't. And I repeat, I didn't know that I'd find you. I had no idea the path would even lead to a cave or mine or whatever the hell this is. Which then led to another delay, because obviously I'd not bought a torch, and had to go fetch one.'

'You're painting quite the picture,' growled Harry.

'The truth can be surprisingly colourful.'

'And harder to believe.'

Askew frowned.

'You're a difficult person to impress, Harry.'

'Don't expect me to change.'

'Shall I continue?'

'You're going to anyway. Shame you didn't bring me any popcorn.'

Another frown, deeper this time, and Harry wondered if he'd pushed too hard. Not that he cared. Being stuck down a mine for so long would make anyone grouchy, so really, Askew was damned lucky he hadn't been stuffed in the old mining cart and pushed headlong into the darkness and whatever waited at the end of it. Hopefully, a hole, a very, very deep one, thought Harry.

'To cut a long story short, I grabbed a torch from a shop in Hawes, raced back over here, found the entrance to this place again, and went exploring. I didn't know what I would find, I just knew that it had something to do with you being missing, that was all. So, believe me, I'm just as surprised to find myself standing in front of you, as you are to find me doing exactly that.'

'How did you know that this place had something to do with me being missing?' Harry asked. 'And where are we, anyway?'

'I'll answer your second question first,' Askew said. 'We are, right now, down an old mine, somewhere in Swaledale, on land owned by Mr Matthew Palmer.'

'Never heard of him.'

'He's an artisan cheese maker in Aysgarth. And he's dead.'

'What was that?'

'Dead,' Askew repeated. 'An odd coincidence, don't you think?'

'What do you mean by dead, exactly?' Harry asked. 'And I don't believe in coincidences.'

'He was murdered,' said Askew. 'Drowned in a vat of milk in the building his business operates from.'

Harry scratched his head.

'This place belongs to a cheese maker? Why? What would he want a mine for? And why would he put me in here?'

'Cheese,' Askew said. 'There's a cave not too far from here, I passed it on the way. At first, I thought that was where the person I followed must have gone, but what I found just a few metres inside the entrance made me think probably not.'

'And what was that?'

'A locked cage full of cheese wheels, all wrapped in linen.'

'This Palmer bloke was cave-aging it?' said Harry.

'Looks that way.'

Harry shook his head, unable to grasp what he was hearing because he couldn't make any connection between it, where he had spent the last few days, and a dead cheese maker.

'At least he's not trying to do that in here,' he said. 'If this is a Swaledale mine, then it's a lead mine, isn't it? Not exactly a safe environment.'

'No, not really.'

'Can't say any of what I'm hearing makes much sense right now,' said Harry.

Askew smirked.

'And to think only a few minutes ago you were convinced you knew the answer as to why I was here.'

'Actually,' said Harry, 'on that, I reckon I still do.'

'How so?'

'The person you followed, I know who it is. I wish I didn't, and my guess is that there's a lot going on that neither of us knows right now, but their identity? Now that, I'm fairly sure about, though right now it saddens me more to say so than it angers me.'

'You going to tell me, then?' Askew asked.

Harry laughed, though the question seemed to be a little too knowing for his liking. And that told him enough. 'You know, don't you?'

'I do,' Askew said. 'Not just because I followed him, but because he called me when I was on my way here, told me everything, well, as much as he knew, anyway.'

Harry's heart sank.

'What did Ben say?'

'A few days ago, he received something through the post, an envelope containing photographs of his partner and information about you.'

'Photographs of Liz? Bloody hell ...'

'From what I could gather, the photographs came with instructions, telling him to kidnap you, and a syringe full of a sedative, I'm guessing, because I can't see how else he could have done it.'

Harry rubbed his neck, remembering the sharp jab he'd felt there before waking up in the cave.

'And the photographs were a threat, then, right?' Harry guessed.

Askew gave a nod.

'Ben had no choice, did he?' Harry said, knowing his brother better than anyone. 'He wasn't going to risk Liz's safety, not for anyone, not even for me. Did he say who sent the photographs?'

'He said he didn't know, just that he couldn't do it

anymore, not with everything that's been going on with you gone.'

Harry rubbed his eyes, weariness suddenly flooding his body.

Askew said, 'You're taking this better than I thought, Harry.'

'He's my brother,' Harry growled. 'Now, let's get out of this cave so that you can give me your phone.'

'And what if I refuse to give it to you?'

'I think I'll just let your imagination answer that for me, don't you? Now, shall we get on?'

29

Alan Cartwright had always been a practical man. Words were not his thing, not those written down, anyway. It wasn't that he couldn't read, just that he preferred not to, which had been a bit of a problem at school. That hadn't mattered though, because he'd always known what he wanted to do with his life and had been fairly sure that reading poetry and reciting Shakespeare was never going to help him achieve it. At what point was understanding Hamlet going to help him use a plumb line? When would being able to recall the best of Dylan Thomas enable him to make sure a wall was straight and true? Never. So, he'd skipped school whenever he could, and as soon as he could leave, he buggered off sharpish to become a builder. After a few years spent apprenticing to various one-man bands, he'd approached his best mate, Brian Suggitt, about setting something up together. Brian was a man equally good with his hands, but whose craft was wood, not brick. And neither of them had ever looked back.

Today was a big day, the end of a job they'd been working on for a while now. With them both being perfectionists, they'd sent the lads who worked for them to the next job already, leaving them to do the final touches.

'You fancy one of these yourself, then, Bri?' Alan asked. 'A nice little cottage somewhere to escape to, now and again?'

If Brian's laugh hadn't said it all, the look on his face most certainly would have.

'And where would I be escaping to, like? And from what? I already live in a place other people escape to, don't I? And though we're both getting on a bit, it's not like we've any urge to stop what we're doing, have we?'

'You could take up a hobby.'

'Like what?'

'Golf.'

More laughter, louder, deeper.

'Have you ever witnessed anything more daft than folk smacking a tiny ball hundreds of yards with a metal pole then going to try and find it?'

'I think there's a bit more to it than that, Bri.'

'I don't.'

Alan chuckled. That was Brian to a T. Zero time for a discussion about things, because he said what he meant and meant what he said, and that was all there was to it.

The cottage had been a full renovation project. A little place with two bedrooms and a small courtyard garden, a view that presented Wensleydale as a fine oil painting to be viewed resting on a now-perfect dry-stone wall, a bespoke oak kitchen, a pretty bathroom with a free-standing bathtub, and a lounge with a wood burner that Alan just knew would quickly become the little home's cosy heart.

The jobs left for the day were really nothing more than a quality assurance check, and they were going around the whole place, ticking things off a snag list, making sure that nothing had been missed or was out of place. They'd found a few things that needed sorting, but nothing too taxing; a dab of paint here, a bit of sanding there, and come the afternoon, they'd both stepped out of the cottage very happy indeed with the work they'd done.

'You ever think of retiring?' Alan asked.

Brian folded his arms as he turned to his old friend.

'Is this you back on with asking me if I want to get myself a cottage to escape to?'

Alan shook his head.

'No, it's not that.'

'Then what is it?' A dark look swept across Brian's eyes. 'Wait, you're not, are you?'

'I'm sixty-eight years old, Bri,' Alan said. 'And you're a year older, aren't you? I know we both work only three days a week now, but ...'

'But what? What's your point?'

'That we should ease up a bit, enjoy life.'

'I do enjoy life. We both do, don't we? And like you've just said yourself, we only work three days a week, don't we? We're basically part-timers now.'

Alan had spent weeks trying to work out how best to approach the subject with Brian, and already felt like he was messing it up.

'I'm not saying we don't enjoy life, because we do, and the shorter week is grand, for sure, it's just that, well, what I'm trying to say is ...'

No words came, because Alan really wasn't sure what he was trying to say at all. Or maybe it was that he was sure, but he just didn't know how to say it. Or perhaps it was something else. Maybe I should just shut up, he thought.

'Sounds to me like you're saying a big load of nowt,' said

Brian, and he rested a hefty hand on Alan's shoulder. 'People like us don't retire. If we do, that's when we die, isn't it? I'd put money on it; if I downed my tools today, I'd most likely not wake up tomorrow.'

'What, so you're looking to keep working as a way of securing eternal life?'

'Don't be daft, of course I'm not! All I'm saying is that I don't want to be one of those blokes who sits around doing nowt, just waiting for death to come knocking. Where's the life in that? Anyway, what's brought all this on?'

Alan wasn't entirely sure what had brought it on, but something had, and he'd been doing a lot of thinking lately. Eileen, his wife, was happy enough that he still worked, because it meant they didn't have to struggle for money, could treat themselves, drive decent vehicles. It kept him busy, and she knew that he needed that, to feel useful, that he wasn't just wasting his life away, that he served a purpose. They'd even been going on their holidays, and abroad! But she'd like to spend more time with him, and he with her, and really that was it, wasn't it?

'I want to spend more time with Eileen,' he said.

'Can't blame you for that.'

'I'm not asking you to, I'm just saying, you know? We're lucky to have got to the age we have, and I'd like to make the most of it, not just spend what's left building stuff for people with more money than I've ever seen or ever will see.'

For a moment, Brian said nothing in reply. Instead, he just stared off for a while, and Alan joined him.

The sky was clear, and the emerald fells around them were like a page torn from God's book on creating Eden. Far off, a curlew called out as it danced in the air, as further on two collies guided a flock of sheep down a narrow lane to a new pasture.

'Maybe you've got a point,' he said at last.

Alan was rather taken aback.

'What?'

'I hear you,' Brian continued. 'We should maybe not be doing as much as we are. I mean, we've got the lads all trained up now, haven't we? We could just oversee things a bit more, instead of—'

The sound of an engine cut Brian off and both he and Alan saw a motorbike pull up next to the van they'd arrived in, which was parked in the small gravel area just at the end of the garden. Beyond that, the lane snaked off towards Askrigg, and Alan rather fancied popping into The King's Arms or the Crown Hotel later on for a pint and a pie.

The bike was one of those off-road types, Alan noticed, the kind people would cover in paniers and take on adventures across deserts and goodness knew where else. There was something long strapped to the side of it as well, but he couldn't make out what it was.

At first, Alan didn't recognise him when the rider removed his helmet and climbed off the bike. He raised a hand and waved anyway, guessing that it could really be only one person, considering where they actually were, and as the figure drew nearer, he realised that his initial confusion was because the huge beard was now gone, replaced with a cleanly shaved face. It was definitely an improvement. The bike was new as well; usually, Smith had turned up in a car.

'Now then, Mr Smith, I think you're going to love it,' he said, and rubbed his own chin. 'I see you've got rid of it then, that huge hedge you've been wearing for so long?'

Mr Smith smiled, laughed, gave his skin a scratch.

'Yeah, I fancied a change,' he said.

'You look right different, like,' said Brian, and Alan saw his old friend narrow his eyes at Mr Smith and lean towards him. 'But not different, if that makes sense? And you don't half remind me of someone. No idea who, though.'

Brian's words caught Alan sharp, because as he'd said them, he'd found himself thinking the same; there was something about Mr Smith that was oddly familiar, now that he'd got rid of the ridiculous beard, but what the hell was it?

'So, you going to give me a tour, then?' Mr Smith asked.

'Right this way,' Brian directed. 'We're just going around doing a final check of everything ourselves, just to make sure it's perfect for you.'

'I'm sure it is.'

As Brian led Mr Smith into the cottage, Alan followed, still trying to get to the bottom of why the man they'd renovated this little place for suddenly reminded them both of someone. Or maybe he didn't, Alan thought. Perhaps it was just the shock of seeing him without the beard.

With a quick look at the lounge, which included a few seconds of almost reverent silence in respect of the beautiful stove, they then made their way through to the kitchen, after which they went back into the lounge and to the stairs.

'As requested, we've installed a gun cabinet in the cupboard under the stairs,' Brian said. 'You shoot much?'

'Never,' said Mr Smith.

The answer rather stunned Alan, and he wasn't sure he'd heard right.

'Pardon?' he said, his eyes flicking between Brian and Mr Smith. 'You've never shot at all? Then why do you want a cabinet for a couple of guns?'

Mr Smith's answer was to hold up a hand, then dash from the cottage, down the path to his motorbike, collect something, then dash back.

'It's for this,' he said, and swung the gun sleeve off his shoulder.

'You own a gun, then? Well, that's something,' said Brian, as Mr Smith unzipped the sleeve.

Well, that at least explains what that long thing was he'd seen strapped to the motorbike, Alan thought, remaining quiet. But something immediately bothered him; if Mr Smith had never shot before, then there was no way he would ever have been able to prove to the police a reason to own one, so where had he got it from, and why? Something here was off, he thought, but what?

'Here we go,' Mr Smith said, now holding in his hands a side-by-side shotgun, the barrels pointing directly at Alan and Brian. 'What do you think?'

'I think you should be pointing that somewhere else, lad,' said Brian, and reached out to place a hand on the barrels and push them down towards the ground.

The barrels didn't shift.

'You don't recognise it, do you?' Mr Smith asked.

Alan was too busy trying to work out what was happening to even register the question. Why the hell was Mr Smith pointing a shotgun at them? What was going on?

'It was my dad's,' said Mr Smith. 'He's not used it in years. Just over three decades since, I reckon, don't you?'

Alan's brain slipped into gear at last, and a very distant memory floated to the surface.

'Wait ... no, you can't be ... I mean, no ...'

Mr Smith didn't move the gun, his body, or even his head, just his eyes swivelled to look directly at Alan.

'Go on,' he said. 'I think you've got it, haven't you? Or would you like a clue?'

'What the hell are you talking about?' asked Brian, his hand now gripping the shotgun's barrels. 'I know this isn't loaded, but you should know better than to point a—'

'I never said it wasn't loaded ...' Mr Smith said, and Alan, for the first time in over six decades, felt something wet and warm flow down his leg.

30

'Matt, it's Harry.'

It took Matt a few seconds to deal with the shock of hearing the voice of the team's beloved DCI. He simply couldn't believe it, not right then, because there was just too much going on already for such a thing to be true. And yet, it was.

'Matt? Matt!'

'Yes?'

'It's Harry, Matt. It's me.'

'I know, Harry, I know,' Matt replied, his words tumbling over themselves, 'it's just that, well, I mean, what the hell's going on? Where are you? Why's Askew with you? And how the bloody hell has he found you before us?'

'Because, as we all know, he's a sneaky, nosy bastard. Aren't you, Askew?'

Matt heard down the line a muffled response from Askew himself. And although he'd probably not put any money on it, he felt sure Harry's voice had given away just a hint of warmth towards Askew, despite what he'd actually just said.

'Not sure that's a good enough reason,' said Matt. 'He was supposed to keep in touch with me, let me know if he knew anything.'

'Damn it,' said Jen, cutting in. 'We saw him at Ben's. Askew, I mean. Totally forgot to mention it. Sorry.'

Matt heard a rustling sound down the line, then Askew's voice came through loud and clear.

'I phoned you when I knew something,' the journalist said. 'Which was about two minutes ago now, I think.'

Matt couldn't believe what he was hearing.

'You mean to say you had no idea where you were going or who you were going to find, is that it?'

'Sort of.'

Harry came back on the phone.

'Matt, I'm over in Swaledale. I've been kept out of the way somewhere up near Crackpot Hall, I think. Askew's bringing me back right now, so I won't be too long; we'll be driving past the Buttertubs in a minute or so, I think.'

Matt still couldn't quite get his head around what he was hearing.

'But what are you doing over there? And why are you even there in the first place? I shouldn't be asking you, I know, because there's no way you can know, is there? And there's been so much going on lately that it's hard to think straight.'

'Askew's told me,' Harry said. 'Two bodies, right? A cheese maker and a farmer.'

'Correct.'

'My guess is that whoever's responsible for what's been going on blackmailed the person responsible for kidnapping me to make sure that I wouldn't get in the way.'

Matt let those words sink in, and as he did so, he realised the rest of the team had gathered around him.

'Blackmailed? You mean there's more than one person involved?'

'Exactly that.'

'But he was here, about half an hour ago, at the Community Centre, the man responsible for it all, Anthony Booker.'

There was a moment of silence from Harry's side of the conversation.

'Explain.'

Matt told Harry about the walker who had found Dicky Guy's body, that he'd met with Jen to provide a witness statement, only it had been so much more than that.

'Anthony Booker wasn't just the witness,' Matt said, 'he was the one who killed him. Confessed the whole thing in his statement.'

'What? Why?'

Matt then explained about what had happened to the vehicles, how the tyres had all been ruined with caltrops.

'He's got some balls, whoever he is,' said Harry.

'It's the whoever he is that's the problem,' said Matt. 'We've no idea, and he was right here; if we'd known, we could've grabbed him.'

'He knew you didn't know,' said Harry, then he asked, 'How are Ben and Grace? And what about Smudge?'

'Smudge is with Grace, and Grace is fine. She even joined in the search when you first went missing.'

'What about Ben?'

Matt stared at Liz, her eyes bloodshot now by the tears.

'Yeah, about Ben,' he said.

'What about him?'

'He's run off. We don't know where. He called Liz, said he'd been involved with something, and that he'd had to do what he did because otherwise she would be in danger. And he said that he told Askew everything.'

'He did,' said Harry. 'Well, as much as he knew, anyway. Matt, it was Ben who kidnapped me ...'

Matt held the phone away from his face and just stared at it in disbelief for a moment. What Harry had just said, well, the same thought had started to cross his mind when he'd been listening to Liz, but it had seemed so completely ridiculous that he'd not been able to accept it. To hear it from Harry was more than a shock, it was almost enough to take his legs from under him.

'You're sure about that, Harry? Ben?'

'Matt, I know it was him. He visited me while I was in the mine. I didn't know it was him right away, but there were signs, and with what Askew's told me, it only confirmed what I'd already guessed. I just need him found now, is that understood?'

'You were in a cave?'

'Yes, I was in a cave, over Crackpot Hall way, like I said, but that's not important right now. We need to find Ben, and we need to stop whoever is out there doing the killing, because my guess is that this isn't over, not yet. Otherwise, why keep me locked underground for so long?'

'We've been trying to tie all the threads together,' Matt sighed, 'but there's just so many of them, and with you missing as well ...'

'Is the team with you?'

'They are.'

'Put me on speaker.'

Matt did as Harry asked and held his phone out so that everyone could hear what their DCI was about to say.

'First, how are you all doing? Don't all answer at once, though. Jen, you first.'

'Er, we're, I mean, I guess we're just happy to hear that

you're safe and well, Harry,' Jen said. 'It's been a hell of a week.'

'Where are you, Harry?' asked Jim, jumping in.

'Swaledale,' Harry replied. 'Woke up in a mine, like I told Matt. Been there ever since. How many days has it been, just out of interest?'

'Three, I think,' said Jadyn.

'Liz, are you okay?' Harry asked.

'No, I'm not,' Liz replied, her voice a little croaky now. 'I don't know where Ben is or why he did what he did to you.'

'Because he had no choice, that's why,' Harry said. 'I'm convinced someone blackmailed him, told him that if he didn't help them, then they'd harm you. That would've been more than enough to make him do what he did. Whether they'd have hurt you or not, is another matter entirely, but he wasn't about to risk it.'

'You don't sound very angry.'

'Oh, I'm angry,' Harry replied. 'But not with Ben. I'm worried about him, is what I am; I'm saving my anger for who's behind it all. Can't blame Ben for what he did, not under those circumstances. None of us can. And we won't be doing that either. Matt?'

'Boss?'

'Can someone let Grace know that—'

'Already done,' said Jen, cutting in. 'I messaged her straight away.'

Another voice thrust its way into the conversation.

'Mr Grimm?'

A pause.

'Er, yes? Who's that, then?'

'I'm DI Ethan Morgan,' Ethan said. 'I've been given the opportunity to join the team for a while, six months at least.'

'Lucky you.'

'He's good, Harry,' said Walker, jumping in. 'Because of course he is, because I've brought him in for you as an extra pair of hands.'

'Replacement for Gordy, you mean?'

'This is temporary, that's all.'

Harry went to say something, but his voice cut out and was then replaced by a thin, high-pitched beep.

'Phone's cut out,' said Matt. 'Signal's dodgy over the tops, anyway. But at least we know he's fine and on his way.'

The phone rang, and Matt answered.

'Harry?'

'Right then,' Harry said, wasting no time, 'I want to know everything, Matt, you hear me? Everything. Don't miss a single detail.'

So, Matt told him, and after a few minutes, as he continued to listen to what the detective sergeant was saying, Harry sent a text.

31

Arriving in the marketplace, Harry could see that not only was the team standing together waiting for him, but a crowd also seemed to have gathered with them as well. Jen, he couldn't see, which meant she was still doing as he'd requested in his text.

'That's quite the welcome party,' said Askew, as he slowed down to pull over just beyond the Fountain. 'Bet you never realised you were so popular.'

'You're a funny man, Askew,' Harry replied, 'just not ha-ha funny. Regardless, I do find myself oddly in your debt. Can't say I'm all that enamoured of the fact, either.'

Askew slowed his car to a dead stop.

'Most fun I've had in months,' he said. 'Now you'd best get out there, because there's a killer to catch, isn't there? And that's what you do best.'

Harry reached for the door handle, opened the door, and as fresh air pushed its way in, Askew spoke again.

'I'm sure you'll find Ben safe and well,' he said. 'If he contacts me again, I'll let you know.'

'I'd appreciate that,' Harry said, then was out of the vehicle, striding over to the team, suddenly very aware that all that time in a cave hadn't done much for his hygiene. But there was no time to be worrying about whether he needed a shower or not, because the simple fact was that he did, he just didn't have the time, not right now.

The crowd that had gathered was full of faces he recognised, as though half of Hawes had turned up to greet him. To his surprise, they actually started to clap and cheer.

'I'd stay well away right now,' Harry called out, as people started to close in, and he pushed on through, his arms outstretched to keep them at bay.

When he finally made it to the team, he didn't stop, just kept on walking, leading them away from the marketplace and towards the Community Centre.

Matt was the first to come up to Harry, his arms outstretched for a hug. Harry held him at bay with a wave of a hand and kept walking.

'You wouldn't want to hug me right now,' he said. 'The way I stink, you might end up taking it back with you to Joan, and she'd never forgive me for that.'

'Need a shower, then?'

'No time. We've a job to do.'

Walker was the next person to approach him, and managed to get him to stop.

'Harry, you've been through a stressful, traumatic experience, so it might be a good idea if—'

'No, it wouldn't be a good idea at all.'

'You don't know what I was going to suggest.'

'That I get myself home and let the team get on with things?'

'Oh, you did know.'

'Detective, remember?'

Those two words made the whole team laugh.

'Yeah, he's fine,' said Dave, stepping forward. 'And I don't care how much you stink, I'm coming in for a hug, and just you try to stop me.'

Harry could see the Community Centre just ahead, and took a step back as Dave approached, trying to dodge what he knew was coming, but then another body shoved itself between them, and a sharp bark rang out like a rifle shot.

'He won't, but I will, that's for damn sure!'

Grace was suddenly in front of Harry, with Smudge at her heels. Before he could do anything about it, Grace grabbed his face with both hands, kissed him, and refused to come up for air for rather longer than Harry had expected. Smudge, refusing to be outdone, jumped up onto her back legs and leaned her front paws against Harry, desperate to reach for his face to give it a good lick, her tail going like the clappers.

'You're right, you do stink,' Grace said, when she finally pulled away, screwing up her nose just enough. 'But bloody hell, Harry, it's good to see you.'

'You too,' Harry replied, and his ruined face did its best to perform a smile as he folded her in his arms and hugged her tight enough to make her joints pop. That done, he then turned his attention to the now desperate Smudge. 'Come here, then, you soft lump,' he said, and dropped to his heels, whereupon Smudge jumped on him and almost knocked him onto his backside.

As Harry wrestled with his dog, and Grace looked on, a cough sounded, loud enough to get his attention.

Harry peered up from where he was wrestling with Smudge and saw a new face staring back at him, perched on top of a tall, slim, well-dressed body.

'Something caught in your throat, is there?'

'DI Morgan,' the tall man said. 'I know it's not my place—'

'Can't disagree with you on that one ...'

'—but shouldn't we be getting on?'

Harry smiled as he saw Jen approaching from the Community Centre carrying a file.

'Who's to say we're not doing that right now?'

Standing up, he looked at Jen, who then handed him the file. 'That everything I asked for?'

'Not completely, because I couldn't bring the board out with me, but there's plenty in there to be going on with.'

Grace leaned in and gave Harry another kiss, this one on the cheek.

'We'll leave you to it,' she said. 'Just don't go disappearing again, you hear?'

Harry gave Grace the quickest of winks, and ruffled the hair on Smudge's head.

'I'll do my best,' he said.

'You'd best do better than that,' Grace replied, and with that, she turned away and disappeared into the crowd.

Harry, with the file Jen had brought to him open in his hands, headed for the Community Centre.

'There's other stuff on the board, obviously,' said Jen, 'but you'll see all that in a minute, won't you?'

'I will,' Harry agreed, his eyes buried in the file now, 'but I'll be keeping this on me for reference and so that we can work on the move.'

A moment or two later, Harry was through the Community Centre doors and then in the office, the team hurrying on behind. He flicked through everything that was in the file Jen had given him: the photos, the witness statements from the cheese producer, everything from Sowerby and the SOC team, and various other notes that had been taken. He was looking for something, he knew that, but he wasn't quite sure what. It was why he'd asked Jen to get him the file, so that he could skim through it quickly, let it all sink in at once. Sometimes, that was the best approach, an avalanche of information, which he would then stir like a thick liquid in a cauldron. Sometimes, if he was lucky, something magical would happen. The evidence would be tumbled together, he'd see bits of it sitting next to things there was no clear connection or relationship with, and through that process, he'd spot something that had been invisible before.

As the team gathered around, Harry just kept flicking back and forth through the file, reading things, putting them back, pulling out photos, shuffling things. Then, as he was going through once again, his eyes flicking up now and again to look at the board, he stopped.

'That can't be right,' he muttered, and flicked back through the file until he found a report by the SOC team on a small pile of rubble that had been found under his Rav. Ignoring that the vehicle had been found nowhere near where he remembered last parking it, up in Beckermonds, Harry scanned the report until he found the thing that had snagged in his head.

'Alpacas,' he said.

'What about them?' asked Matt.

Harry handed Matt what he'd been reading.

'Says there that alpaca hair was found in the mortar in the rubble. Bit weird, that, isn't it?'

'A little. You think it's relevant?'

'I think,' said Harry, 'that it's a perfect example of my detecting rule; you're either looking for something that should be there, but isn't, or the opposite of that.'

'Something that is there but shouldn't be?'

'Exactly. Alpaca hair shouldn't be in the mortar, should it?'

'There are alpacas in the Dales, though, Harry, you know that.'

'Were there any in the early 90s? That's when that report says the mortar was made, and that's based on an analysis of other organic material found in it as well; seeds, insects, that kind of thing.'

'Obviously it wasn't made by someone who knew much about mortar or concrete or whatever it is, then, was it?' said Matt. 'If they did, they'd have been more careful and not had all that other stuff get in there.'

Jen leaned over.

'What was that about alpaca hair?'

'Why do you ask?' said Harry.

'Dicky Guy tried farming them. Tom Sykes mentioned it in passing when we were in the pub having a chat. I didn't think anything of it at the time, didn't even jot it down, I don't think; didn't seem relevant. Tom said Dicky had tried a few things to try and bring some extra revenue into the farm, Alpacas being one of those things.'

Harry handed the file to Matt, but kept out the photos of the rubble, and placed them on a table.

The team closed in.

'These are dates then, right?' he said, dropping a thick, dirty finger onto one of the photos of the rubble. 'Any luck working out what they are?'

'Did I not jot it down anywhere?' Jadyn asked, then walked over to the board. 'Yep, thought I did; here ... We've got a possible April the something, 1982, for the first one, and then a September the something, 1993 for the second one.'

Matt said, 'We wondered if it was a cairn that Dicky Guy built in memory of his son, , but then why would he smash it up and dump it at the side of the road? That doesn't make any sense at all.'

'How do you mean, in memory of his son?' Harry asked. 'What happened?'

'Drowned when he was eleven,' said Dave.

'We've not been able to contact his brother yet,' said Matt. 'Jen and Jim were due to head back to the farm today to see if they could find anything. Won't be easy telling him that he's lost his dad as well, though, will it?'

Harry asked, 'Have you checked the dates from the stones against Dicky's son?'

'I'll give Tom a call about that right now,' said Jen. 'He might remember. And I'll ask him if he's any idea about the brother.'

As Jen stepped away to make the call, Jim said, 'But even if it is something Dicky built to remember his son by, what's it got to do with anything at all? It was just dumped at the side of the road, wasn't it? And it was in pieces. Maybe he just got sick of seeing it, and decided best to get rid of it. You can't blame him for that, can you?'

'Not saying that I do,' said Harry.

'My parents, they thought about doing something like that when we lost my brother. You know, have something on the farm, a memorial or whatever. They couldn't decide what they wanted, and in the end, I think they were pleased they never bothered; that kind of reminder would've been too much.'

'Any other details we know of?' Harry asked. 'Circumstances, that kind of thing? Must've been awful for the family to go through something like that, a child drowning.' Jen glanced over.

'I've got Tom on the line,' she said. 'He thinks those dates sound about right for the death of Dicky's son, Michael.'

'What about the stones being a memorial or cairn or something?'

'He doesn't know anything about any kind of memorial being built anywhere,' Jen said. 'He says that Dicky and his other son, Andrew, they were hit hard by it, but that all Dicky really did was bury the memory of it all. He doesn't think he'd have been able to cope with putting a memorial up. And as far as he was aware, Dicky never ever went back to where they found his son. Just stayed away from it, the memory of what happened too much, I guess.'

'Like with my parents,' said Jim.

Harry beckoned Jen over and asked for her phone, then put it on speaker.

'Tom? This is Harry. I've got the whole team here listening in; hope you're good with that.'

'Glad they found you,' Tom replied. 'And yes, that's fine with me. No secrets here. Where did you end up, anyway? Who took you? What's been going on, Harry? I've heard about Dicky. Can't believe it, really.'

'That's why I'm calling,' Harry replied. 'Just wondering if you know anything about the circumstances of Dicky's son's death?'

'Micky, you mean? He drowned, Harry, poor lad. It was awful. Hit Dicky and his other son, Andrew, really hard. Was never going to do anything else, really, was it? I don't see how anyone can ever truly recover from something like that.'

'How did he drown, though?' Harry asked. 'Just wondering about the circumstances, that's all. Not like there's a lake on the farm. Was he swimming in the River Wharfe and hit his head?'

'No, you're right, that sounds more like what would happen, but he actually drowned during a shoot,' said Tom. 'I know that sounds odd, but it was another of Dicky's ideas to try and get extra money into the farm. He'd tried alpacas, gave up on that, which was no surprise; those creatures haven't got a brain between the whole species, if you ask me. Anyway, he decided to go ahead and breed a few pheasants, see if the land would run well as a shoot. Can't remember when it happened, the exact time of day, like, but I do know that Micky got lost, and he ended up wandering into a spinney that stands in the fields up behind the house. There's a little pond there, you see, and that's where they found him. Tragic.'

Harry tried to get the facts straight in his head.

'So Micky, he wanders off and next, they find him dead in a pond?'

'He was only eleven at the time. He'd been walking most of the day with a few other beaters; there weren't many, like, because Dicky was only keeping it small, wasn't he? You know, trying it out, like, with a few mates. I wasn't on the shoot, though I'd been invited; just had other things to do that day, that was all. Pleased I wasn't, in the end. There were only four guns on the day Micky died.'

Harry noticed Jadyn was writing something in large letters on the board.

'But you don't just drown, do you?' he said.

'No, you don't,' said Tom. 'They found broken branches in one of the trees in the spinney, a tree that hung right over the pond. They reckoned Micky was climbing it and must've just slipped. Cracked his head on a rock or something in the pond, and that was that.'

On the board, Jadyn had written the name *Michael,* then drawn an arrow to the name *Micky*, and had circled the K and the Y in black.

'And you're saying this happened during a shoot?'

'It did, I know that for sure, not least because I was invited, like I said. It was the first and last shoot that Dicky ever held. Never shot again either, not even on his own. No idea what he did with his gun, but I know he never picked it up ever again.'

Something from what Harry had read in all the notes hooked onto what Tom had just said.

'A gun cabinet was found at the house, but there was no gun.'

'Dicky probably flogged it,' said Tom. 'It was a shame, really. I know it was tragic the way he lost his lad, but that shoot could've worked, made him a few extra quid, and he certainly needed it, especially after everything that happened. He was a good shot as well, was Dicky. And it would've run well, too, what with the involvement of the other three who were guns that day.'

'Friends of his?'

'That's right. There was Alan and Brian; they set up that building company you'll have seen around plenty enough, C&S Builders Ltd. That's them, Alan Cartright and Brian Suggitt. And there was Matthew Palmer as well. I think they were all old schoolmates or something. Anyway, he went off to get some city job for a while, I think. Came back and got into cheese, would you believe? Actually, that reminds me, Harry, someone told me there was an accident or something down at the little industrial estate in Aysgarth. That's where Matthew set up his artisan cheese thing, or whatever it is. I've not seen him in years, though. I hope it wasn't anything serious.'

Harry's mind was whirling now, so much so, he almost felt dizzy. He took the phone off speaker and had it up next to his ear once more.

'Tom, appreciate the chat, but I need to go.'

'You'll be out soon though, right, to talk through security with me, James, and Tina? I've a few others who might want to come along and listen in as well. How's The George suit?

Probably throw in some food for you as well, a nice bit of pie and mash, that kind of thing.'

'Sounds good,' said Harry, 'I'll be in touch.' As he went to hand the phone back to Jen he asked, 'Don't suppose you've got any contact details for Andrew, have you, Tom?'

A moment or two later, Harry jotted down a number Tom had given him.

'Dicky gave it to me,' he said. 'They've not spoken in years. I think the death of Micky drove a wedge between them. Dicky just wanted me to have a way to contact Andrew if anything happened.'

'And have you? Contacted him, I mean?'

'Not had a chance; I've only just found out about Dicky myself. I'll try and give him a call now though.'

'That would be good,' Harry said, and handed the phone back to Jen.

'Micky,' said Jadyn, not giving Harry a chance to digest all that he'd just learned. 'Short for Michael, isn't it? And those two letters on the rubble, they're K and Y. So, I think we were right all along, about the cairn being built for—'

Jadyn stopped talking as the whole room turned to stare expectantly at Harry.

'What is it, Harry?' Matt asked.

'The killer, whoever they are, they've already got to Matthew Palmer and Dicky Guy, haven't they? And remember what I said about this not being finished? It's not, and we know that now because of what Tom just told us.'

'You mean C&S Builders?' said Matt.

'They're after Alan and Brian.' Harry nodded. 'That's where our killer's going next ...'

32

Alan, who had always considered himself to be a brave man, someone who would stand up to another, had never known fear like what he felt right then. That he'd pissed himself was no surprise, but he'd forgotten about it immediately, his mind somewhat taken up with the shotgun pointing at him and Brian.

'What do you mean it's loaded?' said Brian, who Alan could tell had yet to notice the growing pool of urine spreading across the recently laid wooden floor. 'Why would it be loaded? And I tell you, lad, if you don't point it somewhere else, I'm going to be ramming it so far down your throat, your balls'll end up sitting in the barrels like two peas in a peashooter!'

Mr Smith was saying nothing, just staring.

'I knew this one was going to be a little more difficult than the other two,' he said. 'That's why I brought the gun with me. I knew Dad still had it in the house, so I didn't need to worry about buying one or anything like that, mainly because I can't, because I don't have a licence.'

'Please,' said Alan. 'Can you just tell us what it is that you want? We've built you this beautiful house. Why are you now threatening us?'

Mr Smith kept the gun steady but turned his head just enough to stare at Alan.

'I'm not surprised you don't recognise me,' he said. 'I'm a fair bit older for a start. And I don't really remember you coming round the farm much after it had happened.'

'After what had happened?' Alan asked.

'Matthew remembered,' Mr Smith said. 'I saw that recognition in his eyes. And Dad remembered, obviously, because it wasn't really something he was ever going to forget, was he?'

Brian screwed up his face in confusion.

'Matthew? Matthew who?'

'Palmer,' said Alan, his eyes on Mr Smith. 'Correct?'

'Very good,' Mr Smith acknowledged. 'Which means, by a process of deduction, you've no doubt worked out who I am as well, yes?'

At this point, Alan could only stare at the man in front of him, because the last time he'd seen him, at a guess, was probably the funeral of his brother, Michael.

'Andrew,' he said. 'What the hell's this all about?'

'You were all responsible,' Andrew replied, as whatever persona he'd adopted as Mr Smith fell to the floor like flakes of the discarded skin he'd just shed. 'You ran the shoot. You should've stopped it, found him, but you didn't, did you?'

'What?' said Alan. 'That's not what happened! We did stop it!'

Andrew laughed.

'I was there, remember? You can't change what happened; you were the ones who organised it. You should've looked after Michael.'

Brian said, 'What, you're Dicky's lad? The one who just sodded off and left him to his grief?'

'I didn't sod off, I had to leave, I had no choice.'

'We've always got a choice, lad,' said Brian. 'And it's like Alan just said, you're remembering it wrong. We did stop the shoot, and we went to look for Michael. We just didn't find him soon enough.'

'That's no excuse!'

'He ran off,' repeated Alan. 'That's honestly what happened. One minute he was with one of the beaters, next he'd just raced off. The beaters went after him, but he was like a whippet, wasn't he, your brother? He was off. He'd not wanted to be on the shoot anyway, that much had been clear from the off.'

'What, so you're blaming him now, is that it?'

'You're the one holding the gun and doing the blaming!' Brian roared. 'The hell is wrong with you? Aren't you listening to what we're saying?'

'You lost him,' Andrew repeated. 'You lost him, and he's dead, and ... and ...'

Alan watched as tears welled up in Andrew's eyes, his whole body vibrating.

'It was a tragic accident,' he said. 'But whatever any of this is, it's not going to bring him back, is it?'

'But he's never gone away!' Andrew roared back, then he smacked the side of his head with his hand. 'He's still in here, isn't he? Always talking to me, always calling me, and he never stops, never stops, just keeps talking and whispering to me, all the time, every day, every night, and I just need it to end, and this is the only way I can do it ...'

Andrew's words tripped over themselves and the tears were running freely now.

'Give me the gun,' said Alan.

Andrew wasn't listening, he was still talking about his brother.

'Since the day he drowned, it's all I've heard in my head, his voice, talking to me! Have you any idea what that's like? To be haunted by the voice of your dead brother? I talk to him every day, just to keep him calm, let him know that everything's going to be okay, because that's all he wants, is all I want, and the only way that can happen is for us to be together again, why does no one understand that?'

Alan was starting to sense that all was not well in Andrew's mind, and that whatever had come loose had been that way since that fateful day all those years ago.

'I do understand,' Alan said, not actually understanding anything at all, really, but just wanting to keep Andrew talking, to give them all a chance to get out of this without someone getting hurt. 'Losing someone is hard. Death, it's not easy to accept, not when it takes those we love.'

'But it was your fault!' Andrew yelled back, and Alan was struck then by how he was no longer arguing with a grown man, but that ten-year-old boy. 'Micky told me! Micky said you got him lost and that he couldn't find you and—'

'Micky can't have told you,' Alan said. 'You know that, Andrew, don't you? That's just what you're telling yourself. You're hearing your brother's voice, but they're your words, your thoughts. It's the grief talking, and that's okay, really, it is, but—'

'They're not! They're Micky's!' Andrew tapped the side of his head again. 'Twins, remember? You can't just break that in two, you know? You can't just pull us apart and expect us to not still be together.'

Alan was having a lot of trouble following what Andrew

was talking about now, and he could see by the look on Brian's face that he'd stopped listening to any of it a long time ago.

'Maybe we can just talk this through? What do you say to that, Andrew? Maybe go for a pint?'

'Talk it through?'

'Yes, just talk,' Alan repeated. 'Maybe if we do that, we'll all have a better understanding of what happened, won't we? That would be good, wouldn't it? Don't you agree, Brian?'

Alan turned to Brian for an answer. The man's face was red, and his jaw was clenched, as he stared wide-eyed at Andrew, rage and disbelief twisting together in his eyes.

'Brian?'

No response.

'Brian, you agree with me, don't you? That we should all just go for a drink, talk this out?'

'Just the three of us?'

'Exactly.'

'You, me, and this git here pointing a shotgun at me?'

'Brian ...'

'Not a sodding chance, mate!'

Brian once again grabbed the barrel of the shotgun.

'And it's not even loaded, is it, Andrew? Now get it out of my face or I'll—'

The sound of the gun going off in such a small space was so loud and so shocking that Alan dropped to his knees, his hands over his ears with the pain of it, eyes closed simply as a reaction to something so violent. And he stayed there for a while, working to control his breathing, hoping that the ringing in his ears would soon stop.

As he thought about what had just happened and how impossible it all was, he felt something on his skin, like a faint mist, and it reminded him of an early morning walk with his wife and dog on the moors. Opening his eyes, he reached up to his face to wipe it, and when he pulled his hand away, he saw that his palm was the deepest red.

33

Having called the number of C&S Builders, Harry had an address of where the owners, Alan and Brian, were working that day, because if that's where they were, then that's where he guessed that the killer was most likely to be. He'd also asked the receptionist if any word had come in from either man, but apparently nothing had, and all seemed normal.

'It's a cottage they've been renovating for a Mr Smith,' he told the team, 'which isn't the kind of name that makes anyone suspicious at all, is it?'

Harry grabbed the file Jen had brought to him earlier, and marched out of the office.

'Where's the cottage?' Matt asked, as he and the rest of the team followed Harry out of the building.

The crowds that had gathered for Harry's return were still hanging around in the marketplace. He really wished that they weren't.

Harry came to a dead stop before they got there and turned to face the team.

'Two things,' he said. 'First, I need volunteers to see if they can't track down Ben. He's an innocent victim in this, and I don't want any more harm to come to him, or for him to go and do something stupid. Liz?'

'Yes?'

'You happy to lead on this?'

'But I'm just a PCSO, I can't—'

'You can and you will,' Harry said, his tone forceful enough to let everyone know there would be no arguing. 'DI Morgan? You'll work alongside Liz, and I think Detective Superintendent Walker would be useful, too.'

Both Walker and Ethan stepped over next to Liz.

'Liz, you know Ben better than anyone else,' Harry said. 'Better than me, now, I should guess. So, use Walker and Morgan and get the lad found, yes?'

'Yes,' Liz replied.

'Off you go, then!'

With that small team dispatched, Harry turned to the others.

'Right then,' he said, 'whatever it is we're dealing with here, I don't want any heroics. Our aim is to get over to the cottage sharpish and hopefully stop something before it happens. Now, let's see if we can't all squeeze into the old Land Rover, shall we?'

Harry handed the file to Jen and led the team over to the Land Rover.

Jim asked, 'But who is it we're after, Harry? Do we even know?'

Before Harry could answer, and as he was climbing up into the driver's seat, Jadyn said, 'It's Micky's brother, Andrew, isn't it, Boss? That's who's behind all of this. Has to be.'

Harry clipped in his seat belt as the rest of the team pushed themselves into the vehicle.

'What makes you think that?' he asked.

'Everything, actually,' said Jadyn. 'The cairn's got his brother Micky's birth and death dates on it for a start, and that alpaca hair links it directly to the farm around the time he drowned. He's already killed two of the four people who organised the shoot, Matthew Palmer, and his dad, Dicky Guy. I don't know how he's been able to pull any of this off yet, but having you out of the picture was clearly a way to keep us otherwise engaged, wasn't it? And to do that, I reckon he must've been in the area long enough to know what to do and how to go about it.'

Yep, Jadyn was going to make a fantastic detective, Harry thought.

'And there's that witness statement,' said Matt. 'The one from that bloke who claimed he found Dicky in the trough, Anthony Booker; that was Andrew, has to be.'

'Of course! The sneeze!' Jen said, her voice echoing inside the tin shell of the Land Rover.

That comment made Harry confused.

'What sneeze?'

'I can't remember who said it, but when we met with Tom, James, and Tina over at The George Inn in Hubberholme, one of them said about how Andrew was the sickly one, always getting colds, fussy with food.'

'And that's relevant because?'

'Because when Anthony Booker came into the Community Centre to give his witness testimony, he sneezed, didn't he? I didn't think anything of it at the time, because he said he'd got a cold from being out on the hill. But it wasn't that at all, was it? It was his allergies.'

'Bloody hell, you're right!' said Matt. 'Billy sodding McCain! He said he couldn't meet at the office because he was allergic to dogs, didn't he? Must've let that detail slip by accident, too busy trying to be Billy to notice.'

'Which means,' said Jen, 'that Billy McCain and Anthony Booker are actually the same person; Andrew Guy.'

As that detail sunk in, Harry started the engine and eased out of the marketplace.

'So, this witness statement, then?' he asked. 'What's in it, exactly? You didn't tell me when you mentioned it on the phone, seeing as we were rushing to get through everything.'

'I've got it here,' Jen said, and Harry heard her shuffling through the file he'd handed her. 'You sure you want me to read it out?'

'Yes,' said Harry.

'Right, then ... It says, "*He's so lonely without me. I know this because he's told me. He tells me all the time. He cries. I don't like it when he cries. I cry, too. I'm lonely without him, too. We talk a lot, because we always have. Even now, as I write this, I can hear his voice, telling me what he wants me to do. It's with me, always. I need it to stop. I need to stop hearing it. The only way to do that is to do to them what they did to him, like he's told me to. Then he will be happy. Then we can both have peace. Then can we both be together again, like we were always supposed to be until they killed him.*"'

Jen paused for a moment, and the Land Rover was silent, expectant.

'It didn't make sense when I first read it,' she said eventually. 'I knew it was a confession, that the killer had been in the interview room, that it was Anthony Booker who was responsible. But I didn't make the connection right then because of everything that was going on, that Anthony was Andrew.'

Harry had been listening, but at the same time, he was already miles down the road, trying to plan what they were going to do when they got to the cottage, wondering what they were going to find.

The team fell quiet, and Harry got on with driving, aware then that in such a confined space, his very unpleasant stink was enough to make his eyes water.

'Sorry about the smell,' he said, and opened a window.

Matt, who was sitting beside him, did the same, after which the rest of the windows were also opened.

'Don't you worry,' said Matt. 'We've all smelled worse.'

'Not sure I have,' said Jen. 'I run mountain marathons for fun, and believe me, we can get pretty stinky doing that. But Harry? You're ripe.'

Soon, they were drawing near to the cottage's location, which was at the end of a thin and winding lane just above Askrigg, the lane becoming nothing more than a dirt track across the moors once it mooched past the cottage.

Harry pulled the Land Rover to a stop, then turned around in his seat to face everyone.

'This is how we're going to play this,' he said. 'We'll get as close as we can without hopefully seeming too suspicious. Not easy in a police Land Rover, but you know what I mean. Then, I, and only I, will head up to see what's what.'

'Can't say any of us are liking the sound of that at all,' said Dave from the very back of the vehicle, squashed up against the door rather uncomfortably. 'What was it you only just said about not wanting any heroics? You can't be going in alone.'

'I can, and I will,' said Harry. 'Andrew has already killed two people. There's a motivation here beyond normal reason; he's blackmailed Ben, threatened Liz, kidnapped me, killed Matthew Palmer and his own father, and judging by what he wrote on that witness statement, is doing it all because he thinks he's being told to by his dead twin brother. He's no idea that I'm free, so seeing me will knock him, and that could serve us well, because it means not everything has gone to plan. Then all I need to do is to try and talk him down, and the emphasis there is on try. Yes, we could do with backup, but also, we all know we've not got time for that. I need everyone to stay out of it, while I go and see if I can bring him in.'

'And what if he refuses?' Jim asked. 'What then?'

'I've been known to make a grown man shit himself just by staring at him,' Harry replied. 'I'm sure I'll think of something.'

With nothing left to be said, he twisted back around in his seat and continued on up the lane, nice and slow.

'That's it, just ahead,' said Matt, pointing through the window.

The cottage was about a hundred metres away, with a van parked in front of it. He pulled the Land Rover to a dead stop, blocking the lane.

'Now, remember what I said, okay? I'm going in on my own and I'll see if I can bring him out.'

'But we can't all just sit here doing nowt, can we?' said Jim.

'And we won't be, either,' said Matt, turning in his seat to Harry.

'Matt ...'

'No, Harry,' Matt replied, his voice diamond hard and unyielding. 'I'll not be hearing any of it, so don't even start. I don't want you giving me any of that senior officer bollocks, you hear? You're not going up there on your own. That's just not happening. I know Ben's got pulled into this, and I know you're not exactly happy about having been kidnapped, but this isn't like when you turned up all hard-edged, jaded city cop. We work differently, and so do you now. Understood?'

Harry couldn't think of a single time that Matt had ever talked to him like that before.

'I can't put you all at risk.'

'Horseshit,' said Matt. 'You brought us here for a reason, so let me tell you what it is, in case you've forgotten; we're a team, remember? A team. We work together. We've spent all sodding week worried sick about you, wondering where you were, what had happened. So, don't you go thinking you can just bugger off now that we've got you back. Just isn't happening, Harry, sorry.'

Harry took in a slow, deep breath, then exhaled even more slowly.

'What do you suggest, then?' he asked.

'We surround the place,' Matt said. 'Simple as that. Then, if Andrew makes a break for it, we have him.'

'I don't like it.'

'I know, but that's the way it's going to be. Everyone? Out, and be quiet about it!'

Harry sat in the driving seat as the rest of the team clambered out of the Land Rover.

Matt came around to Harry's window.

'Come on, then,' he said. 'You're the one in charge, remember?'

'You sure about that?'

Matt opened Harry's door.

'I'm still going in on my own,' Harry said.

'No arguing on that point,' Matt replied. 'Just wait till we're all in position, like, okay?'

'Doesn't look like I've any choice, does it?'

'No.'

Harry stayed where he was, as Matt directed the rest of the team, then watched as they fanned out, careful to keep themselves out of sight of the cottage. When they were all in place, he caught a quick wave from Matt, and took that as the signal to get moving.

With the cottage ahead of him, Harry started walking, when the sharp crack of a gunshot burst into the moment and blew to pieces not only his own plan, but Matt's as well. And with a bellowing roar to the team to have everyone stay exactly where they were, he sprinted towards the cottage.

34

With no thought at all for his own safety, Harry threw himself through the open front door of the cottage, only to lose his footing on a spreading pool of blood on the floor, slip, and tumble to the ground.

He saw a man standing in the middle of the room, a shotgun clasped loosely in his hands, another cowering on his knees, and a body lying on the floor minus most of its head.

'Andrew,' Harry said, his eyes firmly on the shotgun he was holding, even more desperate now that the team obeyed his last shouted command to stay where they were. 'Don't do anything else you'll regret. It's over. All of it. Understand?'

Andrew stared at Harry.

'This isn't how it's supposed to happen,' he muttered. 'Shooting him ... That wasn't ... They're supposed to drown ... like Micky ...'

Harry raised his hands in an attempt to keep Andrew calm and to show him that he meant no harm.

'Andrew ...'

'Then ... then I can join him, can't you see? I can be with my brother again, like he wants, like I want. That's what has to happen. It's why I came back!'

'Let's just talk this through,' Harry said.

'I need to be with him, with Micky. I should've been with him. We could've gone together then, couldn't we? Been together forever.'

Harry had zero idea what Andrew was talking about, but the fact that he was talking was enough.

'Come on, Andrew,' he said. 'Just you and I, okay? Let's talk about Micky, about—'

Andrew swung the shotgun around and aimed it at the other man in the room.

On his heels now, Harry launched himself at Andrew, aiming for his waist in the wild hope that he would knock the gun out of the way and bring the man down in one swift movement.

The gun went off as Harry connected with Andrew, and his ears rang with the sound of it, as the sharp stink of the propellant from the cartridge mixed with the metallic tang of blood.

Landing hard, Harry tried to hold on to Andrew, but Andrew kicked Harry away from him and was on his feet and out the door, while Harry was still trying to scrabble for purchase on the slick floor.

Harry glanced over at the other man in the room, expecting the worst, relieved to see that the shotgun blast had gone wide of its target, and made a nasty mess of the wall, the shotgun itself lying on the floor, the man unharmed, physically at least.

'I'm with the police,' Harry shouted, because that was the only way either of them could hear past the ringing in their ears. 'Stay here. I'm sending someone in to help. Understood?'

The man, who was in exactly the same position he'd been in when Harry had skidded into the room, gave the weakest of nods, and that was enough for Harry, who sprinted out of the door. He exited the cottage just in time to see Andrew, who was sitting on a motorbike he'd not spotted from where he had parked the Land Rover, kick Matt away from him as the detective sergeant tried to wrestle him off. He yanked the throttle hard and sped off, not down the lane towards the Land Rover, but up it, past the cottage, and into the moors.

Harry raced down to check on Matt, aware of the sound of Andrew's motorbike fading into the distance as he headed off up into the moors.

'I'm fine,' Matt said, 'but you should have a look at yourself for a moment, like something out of a horror movie. I hope none of it's yours.'

Harry looked himself up and down, saw that his clothes were dark with blood, then noticed the rest of the team gathering around.

'It's not mine,' he said, his eyes glancing around the faces staring at him. 'We've one dead, and one in shock in the cottage. It's a mess in there. I slipped in the aftermath of that gunshot we heard.'

Jadyn turned to head towards the cottage.

'No!' Harry called out. 'Jadyn, everyone stay here.' He looked at Matt. 'No one needs to go in there other than you. Understood?'

Matt gave a nod.

Harry looked at the rest of the team.

'Cordon this place off, put in the usual calls; SOC Team, ambulance, everything.'

'What about you?' asked Dave.

'I'm going to need the Land Rover,' Harry replied.

'You won't catch him.'

'I don't expect to.'

Harry's mind had been working on what Andrew had said to him in the cottage about Micky, about how he should have been with him when he drowned, how he wanted to be with him now, once everything was done. And he could still hear the words Jen had read to them all in the Land Rover, Andrew's own penned confession.

'I think everything Andrew's done is to allow him to join his brother,' Harry explained. 'Tom said Micky drowned in a pool in a spinney just out behind the farm, didn't he? I think that's where Andrew's going. I think he's had enough of his brother's voice in his head, and all of this is about silencing it.'

'Silencing it?' said Matt. 'How?'

'He's going to drown himself in the same pool that took his brother.'

Harry didn't give anyone a chance to argue or discuss what he'd just said, turned on his heel, and ran down to the Land Rover, only to find that when he arrived and yanked open the driver's door, the rest of the team had followed.

'You need to get up to the cottage,' he said, barely containing his frustration. 'Cordon off the area, make the phone calls, there's a witness, and there's a body ...'

'We know all that,' said Matt, his own frustration as barely restrained as Harry's, 'but I can't be having you disappearing again, can I? Grace would never forgive me, Harry, and neither would Smudge for that matter!'

'I need to get to Dicky's farm, Matt,' Harry said, his words forced out through clenched teeth. 'Right now, before Andrew—'

Then Dave spoke up.

'I'll come with you.'

Harry did a double-take, as did the rest of the team.

'What? Why? No, don't answer me that, because you won't be, Dave, you'll be staying here, as ordered.'

Dave's reply was to march around to the passenger door and climb in.

'Well?' he shouted at Harry, leaning across from where he was now sitting. 'Are we going, or what? Shift your arse!'

Swearing under his breath, Harry gave a nod to Matt.

'I'll be in touch,' he said, and started the engine.

Unable to turn around in the lane, Harry drove up the way that Andrew had gone on the motorbike, but instead of following him up into the moors, he spun the Land Rover around on the grass behind the cottage, then headed back down the lane.

'Back over to Wharfedale, then?' Dave said.

'Now's not the time for chit-chat,' Harry grumbled in reply.

'Thought about living over that way myself, you know,' Dave continued, ignoring Harry. 'Still don't know why I didn't. I think life just got in the way, really, and it was a little extra to the journey when I was working offshore. That was probably it, wasn't it?'

'Probably.'

'Beautiful dale, though, isn't it? I love that view when you roll over the top of Beggarmans Road and you can see all the way across to the Three Peaks. You climbed those yet at all?'

Harry was having difficulty concentrating, not just on the road, but what Dave was saying, and his own internal map of the Dales; with no satnav to speak of in the Land Rover, and no way to secure his phone and use that, he had no other choice.

'Which way are we going, then?'

Dave's question barged into Harry's mind at the same time as he was mulling the question over himself.

'We either go via Aysgarth, and drop down from there, through Thoralby, then along through Bishopdale,' he said, 'or we head back up the dale, out of Gayle, and up Beggarman's Lane.'

'Six and two threes, really, isn't it?' Dave offered. 'I wouldn't like to put money on either route being quicker.'

'I'm not asking you to.'

'Good job, then, isn't it? Because I wouldn't. Not a gambling man, you see, Harry; that's a mug's game. Though, saying that, I have put a few quid on the horses now and again, not that I've ever won out, like.'

'I reckon I know the route over Beggarmans better than the other,' Harry said. 'We'll head that way as I'll be able to make the most of knowing the route and push a little harder.'

Dave gave a loud tut.

'And what was that for?' Harry asked.

'Knowing a route doesn't make you better at driving it, it just makes you complacent,' Dave said.

'Does it now?'

'It does.'

'Then what do you suggest?'

If Harry was honest, he was asking questions but not actually listening to the answers. He had given no real thought to how Andrew was going to make his way over to his father's farm, what route he might take, so for now, was focused on just getting there as quickly as he could, and he sent them skipping through Askrigg, and on towards Bainbridge, with little else on his mind.

'What about Stalling Busk?'

Dave's question caught Harry off guard.

'What about it?'

'That's more direct, isn't it?'

'It is?'

Harry tried to visualise where the tiny hamlet sat in the Dales, but couldn't work out what Dave was getting at.

'If we head out the back of Stalling Busk, take High Lane over the tops, then we'll drop down just above Cray, won't we?'

Now Harry knew what Dave was thinking.

'You mean go off-road?'

'You're in the right vehicle for it, aren't you? It's more direct that way. And once we're over to Cray, you're on the main road to Yockenthwaite. And did you notice that motorbike that Andrew was riding?'

Harry did his best to remember.

'I think so,' he said, not entirely sure that he did.

'One of those long-distance off-road expedition types, isn't it? Means there might even be a chance that he's taken that route himself. We might even catch him, Harry!'

'Slim chance of that,' Harry said, but he knew that what Dave was saying had enough merit to be taken seriously.

'You really think it'll be quicker?'

'I wouldn't bet on it, because, like I've just said, I'm not a gambling man, Harry, but this old truck will fare better that way than it will on tarmac.' Then, quite to Harry's surprise, Dave winked at him. 'It'll be more fun as well, won't it?'

Bainbridge green was ahead. Harry had to decide now; either turn right at the junction and head to Hawes, or go left, through the village, over the bridge, along the side of the Roman fort, then off the main road and towards Stalling Busk.

Harry hung a left.

'Bloody hell, Harry!' Dave roared, as the vehicle swerved sharply to the left to a chorus of squeals from the tyres on the road, and he was sent tumbling towards Harry.

Harry ignored Dave's complaining, and soon they were off the main road.

Dave reached up to grip the handle above the door and braced his feet in the footwell.

'You always drive like a lunatic, then?' he asked.

Harry's answer was to drop a gear and push the engine harder, forcing it to scream at him as it chewed up the road ahead. Then the inky black depths of Semerwater came into view on his right, and the view brought back memories of when he'd thrown himself into those waters, and then eventually persuaded Ben to do the same.

The thought of Ben, of what hell he must've been going through to do what he did, twisted Harry's gut.

'Dave, can you message Liz for me, just to check how she's doing with finding Ben?'

Dave pulled his phone out of a pocket, but as he did so, Harry hit both a bump and a bend in the road, and Dave's phone went spinning across the cabin and cracked Harry hard in the face.

'Bloody hell, Dave! What are you doing?'

The sharp pain of the phone's impact died quickly, but Harry rubbed at his cheek anyway.

'Well, if you weren't in such a hurry ...'

'How the hell else am I supposed to get to where we're going in time if I'm not in a hurry?'

'Well, we'll be no bloody use if we end up there in pieces or not at all, will we?'

Harry opened his mouth to say something, but instead shut it, reached down to his feet to grab Dave's phone, then handed it over.

'Liz,' he said. 'Now.'

Dave sent a message as, just before turning down towards Stalling Busk, Harry took a left off the main road, and shot them forwards onto High Lane, the Land Rover's tyres almost grateful to be off the tarmac and onto something a little more to their liking.

The first part of High Lane was straight and fast, and Harry knew he was pushing it, as gravel and rock spat out from beneath the tyres.

'Don't hang about, do you?' said Dave. 'If you ask me, your style of driving suits this kind of road a little better; I almost feel safer.'

Harry would've laughed at that if he hadn't been so focused on the road ahead.

Dave's phone pinged.

'Is that Liz?' Harry asked. 'What has she said?'

Dave stared at his phone screen.

'They've got him,' Dave said, then added, 'Bloody hell, Harry! They've got him!' before reinforcing his joy at the news with a swift punch to Harry's arm.

'Are you trying to break me, is that it?' Harry snarled, snapping a look at Dave. 'First you throw your phone at me, then you punch me?'

Dave wasn't given time to answer as the lane began to twist, rising into the fells like a snake advancing on its prey.

Despite everything that had happened that week, and what they were now dealing with, Harry found himself enjoying the journey as he coaxed the Land Rover deeper into the hills. Even in the darkest of times, the fells were things of such breathtaking beauty that he was forced to stare in awe. Even on the bleakest of days, he found them to be a comfort, as though their quiet majesty was all that he needed to keep going. Dave's barked news about Ben had also given him a much needed lift. He was about to ask what Liz had said specifically when Dave gave a shout.

'Gate!'

Slowing down, Harry came to a stop, and without being asked, Dave jumped out and dashed to the gate, opening it swiftly. Harry drove through. Dave closed the gate behind him, then jumped back in.

'There's a few more,' he said, as Harry drove on. 'Next one is just beyond those mountain bikers ahead.'

Soon passing the small group of mountain bikers, Harry couldn't help but notice how some of them looked at him with envy, particularly the one at the back of the group, who seemed to be huffing and puffing his way to a heart attack.

'So, what did Liz say about Ben, then?' he asked, as he approached a rather stubborn sheep, which refused to move from its sitting position in the middle of the lane. 'Where was he? How did they find him?'

Harry slowed down, stopped.

'They didn't, Askew did,' Dave answered.

Had Harry been drinking, he'd have spat out whatever was in his mouth.

'Askew? You're kidding me!'

Dave shook his head, then lifted up his phone for Harry to see the screen.

'I can't read that,' Harry said.

'You'll just have to take my word for it, then, won't you?' Dave replied. 'All Liz says is that Askew brought Ben in. They're at the Community Centre, and he's being looked after.'

The sheep still hadn't moved, so Harry pulled on the handbrake, put the Land Rover in neutral, and opened the door.

'You're sure it was Askew?' he asked, climbing out.

'I can read, Harry,' Dave answered.

Stunned by this news, Harry walked over to have a word with the sheep, only to have it slowly stand up before walking directly towards him, sniff him momentarily, then carry on down the lane as if nothing had happened.

Back in the driving seat, Harry continued on, taking them at last over the top, then down a twisting section of track where the way had been partly eroded by rushing water to the bedrock. The Land Rover bumped and thumped its way over the rocks, at one point sending Dave up into the roof with a dull thud. Harry didn't even bother trying to disguise his laugh.

'It's not funny,' Dave said, rubbing his scalp.

'Funniest thing I've seen in months,' Harry replied.

At last, the main road came into view, and they were back on tarmac, through Cray, and on towards Yockenthwaite. Hubberholme barely noticed them as Harry bounced the Land Rover past The George Inn.

'We're here,' he said, as they arrived at Dicky's farm.

Harry turned off the main road, then followed a gravel lane through to the main yard, and parked up.

'There's a barn over there,' Dave said, pointing through the windscreen. 'If we're here before Andrew, we don't want him getting spooked, do we?'

'Good plan,' Harry said, understanding exactly what Dave meant, and he quickly reversed into the barn, hiding the vehicle in the thick gloom inside.

Leaving the Land Rover in the barn, and closing the large, weatherworn door behind them to keep it fully out of sight, Harry led Dave into the farmyard.

'Now what?' Dave asked.

'We need to find the spinney,' Harry said. 'The one

Michael, Andrew's brother, drowned in. Everything started here, so this is where he has to be.'

'You're sure of that?'

'My gut is,' Harry replied, and with that, he walked away from the barn and up into the green paddocks behind the farm, Dave following on behind.

35

The cordon tape was still flapping in the wind, a thin and feeble reminder to the world that the trough it encircled was where something terrible had taken place. But it wasn't to that which Harry was drawn; he needed to find the spinney, because that was where Andrew would head, he was sure of it.

Harry came to a dead stop.

'What is it?' Dave asked.

Harry looked all around, saw various small clumps of trees huddled together in the fellside. Some were barely two or three trees together, and he couldn't see them having sufficient space beneath them to hold a pond. A few others were larger. Though, one particularly so, which meant he counted that out right away, as it had clearly moved beyond being a spinney and into a full-sized wood.

'Michael drowned in a spinney,' Harry said, 'but which one is it?'

Harry watched as Dave stared out across the fells, rubbing his chin thoughtfully.

'Well, there's too many for us to be looking at each one, aren't there?' Dave said.

'Exactly what I was thinking,' Harry agreed. 'We need to narrow it down.'

'If he drowned, then there's water, right? And I know I'm stating the obvious there, but look up there, and over there as well ...'

Harry followed to where Dave was pointing one of his huge, meaty fingers.

'What am I looking at?' Harry asked.

'Streams,' Dave said. 'There's one over there, going into that little crop of trees, and another over there, going into that other spinney.'

Harry saw what Dave was talking about; the thin silvery lines of streams tumbling down the fell and into the spinneys Dave had spotted.

'Those streams lead somewhere, don't they?' said Dave. 'My guess is a pond.'

Harry pointed to the spinney on the right.

'You head there,' he said, 'and I'll take the one over here on the left. Go quietly. If Andrew's there, don't attempt to speak to him or arrest him. Just call me, and I'll come.'

'And you'll do the same, right?' Dave asked.

'Absolutely.'

The look Dave gave Harry in reply was enough to tell him that he didn't believe him.

'And if he's not there, but a pond is?' Dave asked.

'Wait,' Harry replied. 'If both spinneys have ponds, then we need both covered. From here on in, we're playing by ear.'

'How long do we have to wait?'

'As long as we need to,' said Harry, and with that, gave Dave a gentle slap on the shoulder, before turning and heading for the other spinney.

The walk to the small clutch of trees wasn't long and, under different circumstances, Harry would've enjoyed it, especially if Smudge had been with him. He wondered how his dog was doing, had no doubt that she was warm and comfortable back home with Grace and Jess, but did she miss him? And why did he care? That thought made Harry laugh, because he couldn't quite believe that it mattered to him so much, the attention of a dog he'd rescued from a puppy farm during an investigation he, even now, tried to forget.

Entering the spinney, Harry's world turned dark, the thick foliage of the trees sending the world at their feet into gloom. It was chilly, too, but not unpleasant, and after the hard drive over and then the brisk walk up to where he now was, he welcomed it.

The trees were a motley collection of various types, he noticed, not that he could identify any of them all that accurately. One was an oak, he was sure of that at least, another a sycamore, and there was a fir tree or two, but the rest he had no idea about. They stood leaning into each other like drunks waiting for a taxi, and the wind through their branches sounded like the soft sighs of the very tired.

Pushing deeper into the grey light, Harry at last came upon a small pool of water. He wasn't quite sure what he'd been expecting, but in many ways, it wasn't this. The pool looked about as dangerous as a spilled glass of water. Its edges were lined with the soft, mottled browns of leaf litter, and long, green fronds of grass floated in the water like the hair of a corpse.

That image alone was enough to have Harry stop and, for just a moment or two, feel the ghostly atmosphere of the place chill him a little. He tried to shrug the sensation off, but he couldn't, the atmosphere at once oppressive and filled with menace.

He stared again at the pond, trying to focus on the job in hand, ignoring the prickling sensation at the back of his neck. At one end, he saw large fronds of fern draped over the dark water like they were looking for something in its oily depths, or waiting for something to rise out of it. The very blackness of the water gave Harry the impression that the pool was considerably deeper than he suspected.

At the other end of the pool, he spotted an area of disturbed dirt and a collection of stones half buried in the black, peaty soil. He searched for a long stick, gave the water a poke, disturbing its mirrored surface. The stick went in further than he'd expected, causing him to stumble forward a little, having expected it to hit the bottom before it actually did, almost as though the pool was gobbling it up hungrily.

Aware that his imagination was at risk of running away with itself, Harry pulled himself back up to stand tall amid the trees. He was a logical man, had seen horrors the likes of which few would ever, thankfully, know, and he wasn't about to let himself get spooked by a gnarly collection of bramble-choked trees.

A sound cut into the moment and Harry looked back the way he'd come, through the trees, and down towards the farm. A motorbike was approaching, carving its way up the fields towards the spinney he was in, and he sent a message to Dave, receiving a reply almost immediately: *Spotted. On my way.*

Harry was as relieved as he was saddened to see Andrew. That he'd guessed where the man had been heading said something about his own detective skills, and he was happy with that. But it bothered him that Andrew's life had led him to this, to come back here, and do what he thought or believed had to be done.

Hearing the engine at last die, Harry moved away from

the pond and stepped behind a tree, the base of which was hidden by a thick clump of ferns. He dropped down, hidden from sight, but able to watch Andrew approach. The last thing he wanted to do was spook him, and risk sending him running back to the motorbike to take off again, or to do something foolish.

Though what that might be, Harry wasn't entirely sure what that would be, but after hearing what Andrew had written as his witness statement, he could guess.

As Andrew drew closer, Harry didn't see a man buoyed by what he'd done. He was crying, the sound of his sobbing deep and hollow. There was no sense of victory in the way he walked up the hill towards the spinney. No, Andrew was a man broken by his deeds. The weight of it all turned his walk into little more than the shambling stumble of someone who could barely stay on their feet.

As Andrew entered the spinney, Harry could see that he was spattered with blood, and that brought to mind the shocking scene he'd stumbled in on at the cottage, before Andrew had fled. His shoulders hung low, his back bent over as though straining under the weight of an impossibly heavy sack. Though his crying was quieter now, the tears still ran free, cutting thin, white furrows through the blood and muck on his face. Harry realised that he'd not seen a helmet on Andrew as he'd sped off; the blood would've dried quickly in the wind, and the dirt from whichever route he had taken to get here had coated his skin with ease, made darker still against the desiccated remnants of the shotgun blast.

Walking towards the pond, Andrew came to a dead stop at its edge, and knelt where Harry had seen the buried stones. Harry readied himself to come out from his hiding place and approach, but saw Andrew scraping away at the dirt, looking for something. Harry held back, observing, as

Andrew removed something from the hole he had just dug. Harry couldn't quite see it from where he was crouched, but knew that it was important, not just to Andrew, but to the investigation.

As he pulled the still hidden item from the clutches of the peaty soil, Andrew's crying grew momentarily louder, turning into the wail of a heart broken by years of pain and confusion. Then he brought it under control, the sobbing faded, and he started to talk. Not to himself, Harry realised, but to someone else, someone who still haunted not just the spinney, but Andrew's mind; Micky, his long-dead brother.

'I'm sorry, Micky, I did the best I could. I really did. You know that, don't you? You must, because you were with me through it all, saw it, heard it. But it all went wrong in the end. I didn't mean it to. I planned it, didn't I? Moved back here like I said I would, became someone else so that no one would know who I was, or ask any questions. But Brian, he wasn't listening, and it all went so badly. I was ready to get them into their van, bring them here, but then the gun went off. You said to load it, so I could frighten them if I needed to. I did like you said, but you saw what happened, didn't you? And that detective, the one that I told you about, he got out somehow. He turned up at the cottage and I had to escape and Alan, he's ... he's still alive, Micky. I'm sorry... I can't ... I can't do this anymore ... I've done enough, haven't I? Please? Can I come now? Is that okay?'

The crying started again, and those last few words worried Harry about what he would do next. He had to let Andrew know he was there and bring this to a close at last. Rising to his feet, slowly, quietly, he made his way out of his hiding place, then over to the pond.

'Andrew?'

On hearing Harry's voice, Andrew jumped to his feet. He

was clutching something close to his chest, the things he had unearthed by the pond. Harry saw a metal tin maybe half the size of a shoe box, a sheet of something in a see-through bag, and something else, too, though he couldn't make out what it was. The keys to the motorbike, he guessed.

Andrew stared at Harry, eyes wide like an owl's.

'What? Why are you here? How? It doesn't make sense! You were at the cottage!'

Harry didn't move, just stood his ground, and lifted his hands, palms down, in an attempt to keep Andrew calm and show that he meant no harm.

'You need to come with me, Andrew,' he said.

Andrew didn't move, still staring.

'There's no way you could've known I'd be here, no way at all! It's impossible. You should still be in the cave, like I planned.'

'Doesn't matter right now how I knew, Andrew,' said Harry, focusing on repeating the man's name to try and ensure that he didn't see him as a threat. 'Just that I did. And here I am. Now, how about we have that talk I mentioned back at the cottage?'

Andrew shook his head, clutched what he was holding even tighter to his chest, as though afraid Harry was going to take it from him.

'I don't want to talk, not to you, not to anyone. I don't need to. I just need to be with Micky, that's all, that's what matters, me and Micky. That's all that's ever mattered.'

'Is that the pond where Micky died, Andrew?'

The question sat alone in the air, unanswered, but that was answer enough, thought Harry.

'Do you really think your brother would want you to do any of this? It's over, Andrew. You know that, don't you?'

'It isn't, it can't be. I've still got something to do. Alan ...

He escaped … I messed up, I know I did, but Micky understands, and I can go now, can't I? I have to, I have to go.'

Whatever Andrew was talking about, Harry didn't like the sound of it at all.

'Whatever it is you've come here to do, Andrew, I won't let you.'

When Andrew spoke again, his voice was louder, not with anger, but pain, a torment he'd suffered for decades, since he'd lost his brother, Harry guessed.

'I have to! It's the only way! I can't go on just listening to him, can I? You don't know what it's like, his voice in my head. I can't escape from it, even when I'm asleep!' Andrew tapped the side of his head with his clenched left fist, as though trying to knock something free. 'I've tried to drown it out with alcohol, with drugs, but it's still there, sometimes even louder! It's all I hear, all the time, day and night, day and night, day and night! Micky talking to me, Micky whispering, Micky telling me what to do, calling me. It's too much!'

Harry took a small step forward.

'Then let's make it stop, Andrew, you and I, how does that sound? Just let me take you in, and we'll have a talk, okay? About you, about Micky, about all of it. Talking helps, believe me.'

At that, Andrew laughed.

'Believe you? What do you know about it, about any of what I've gone through, what I've done? You've killed people, I know you have, but it's different, isn't it? You were a soldier, that was war, but this? It was personal. I had to do it, to get justice for Micky.'

Another step. Andrew was almost within reach.

'Ben told you a lot about me, then,' said Harry, changing tack now. 'You got the job at Palmer's place in Aysgarth, and I guess you saw an opportunity with Karen when you found out she was friends with Jen. I'm sure you'd have found another way to work out how to take me out of the picture, but that was clever work there, Andrew. Impressive, really.'

'I don't want to talk about it!'

'That allergy must be pretty bad if you had to get Ben to kidnap me, though, just so you wouldn't have to be near my dog.'

'I couldn't risk it,' Andrew replied. 'It would've gone wrong if I'd done it. But I didn't hurt you, did I? You were safe. And I didn't hurt Liz, either; I just needed Ben to do what I told him to do.'

'He didn't know it was you, did he? Still doesn't, at a guess. But then how could he? You've had to be so many different people to do this. It must be confusing, especially for you.'

'Micky helped me plan it all. He was always the clever one.'

'I doubt that,' said Harry. 'Strikes me that you're very clever indeed to do what you've done. Which is why we need to talk it through, Andrew, get to the bottom of it. You understand that, don't you?'

Andrew backed away a little, shook his head, then looked around him, his eyes flicking from tree to branch to pond.

' Micky and I talk about this place all the time, what happened here, him dying, leaving me alone, how it was their fault, that they lost him and he ended up here and drowned.'

'Please, Andrew,' Harry said, keeping his voice soft and calm. 'Micky can't tell you what to do. He's not in control of you. He's not.'

Andrew, clutching the tin and sheet under his right arm, lifted his left fist.

'I don't care! Not anymore! I need to sleep, I need to have some peace, and I need to see Micky again!'

'Micky's dead, Andrew. It's just you and me. So, please,

just come with me. That's all I'm asking, okay? That's all you have to do. Just come back with me, and we can talk.'

As Harry was talking, he caught movement at the edge of the spinney; Dave was creeping through the trees, and for a man of his size, doing so with astonishing skill, making not a sound.

'I don't want to talk and I don't want to come back. I want to go! I have to!'

'Andrew ...'

With no warning given, Andrew lifted his fist into the air, and it was only then that Harry saw it was clutching a syringe.

'No!'

Harry threw himself across the remaining distance between them, but as he did so, something else slammed into Andrew, driving him to the ground, and sending everything he had been holding to scatter across the woodland floor.

'I've got him, Harry! I've got him!'

Harry scrambled onto his knees through the dirt towards the two men.

'Dave! He's got a syringe! Left hand!'

Andrew kicked out, catching Harry hard in the face, sending him sprawling.

'Hold him, Dave! Bloody well hold him before he—'

Andrew swept an elbow back, catching Dave hard across the jaw. He jumped to his feet, grabbed hold of the tin he had been carrying, and dashed over to the edge of the pond, left hand raised.

Harry saw the syringe.

'Andrew, don't!'

Andrew smiled weakly, gave a shrug, hammered his fist into his neck, then threw himself into the pond, at the same time opening the tin he had been holding.

Harry watched as a fine dust billowed up into the air just as Andrew broke the pool's still surface.

Without a second thought, Harry jumped into the pool with him, and dragged him to the edge of the water.

'No, you bloody well don't! Not on my watch, you hear? Not on my bloody watch!'

Dave stumbled over to help, grabbing an arm to heave the now sodden Andrew from the water.

Falling backwards, Harry and Dave heaved Andrew out of the pool and crashed in a tumble onto the soft floor of the spinney. Harry pushed Andrew off and quickly moved next to him on his knees, checking his vital signs.

'Andrew, don't you dare! Don't you let Micky win, damn it!'

Andrew wasn't breathing.

'Come on, you bastard! Don't bloody well die on me! I won't have it, I won't!'

Harry checked Andrew's vital signs, felt a pulse, pulled him onto his side. Andrew coughed, spluttered, and water spewed from his mouth.

As Andrew coughed, Harry slumped back, suddenly exhausted. He glanced over at Dave, who, like him, was soaked through and covered in mud and weed from the pond.

'Here,' Dave said, and held out his hand to Harry. In it was the syringe, the needle though, was missing. 'Must've snapped it when I threw myself at him.'

Harry took the syringe, then spotted the tin Andrew had been holding. The tin still contained a little of the dust he'd seen spill into the air, though what was left was doing its best to escape, caught as it was in the breeze weaving through the trees.

'Micky?' said Dave.

Harry reached over and snapped the lid of the tin shut on whatever remained of Andrew's brother. Then he caught sight of the sheet he'd seen Andrew holding, trapped as it was in some brambles just an arm's reach away.

As Andrew continued to recover, Harry released the sheet from the thorns that held it. Lit by the faintest speckles of sunlight breaking through the tree canopy above, he started to read.

36

Harry was back in the office, staring at five identical envelopes. One had been found amongst the rest of the post at Matthew Palmer's place in Aysgarth, another had been discovered at Dicky Guy's farmhouse, and a third, at Harry and Grace's. The final two had been found in one of Andrew Guy's jacket pockets when they'd finally managed to get him back to Harrogate to process him and work out what to do next.

The whole thing was a royal mess, and the thought of the paperwork alone was giving Harry's stomach a twist. But more than that was the tragedy of the events, how something that had happened so long ago could have had such awful repercussions all these years later.

The events of those few, terrible days, from the moment Harry had been kidnapped, to when they'd prevented Andrew from joining his long-dead brother, up in the spinney behind his father's farm, were getting on for a week ago now, and the letters had only just come to light the day before.

With everything that had been going on, Harry's own letter had been forgotten, because he was never one to hurry to open his post at the best of times. The ones Andrew had on his person at the time of his arrest had been stowed away with the rest of his personal belongings. It was only when he'd received an image from the SOC team of the letters found at Palmer's place, and at Dicky Guy's farm, that Harry had remembered seeing a similar-looking letter back home.

Though Harry had been the one to apprehend Andrew, it was Matt and Jen who had taken him in. Matt had been with Harry when the image of the letters had come through, and he'd recalled seeing two other such letters in with Andrew's things before he had been placed in a cell.

Sitting with Harry were Matt and Jen, the rest of the team either not on shift, and thus enjoying a much needed break, or out and about up and down the dale. Liz had been allowed to take a couple of days off at short notice, so that she could just be around for Ben, as he came to terms with what he'd done. Where he stood with regards to the whole investigation was still to be decided, but as far as Harry was concerned, and Walker for that matter, he was a victim as much as Harry had been. That he'd gone so far as to sort a replacement key for Harry's Rav demonstrated just how panicked and stressed he had been. Harry knew that it was an unnecessary part of the whole kidnapping, but then people don't generally think straight when under such duress.

Ben was not party to any of the crimes Andrew had gone on to commit and had only acted as he had under appalling coercion. If anything, the only person who could actually press charges was Harry, but he wasn't about to do that to his brother. What Ben needed more than anything was support, and that's what he was going to get. What had astonished Harry the most, however, was that someone very unexpected had been around to visit Ben and check up on him; Askew, the journalist.

'Askew?' Harry had said in amazement, when he'd popped round to check up on Ben. 'He visited you?'

'Brought chocolates, too,' Ben had replied. 'And some magazines. He's actually alright, Harry. You should give him a chance.'

That Askew had been the one to bring Ben in when he'd run off had baffled Harry, and he'd still not got to the bottom of how or why. Somehow, his brother had trusted the journalist enough that when Askew had called to reassure him that everything was okay and to stop trying to run away, he'd told him where he was. He hadn't got far at all. Having grabbed a few days' worth of food from home and a sleeping bag, he had hidden himself away in a tumbledown ruin of a barn out beyond East Witton.

'You going to open it, then?'

Matt's voice knocked Harry from his thoughts.

Only Harry's envelope remained unopened. The other four were in clear evidence bags, their contents easy to view.

Harry picked up one of the bags, checked what was inside again.

'Mine will be the same,' he said, placing the evidence bag down again.

He had read Andrew's letter to his long dead brother, the one he had buried by the pond. It had affected him more than he would dare to ever admit, and had spoken of it to no one, merely handed it in as evidence, and left it at that.

The other four envelopes had contained handwritten letters from Andrew to those he blamed for the death of his brother. That his victims would never read them was, Harry believed, all part of the theatre of what Andrew had been about. Andrew, he thought, hadn't meant for any of the letters to be read until his work was done and, as well as Matthew, Dicky, Brian, and Alan, he also lay dead in the pond in the spinney.

'Might not be, though,' said Jen. 'Why would Andrew have sent it to you?'

'I could ask him.'

'And where's the fun in that?' asked Matt.

'Fun's overrated.'

At that, Jen punched Harry softly on the arm.

'You're very good at the whole grizzly bear with a thorn in his paw act, but we know you now, Harry. Remember that.'

'And what's that supposed to mean?'

'You're a big softy,' Jen smiled.

Harry picked up the envelope, slipped a finger under the flap, and eased it open. He then removed the letter, and started to read …

Dear Harry,

I'm sorry for coercing Ben into doing what he did; kidnapping you, drugging you, locking you in that cave. I hope you weren't too uncomfortable. It had to be done, not because I thought the team would be useless without you, but because I needed them looking elsewhere while I did what I had to do.

Your disappearance was a distraction, and one I really only thought of when I realised Karen was friends with Jen, and I ended up meeting Ben merely by chance. Making use of the mine near the cave Matthew had purchased was too good an opportunity to miss.

What you don't know, though, is that I had other plans. I'd done my research before returning to the Dales, and I wanted to make sure that when I finally got around to doing what Micky wanted me to do (and I make no apology for any of it), I would succeed.

I have learned in my short period of time back in the Dales that you, Harry, are an important member of the community, that you are, dare I say it, loved. I learned about your past as well, and I used some of that to make Ben think it had caught up with you, and that is what leads me, really, to the point of this letter; I hadn't planned on writing to you at all, but it seems only fair, all things considered. I have some paper and a few envelopes left, so why not? And it seems a shame to waste them, considering how much they cost.

This, my final letter, is a warning; to you, Harry, and to Ben, and to your new friends up here in the quiet safety of the Dales, because I have uncovered something, perhaps even disturbed a hornet's nest, and I feel it is my duty to bring it to your attention.

I never intended you any harm, and still do not, but what I share with you now I cannot rightly go to meet my brother in death knowing that I have not told you.

Harry ... your father, if he could ever be described as such, has an older half-brother.

How I found this out is unimportant, that I did is considerably so. But suffice it to say, in my line of work as an accountant, I have perhaps helped certain people hide money well, and washed it clean.

I do not know why this information was never shared with you. All I can assume is that whatever happened between your father and his older brother, in those years before he met your mother, was enough for them both to forget the other. That is, until now.

He is old, Harry, and ill. His one wish was to make amends with his brother before the end. He is now aware that this will not happen, that his brother is dead, and that his death can be tied to you.

I do not know what action he will take, or if he is now too ill to even think about doing so. I don't even know his name, because in his line of work, which made your own brother's criminal activities look like the work of a child, his security and success have been secured by his own anonymity.

I am sorry, Harry, for being the bearer of such news, but I hope that by sharing it, you can think better of me.

Yours, Andrew

HARRY FOLDED THE LETTER, and slipped it back into the envelope.

For a moment or two, no one said a word. Jen and Matt simply stared at the letter Harry had just read aloud, as though unable to look at him and meet his gaze.

'You okay there, Harry?' Matt eventually asked, breaking the silence.

Harry lifted his eyes to meet Matt's, then took out his phone and pulled up a number.

'You calling Harrogate?' Jen asked. 'I don't blame you after reading that; we need to speak with Andrew, get to the bottom of whatever the hell that was all about.'

'You don't believe any of it, do you?' Matt asked. 'Think of what that man's done. This is probably all just part of whatever game he was playing, some kind of final act, though I sure as hell don't know why.'

Harry put the phone on speaker as he waited for the number he'd dialled to connect.

'Not Harrogate,' he said, looking at Matt and Jen.

'Then who?' Matt asked.

Harry waited a moment longer, then a voice answered his call.

'Harry? You do know you're interrupting me in the middle of a very important mug of tea, don't you?'

Harry grinned, and felt the muscles in his face complain as he did so.

'Hello, Jameson,' he said. 'You got time for a chat?'

For more SHOCKING REVELATIONS scan the QR code and grab the next book in the series, where BAD DEEDS mean death in the Dales!

You'll also be able to access free Harry Grimm short stories and sign up for my VIP Club and newsletter.

ABOUT DAVID J. GATWARD

David had his first book published when he was 18 and still can't believe this is what he does for a living. Author of the long-running DCI Harry Grimm series, and the new DI Haig Crime Thrillers, David was nominated for the Amazon Kindle Storyteller Award in 2023. He lives in Somerset with his two boys.

Visit www.DavidJGatward.com to find out more about the author and his highly-acclaimed series of crime fiction.

facebook.com/davidjgatwardauthor

Printed in Dunstable, United Kingdom

65447849R00167